HOPE ISLAND

A gripping murder mystery full of twists

JACKIE ELLIOTT

Coffin Cove Mysteries Book 3

Joffe Books, London
www.joffebooks.com

First published in Great Britain in 2022

This paperback edition was first published
in Great Britain in 2022

Cover art by Stuart Bache

ISBN: 978-1-80405-210-5

For Dad

PROLOGUE

1975

Essie George lay her head against the bus window and turned her face slightly, so she could feel the cool glass against her throbbing cheekbone.

Think of all the dirty hands that have touched that glass, Melissa.

Essie could hear Grandma Nora's voice in her head, and she cried. Tears squeezed out from her swollen eyes and trickled over the scratches on her face, the salt making her wince.

Grandma Nora wouldn't recognize her now. Essie had seen her face for a split second in the cracked mirror of the gas station washroom. A distorted monster had gazed back at her. Essie's eyes were already blackening. The rims of her glasses — miraculously unbroken — had been jammed across the bridge of her nose when she'd slammed face first into the gravel. She touched her lip and ran her finger carefully over her gums, probing for loose teeth. There were none. Another miracle, as Essie could still taste the grit in her mouth from her gasps for breath and futile attempts to scream. One side of her face looked red and bloated from the punch which had initially stunned her. There were smears of blood everywhere, whiplashes from the undergrowth, when she'd finally made her escape.

1

Grandma Nora had been right about everything. Why hadn't she listened? Why wasn't she back safe on the mainland helping Grandma prep food in their tiny diner and rocking her baby sister to sleep? Grandma had warned her, and she hadn't listened.

It had started with a boy.

"That white boy's only after one thing, Melissa. He has no respect for a native girl. He'll use you and throw you away," Grandma Nora had said.

Essie hadn't believed her. The boy had been respectful at the beginning. She remembered their first meeting as clear as anything.

He walked into the diner and ordered fried bread, this golden boy with white-blond hair and eyes as blue as the sky. He paid and thanked Grandma Nora politely and waited quietly for his order.

Essie delivered it, blushing as she set down the fried bread, still warm, with the grease staining the paper bag.

He smiled at her and asked her name.

"Essie," she whispered.

"Cool."

The boy became a regular visitor to the diner. Essie waited for him, an excited feeling in her stomach every time the door jangled. Gradually, their conversations moved beyond a polite exchange, and Essie no longer blushed every time he spoke to her.

She learned many things about the boy. He stayed with his uncle during the summer, while his parents worked in Ottawa. He loved baseball, fishing and the ocean.

Shyly, Essie told him about her life. She was a good student. She lived with her grandmother and baby sister. When she wasn't at school or studying, she worked in the diner. Sometimes, her Auntie Connie would take her to see a movie. Her greatest wish was to see the ocean.

One day, the boy arrived, but didn't order fried bread. He took Essie by the hand and told her he could make her wish come true. He could show her the ocean. She stared at him and flung her arms around his neck.

"We'll go camping," he said. "I promise you, it will be so much fun. Will you come?"

Of course, Grandma Nora forbade her to go with the boy. When Essie protested, her grandmother refused to listen. Finally, Essie turned to her Auntie Connie.

"Help me," she begged.

Auntie Connie helped. She loaned Essie a bag she'd made herself, decorated with intricate beadwork, and a long skirt made of a shimmery material that glinted in sunlight. She invited Essie for a sleepover. Early in the morning, when the air was still fresh, and the sun had just crept over the horizon, she gave Essie a hot cup of tea while they waited for the boy to show up.

"Don't worry about Grandma," she said. "Go on an adventure. Every young girl must experience the world." She kissed Essie's forehead.

Now, huddled on the bus, her limbs aching and her jaw throbbing, Essie remembered that her gut had told her something was wrong. She wished she had taken notice.

* * *

"That's an awesome bag," a voice said behind her, when Essie scrambled into the boy's camper van. She turned to see another girl lounging on the back seat, smoking a cigarette. Blonde hair fell in long curls over her face. The girl was dressed in shorts and a top that showed the lacy edge of her bra. Her legs were tanned and slender, right down to pink-polished toenails. She was perfect. The girl reached out and took Essie's bag. She fingered the beadwork.

"Indian, right?"

Essie didn't know what to say. She snatched her bag back, feeling her face grow hot.

The girl laughed, but it wasn't kind. She reached out and stroked Essie's long black hair. "Pretty," she said. "What a pretty thing you are."

3

It was then that Essie's gut had churned, warning her. But she hadn't listened.

* * *

Later in the journey, Essie forgot her bad feeling. The camper van made two more stops to pick up two more girls, and Essie convinced herself that the perfect girl in the back seat was no more special than anyone else on this trip.

It took all day to reach the west coast of Vancouver Island. They had to take a ferry from Vancouver. The camper van was decorated with psychedelic swirls of colour and attracted disapproving glances from other travellers. But the boy didn't care and turned up the volume on the radio. The camper van blasted out music and Essie sang along with the others but declined the joint that was being passed around. The boy and his friends laughed at Essie's excitement when she saw the ocean. As they lounged in the van, hooting and hollering at the ferry staff, Essie hung over the railing and breathed in fresh sea air. The ocean was beautiful.

Everything had changed in an instant.

It was late afternoon. The boy had driven the camper van for hours across Vancouver Island on narrow roads. They finally stopped for gas and beer.

"Next stop, the beach!" The perfect girl jumped out of the van. Essie followed her and stretched her legs as the boy paid for gas.

A girl dressed in a brown tunic ran out to wash the wind-screen with a mop on a pole. Essie helped her.

The girl looked in awe at the camper van. "It's so cool," she said. "Are you hippies?"

Essie didn't know, but she smiled and nodded.

They got back in the van again, and fifteen minutes later, they stopped in a gravel parking lot, surrounded by thick brush and brambles. Essie climbed out, forgetting how tired she was. Above her, a seagull cried and circled, casting shadows in the sunshine.

Leaving the others behind, Essie found a dirt pathway through the undergrowth. The tangle of bushes gave way to rolling sandy dunes. She pulled off her sandals and gasped as her feet sank into hot sand, but the scramble to the top of the dunes was worth it.

For as far as Essie could see, flat, dark sand stretched until it met the crashing surf of the Pacific Ocean.

"Welcome to Long Beach," the boy said behind her. "Next stop, Japan! Crazy, eh?"

Essie laughed out loud and started to run. She ran and ran, shrieking with delight when her bare feet were finally immersed in the frigid ocean. She bent over, panting and laughing at the same time. Essie didn't think she had ever been so happy.

* * *

Later, Essie curled up on a blanket, next to a campfire the boy had built from driftwood.

The glow of the fire had attracted other people, and Essie lay back, lulled by the sound of laughter and the strains of guitar music.

She'd refused beer. She was feeling lightheaded from the wafts of pot in the air.

* * *

When she opened her eyes, she was still lying on the blanket. The fire had reduced to embers. It was dark, but stars illuminated the summer night sky. Essie shivered and stood up, wondering where the boy and his friends had gone.

Stumbling a little, she made her way back to the parking lot. The camper van was still there, to Essie's relief. There was no movement. Essie tentatively touched the door handle. Maybe she could sleep in the front seat. And she'd left her bead bag inside. Auntie Connie had made that for her.

The first blow came from the side. It threw Essie off balance, and she slammed into the side of the van.

Then she was on her knees, gasping for breath, as her lungs emptied like burst balloons.

There was no time to recover or scream.

Someone grabbed a handful of her hair and slammed her face into the gravel.

The attacker ground her head into the earth. Essie fought for air.

"Dirty little bitch," a voice hissed. "Dirty little squaw bitch."

For a moment, the downward force on her head and neck lessened. The moment of reduced pressure was enough for Essie. She squirmed and broke her attacker's grasp.

It wasn't over.

As Essie struggled to get to her feet, another body blow sent her flying. Hands grabbed her legs, nails dug into her thighs and snatched at her blouse.

Suddenly, she heard Grandma Nora's voice in her head.

Time to run — run!

Essie gathered all the strength she had to propel herself upright, and then forced her legs to move. She had to run as fast as she could.

She thought she could hear heavy breathing behind her, so she kept going even though her lungs were on fire. She soon found the road and her eyes adjusted to the darkness.

Which way?

Essie looked wildly around her. What if her attacker went back and got the camper van? They would find her for sure. She had to get off the road, so she plunged into the undergrowth and found herself in a tangle of brush and spindly trees. She couldn't tell if anyone was following her. All she could hear was her own blood rushing in her ears and the echoing cracks of her feet on dry twigs and leaves. She forced herself to keep going, ignoring the vicious sting of branches on her bruised face.

Essie felt like she'd been running for hours when she finally reached tarmac again. She sank down into a ditch to rest.

She wanted to sob, but she knew she had to stay calm. She tried to remember which way the camper van had driven earlier in the day. It seemed like a lifetime ago.

In the velvet darkness, Essie made her decision. If she turned left, she would eventually reach the gas station, the one they'd stopped at earlier. She might be able to get help.

It took another hour or two before she saw the sign. Progress had been slow, because she had dropped in the ditch, lying as flat as she could, every time vehicle lights had flooded the road.

Although the gas station was lit up, the tiny store was closed. Essie began to panic. Where would she hide? She ran around the wooden building and found a small washroom with two stalls. The smell of urine made her gag, but it was safer here than being out in the open, so she went into one stall and sat on the closed toilet lid, wondering what to do next.

She didn't think she had any broken bones, except maybe a rib. It hurt to breathe. The most pain came from her face. She touched her cheekbone. She was certain it was broken. She slid on to the dirty floor and curled into a tight ball, hugging herself.

Her body tensed every time she heard a car. But finally, she closed her eyes and crouched in the corner of the stall. She was exhausted.

"Hey, are you OK?"

Essie woke with a yelp of fright.

It was the girl in the brown tunic. She smelled faintly of bleach and had a mop and bucket in her hands.

"You're the girl from yesterday," the girl said. "You were in that hippie van. What are you doing here?" She bent forward and dropped the bucket, slopping water on the floor. She clapped her hand over her mouth in horror. "Oh my, what happened to you?"

Essie opened her mouth to speak, but all that came out was a croak.

"Oh my," the girl said again, and hopped from foot to foot. "You can't stay here, no, ma'am — my dad, he don't like Indians, and he don't like hippies. And you're both."

"Help . . ." Essie tried to speak again.

"You wait there. Don't go outside, he's sweeping. We don't want him to see you. I know what to do."

After an anxious look and another entreaty for Essie to stay where she was, the girl left.

Essie struggled to her feet. There was a cracked mirror hanging on the wall, and a single tap over a drain. Light came in from the open door and it was then that Essie saw her damaged face. Trying not to cry again, Essie turned on the tap and splashed some cold water on her face, arms and legs. There was a pile of brown paper napkins on a ledge, so she dried herself off and waited for the girl to return.

When she came back, she was holding something. She looked at Essie. "You look better," she said. "Here." She opened her hand and held it out to Essie.

Essie stared at her.

"Go on, take 'em," the girl urged.

Essie took three crumpled bills, two one-dollar bills and one two-dollar bill.

"I didn't steal," the girl said. "I took 'em from the tip jar. That's my money. Rich people leave tips and I get 'em all. That's enough for the bus to Coffin Cove. Here—" she took another crumpled piece of paper out of a pocket in her tunic — "Here's what you need to know. That's for girls like you. Girls in trouble," she clarified. "Wait here. In a few minutes, the bus will get here. I always get Larry a coffee. When you hear me call 'Larry's here!', you run out and give Larry three dollars. You know how to count?"

Essie nodded.

"Then read that note. Oh — can you read?"

Essie nodded again.

"Good. You do that, and you'll be safe. I've done this before," she said proudly. "Helped girls in trouble, that is.

You're my first Indian, though." She looked Essie up and down as if she were an exhibit.

Essie didn't care.

It all happened as the girl had planned. Essie heard the rumble of the bus pulling in at the front of the gas station. She could see the back of it from the door of the washroom. The engine noise subsided to a low grumble, and then Essie heard the girl call out in a singsong voice, "Here's Larry, ready for his coffee!"

Essie pushed her stiff legs forward. She got to the bus door, which swung open. A dour man looked at her. "What have we here?"

Essie didn't answer, just held out the crumbled bills.

He grabbed them and gestured with his head to the seat. "You get to the back. You stay there, mind."

Essie climbed the two steps and then felt a hand on her shoulder. It was the girl from the gas station.

"When Larry calls out 'Coffin Cove', that's your stop."

Essie nodded. "Thank you," she croaked.

The girl patted her shoulder. "I hope you're all right, Hippie Indian." She turned and stepped down off the idling bus, just before the doors slammed shut and the engine roared into life.

Essie looked out of the bus window but didn't see the scenery that had captivated her before. Was it really just yesterday she'd been laughing and in love, excited to see the westernmost tip of Canada for the first time? That girl had been joyous and free. Now she was hollowed out. She was different.

As the bus rattled and shook over the pitted road connecting the west coast of Vancouver Island to the east, the first waves of shame overwhelmed her. How could she face Grandma Nora now? Hadn't she been warned? What a fool she'd been. Stupid. Stupid. Stupid.

But smart enough to get away. Smart enough to still be alive.

Essie looked at the crumpled piece of paper in her hand.

What was to become of her? Would Grandma Nora look for her? How would she know where to look?

Panic welled inside her and she clenched her fists to keep herself from crying again.

She read the note, and one word made her cracked lips form a slight smile. Maybe it would be all right. She lay her face against the cool glass once more and felt the first glimmer of hope she'd had that night.

CHAPTER ONE

A flat barge glided with the tide into the shallows, and two men lowered a ramp on to the stony beach. The bulldozer's engine spluttered into life and the vehicle moved slowly off the barge on to Hope Island.

The barge made two more trips between Coffin Cove Government Dock and Mercy Beach on the north side of the island, delivering heavy equipment and men in high-visibility jackets. The task was simple: dismantle the crumbling lighthouse and caretaker's cottage on the easternmost point of Hope Island.

The lighthouse was one of the first erected in British Columbia, financed by the British government and illuminated in 1880, to warn inbound steamships of the rocks that lurked beneath the ocean's surface at the entrance of Coffin Cove. It had worked well at first. There were relatively few marine "incidents" until the 1930s. The lighthouse keeper had enjoyed an "extra" salary from rum runners, who needed pitch darkness to escape Canadian waters and deliver illegal booze to Prohibition-era USA. Coffin Cove was home to some of the best hooch to come out of British Columbia, and it was a lucrative sideline for the local economy.

After Prohibition was repealed, there were only three more permanent lighthouse keepers, until the municipality of Coffin Cove argued with the provincial government over the maintenance of the lighthouse. Neither party was willing to bear the cost.

In the late sixties, the lighthouse and the caretaker's cottage were abandoned. And so, the two buildings slowly deteriorated and crumbled over the decades until an environmental group complained about ocean pollution from the decaying structures. The complaint had landed on Mayor Jade Thompson's desk.

The first female mayor of Coffin Cove was nearing the end of her first year in office. The last few months had been a traumatic time for the town and for Jade specifically. Four citizens had been brutally murdered, and Jade herself had been kidnapped.

Jade was a strong, resourceful woman who'd experienced trauma in her life before. She knew it wasn't weak to ask for help. Regular counselling sessions and focusing on her work as mayor had helped her through the worst of the aftermath.

Unfortunately, Coffin Cove hadn't fared as well as Jade. Until the murders, Coffin Cove's economy had been slowly picking up. Jade had encountered a resistance to change — she'd expected that — but some of the townsfolk resented a woman holding the most powerful elected office in town and had purposefully set out to sabotage Jade's projects.

There had been a hiatus when Jade was kidnapped. She would be forever grateful for the community members who had formed search parties to save her. But now the town had slumped back into a resentful apathy, especially as the murders had squashed the last of the summer tourist trade.

The city had no funds for environment remediation work. Jade sighed and hoped if she wrote a placatory letter, Hope Island might be off the environmental group's radar, at least for a while. Then she had an idea. She made a call and arranged to meet a friend for coffee.

Chief George Timms of Lhihw Xpey, Three Cedars First Nation, had already ordered coffee and muffins from Hephzibah when Jade arrived at the café. He'd become an ally when Jade had reached out to him in the first weeks of her tenure, asking if they could work together on various projects. He'd been wary at first, given her predecessor had reneged on several deals. Jade had persisted, and the chief and the mayor were now often seen in Hephzibah's Café. Jade had learned a lot from Chief George. He was a quiet man with a dry sense of humour.

He stood when Jade approached the table and shook her hand. "Mayor," he said, "I ordered coffee. I hope that's OK."

She sat. "Of course. Chief, I have an idea — a proposal, I suppose—"

"How are you?" Chief George interrupted, ignoring her opening sentence. "You look tired." He sipped his coffee.

"I am working quite hard," Jade admitted and smiled. "How are you?"

"That's better," Chief George chuckled.

After exchanging pleasantries, Chief George finished his coffee. "Now, tell me about your proposal."

Jade explained her idea. Chief George listened without interrupting until she had finished.

"I can see this would be beneficial to Lhihw Xpey." He rubbed his chin thoughtfully. "Snuneymuxw First Nation has a similar arrangement for Newcastle Island. It could work."

Jade was pleased. The chief was referring to the Nanaimo First Nation, who were stewards of Newcastle Island, or Saysutshun. The Three Cedars band operated a small ferry to and from Nanaimo and Newcastle Island and provided cultural and historic tours. The venture had been a great success, and Jade aimed to replicate this with Hope Island.

An hour later, Jade and Chief George shook hands. It had been a productive meeting.

A month later, and Three Cedars First Nation and the city of Coffin Cove signed a memorandum of understanding.

Three Cedars would have sole stewardship of Hope Island, including the maintenance, and the city would receive tax dollars and a small percentage of tourist dollars. It was a win-win.

* * *

The contractors, hired by Three Cedars First Nation, worked slowly and diligently on Hope Island, gently retrieving rubble and concrete with a large mechanical claw. The lighthouse was easy to remove — it had crumbled. This was a straightforward clean-up job for the crew. The old caretaker's cottage would require more planning.

At lunchtime, the foreman waved for his men to take a break. The sun was high and even though it was nearly fall, the heat was more like that of an August day.

The foreman ate his sandwich on the beach, enjoying the breeze from the ocean. A movement out of the corner of his eye caught his attention. He stood up and watched bushes rustle, as if an animal were retreating. Were there bears on the island?

Then he remembered. A single man, a recluse called Joshua Moore, inhabited the island. The gossip was he'd been a draft dodger during the Vietnam War and had hidden on the island back in the seventies. When President Carter pardoned all the draft dodgers years later, Joshua had stayed.

Was that him in the bush?

The foreman wondered what would happen to Joshua Moore now that Three Cedars First Nation effectively owned Hope Island. He shrugged. Wasn't his problem.

There were twenty minutes before he had to round up the guys and get them working again. He walked over to the worksite to inspect the morning's progress.

The lighthouse had severely eroded over the years, and the crew had cleared most of the loose stonework. The roof of the caretaker's cottage was caved in, and the south-facing wall had crumbled.

The foreman walked around the cottage, running his hands over the granite. It was beautiful stonework. He wondered if he could salvage some. He peered into the cottage. Under the dirt and debris, he could see reddish stone floors. Taking care, he stepped through the gap in the wall for a closer look. If the tiles were in decent condition, they'd make a wonderful patio.

Inside, the cottage was damp and cool. Only one half of the flooring was tile. The rest was rotting floorboards. He edged in, testing each step, until a loud creak and a cloud of dust stopped him. He pulled his foot back just in time as the floor disintegrated.

"Damn it," he muttered. He knew better than this. The place could collapse at any minute. He turned to retrace his steps. As he did, he noticed a rag poking up where the floorboards had once been. Unable to contain his curiosity, he crouched down.

"Well, I'm damned," he said. When he brushed off the dust, he could see the material was covered in intricate beadwork.

"Shit," he said. "Artefacts."

He heard a creak behind him.

"We'll have to stop work and report this." He stood. "Damn sure this is Indian . . ." As he turned, he saw a small man with leather-brown skin and dishevelled white hair gazing at him through the gaping hole in the wall.

"Who the fuck are you?" the foreman shouted, more out of shock than anything, before he remembered about Joshua Moore.

Quick as a flash, the small man disappeared from the hole. Forgetting to be careful, the foreman rushed towards the wall. "Hey, sorry, Mr Moore!" he called.

Before he could stop himself, he heard a splintering sound, and he felt himself falling. His arms flailed in the air as he made a futile attempt to regain his balance, but he crashed on to the remaining floorboards, which, mercifully, stayed intact.

The foreman lay there for a minute, hoping he hadn't broken any bones. How would he explain himself? First rule of safety: don't go poking around in condemned buildings. After stretching each limb carefully and allowing the adrenalin in his body to subside, the foreman moved himself into a sitting position. Nothing broken.

The wooden floorboards had given way completely where he'd stepped. Under the flooring was a cavity, maybe half a foot high, the foreman estimated, and then just dirt and rock. He heaved himself up and realized he was still clutching the piece of material. He looked back to see where he had found it in case the fall had uncovered any more artefacts.

"Shit," he said again when he saw what was lying in the hole. "Shit."

CHAPTER TWO

The early morning sea mist that had rolled in and blanketed Coffin Cove was clearing. It was turning into a crisp, blue day. The heat of the summer months had been oppressive but cooler temperatures and a fresh breeze had arrived with September. It wouldn't last long.

Andi Silvers lingered on the porch, looking out at the ocean, knowing soon the weather would change again. She was facing her third winter in Coffin Cove, and the relentless rain had been the consistent factor of the last two years.

Andi wasn't in a hurry to get to work. She opted to enjoy the fresh morning as long as possible, so she lingered in her chair, breathing in the ocean air. In a while she'd walk to the office, with a quick detour to pick up a coffee.

Jim Peters, her boss at the *Coffin Cove Gazette*, had not been a stickler for punctuality lately. The community had been quiet after a chaotic spring. Coffin Cove had lost four of its citizens to brutal murders before the perpetrator himself was shot and killed. Andi had been in the thick of the investigation and had helped solve the traumatic case. Although it was all over, the tension in Coffin Cove had been palpable throughout the summer. Even now, four months later, the town was subdued and sullen, the heavy atmosphere impervious even to the refreshing late-summer weather.

Andi felt the taut aftermath more than most. She had discovered one of the murder victims outside her old apartment above the Fat Chicken pub. She had managed to compartmentalize the horror, pushing it to one side while the "journalist" section of her brain focused on the story. But once the murders had been solved and her articles written, the delayed shock had set in. Jim had encouraged her to take time off. He'd also advised her to see a counsellor, and although Andi was unconvinced that talking to a stranger would make her feel better, she'd sat through a few appointments.

In the end, her healing had started when she'd moved out of her apartment and stopped reliving the horror of discovering Nadine Dagg, the murder victim, with her throat cut at the bottom of the stairs leading to her home.

Andi had moved all her belongings into the spare room of Hephzibah Brown's cottage, on the aptly named Seaview Road. Hephzibah owned the only café in town, and she had become one of Andi's closest friends.

"This is your home now," she'd said to Andi, "until you want to make a change."

Andi loved living with Hephzibah. She had felt instantly at home. She hadn't got many belongings, and she had soon settled into the compact attic room, happy to trade space for a spectacular view of Coffin Cove.

The cottage sat on the side of the hill with a cluster of other small clapboard homes, which had originally housed coal miners and their families over a hundred years ago. Some cottages had been vacant for years and had fallen into disrepair, but Hephzibah's was picture-perfect. Harry, Hephzibah's brother, owned the house, and had renovated it before deciding he was happier living on his boat and renting it to his sister. She'd added a garden and had cluttered the rooms with her artwork and craft projects. The kitchen smelled of heavenly home-cooked food, and Hephzibah always found the time for a coffee and a chat. Andi had spent many hours pouring out her heart to the kind-hearted woman, who listened without judgment.

Hephzibah had helped in another way, too. In the weeks after the murders, Andi had blotted out the trauma with wine. Every evening, she'd craved the first loosening of the ache in her shoulders and jaw as the alcohol hit her bloodstream. Wine dulled her senses, and she could disconnect with reality for a while. But then she'd wake up in the early hours of the morning, her sheets damp with sweat, and her mind in overdrive. Each morning, she'd drag herself out of bed, hungover and depressed.

One evening, Hephzibah put her hand on Andi's arm as she was reaching for the corkscrew.

"Could you help me with something, please?" she'd asked.

Andi, slightly irritated, had agreed and followed Hephzibah outside.

She'd gazed round in amazement. Andi had taken little notice of the fenced garden at the back of Hephzibah's house. The garden was extensive, divided into three areas. There was a tiny lawn bordered by flower beds. Roses competed with lilies and lupins, and large clumps of daisies and lavender. A greenhouse stood on a gravel area, and Andi had seen it was crammed full of tomato plants, and one large strip was given over to vegetables.

"This is beautiful, Hep. When do you find the time?"

Hephzibah had laughed. "I do a little every day. Pull a few weeds, water and keep it all tidy. I make it part of my working day. All the veg I use for soups and stews for the café, and the rest fill my freezers and cans for the winter. Harry brings me fish and game, so it's a huge saving. But you're right, it is a lot of work. Which is why I need your help."

"Me? But I've never gardened in my life." Andi had frowned. "I could mow the lawn, I suppose."

"Nonsense. I've got some weeding for you. Come on, Andi," Hephzibah had said gently. "Spending every evening downing a bottle of wine? It's not helping. You need to get out of your head. Just focus on *doing* something."

Andi had nodded and agreed to try. Hephzibah was right. She couldn't carry on like this. The wine habit had to be broken. But *gardening*? She wasn't sure. But she couldn't refuse Hephzibah, who'd been so generous.

Reluctantly, Andi had pulled on a pair of gardening gloves and crouched down to pull weeds between rows of carrots at Hephzibah's direction.

Twenty minutes later and she'd cleared an entire row, but her back was hurting, she was sweating, and it felt like a thousand mosquitos had bitten her.

"Having fun yet?" Hephzibah had laughed.

Actually, Andi had thought, it wasn't too bad at all.

The next evening, Andi had stopped outside the Fat Chicken to buy a bottle of wine. She had walked to the door, hesitated, and turned around.

"Not tonight," she'd said out loud. The evening gardening became a habit and had helped more than the counselling. Sometimes Harry joined their evening gardening sessions. He'd split logs and stack them ready for winter, while Hephzibah and Andi fussed over the vegetables.

With a groan, Andi wrenched herself away from Hephzibah's porch. She had a job to go to, after all. She slung her bag over her shoulder, clicked the gate shut behind her and took her time ambling down the quiet streets to the boardwalk and Hephzibah's Café.

* * *

"Here's your coffee."

"Thanks." Andi smiled up at Hephzibah. "Hey, what's this? New mugs?"

She pointed to the mug of coffee Hephzibah had just placed in front of her. Instead of one of the usual mismatched, worn pieces of crockery, it was brand-new and shiny, with *Hephzibah's Café and Bakery, Coffin Cove* printed on it.

Hephzibah sighed. "I've been trying to shine the place up a bit. You know, new crockery, repair the chairs, revamp the menu, that kind of thing. I will have competition soon, when the Fish Plant opens, and the museum gift shop will serve coffee."

"Hep, it'll be completely different. People come here for you and all of this." Andi waved her hand around the comfy oceanfront café. "Everyone loves your baking, and we love you," she said loyally, meaning every word.

"Thank you for that. But I can't be complacent. In a few days, I'll be offering free Wi-Fi too." Hephzibah pulled a face. "Then everyone will be looking at their phones and not talking to one another. Still, that's progress, I suppose."

It was true. Andi knew Hephzibah was right to be thinking about the future, even if it meant some uncomfortable changes. The Fish Plant was the recent development at the other end of the oceanfront. The old fish processing plant had been redeveloped to create some sea-view apartments and commercial space for a visitors' centre, the Coffin Cove Museum and Gift Shop and other boutique stores, which hadn't yet moved in. The grand opening and renaming of the building were slated for December, so business owners could make the most of the Christmas season.

"You know, you could just make coffee at home, and fill a flask for the day," Hephzibah said. "You don't have to pay for it here. And—" she gestured to a new shelf — "you could purchase one of my new thermos flasks."

Hephzibah sat in the chair opposite Andi and took a sip from her own mug of coffee.

"That's true, I could." Andi smiled back. "But it's not the same as taking a break here. Plus, I get to find out what's going on in the town if I hang out long enough. It's part of my job. I'm sure everyone will still drop in here to catch up on the important news of the day, even with the Wi-Fi."

"Is that right? Does Jim agree?"

Andi shrugged and laughed, thinking of her boss at the *Coffin Cove Gazette* and his disdain for local gossip. "Maybe not," she conceded. "By the way, I love the new flasks. But don't change everything, Hep."

The café was a sanctuary for many of the town's residents. Coffee was ready for the early shift at the pulp mill, or for the few commercial fishermen who still tied up their boats at Government Dock. The easy chairs at the back of the café, with their comfy sag, were near to the wood stove and the bookcase. Andi had lost many winter afternoons huddled with a book while rain pelted outside.

Hephzibah reached across the table and grabbed Andi's hand, jolting her out of her daydreams. Andi tried to pull it back, but Hephzibah hung on, laughing. "Aha! I see dirt underneath these fingernails," Hephzibah said. "Gardening this morning, were we?"

"Well done, Sherlock." Andi removed her hand, feeling self-conscious, but laughed with her friend and roommate, anyway.

"How's Jim these days?" Hephzibah asked.

"Same. Bit quieter than usual, but we've all been quiet lately, I suppose. Not missing any excitement, anyway."

"I don't believe that for a minute." Hephzibah said with conviction. "You thrive on excitement."

Andi stared at her friend, irritated for a moment. "What do you mean? Don't you think I've had enough of all that for a while?"

"Oh, I know it's been tough, Andi. But you can't stay in the garden for ever. It's not who you are. You thrive on finding stories, investigating and poking around dark places. Time to get back to work, girl. Really get back to work, I mean. Not just making an appearance at the office." Hephzibah was smiling, but her tone was firm.

Andi knew her friend was right. She'd been in hiding. She was scared to admit it, even to herself, but she was wondering whether journalism was right for her. If she fell apart every time a story was too brutal or dangerous, what kind of investigative reporter was she? She knew other journalists who literally ran towards gunfire to get a story. The problem was, if she wasn't a journalist, what the hell would she do with her life?

Hephzibah patted her hand. "Just think about it, Andi. Don't give up." She got up as a customer came in, and left Andi alone with her coffee and her thoughts.

A few years ago, Andi knew exactly what she wanted out of life. She was a city girl with her entire future mapped out as a high-profile investigative journalist for a national media organization. A broken love affair with the married assistant editor and a serious error of journalistic judgment had led to her firing and a move to the *Coffin Cove Gazette*. Jim Peters was the only editor who would give her a chance.

Lately, Jim had been badgering her to take on more of the administrative duties at the *Gazette*. But Andi preferred to write articles and interview people. She disliked drumming up advertising business and doing the monthly accounts.

But Jim had said a while ago, "Someday I'll retire," and he'd waved his hand in the air around the office. "All this could be yours one day."

Andi had never been sure if she saw her entire future as the senior reporter and editor for a small outfit in a tiny backwater like Coffin Cove. When she'd first arrived, she'd viewed the job as a stepping stone to regroup and work her way back to a national newspaper. Now she did not know what she wanted.

Hephzibah came back to the table and sat down again. "Did you hear Peggy Wilson is running around saying we should fire the mayor?"

"No. Why? And is that the best gossip you have?" Andi pushed her worries to the back of her mind.

"Afraid so. It's been quiet around here for the last few weeks, and I'm glad. But Peggy thinks Jade Thompson sucked us all in with the fish plant development. Peggy says all she has is an increased property tax bill and less business than usual this summer. She says it's a disgrace. And now she's furious about the Hope Island proposal."

Andi sighed. People had such short memories. It was only a few months ago the whole town was out searching for their first female mayor, Jade Thompson, who could have easily been another murder victim, if it were not for the community working together with the police.

The townspeople had voted Jade Thompson in on a promise to keep Coffin Cove solvent and free from the threat of being absorbed by the nearby city and district of Nanaimo. Everyone had been on board with her plans, and most people loved the fish plant renovations. The old warehouse and rusted-out pier had been an eyesore. But, so far, the prosperity had not been forthcoming. Public sentiment was turning against the young mayor, especially now Jade Thompson had announced plans for a new development on Hope Island, which was about a twenty-minute boat ride from Coffin Cove.

"I feel badly for the mayor." Hephzibah was still talking. "She worked so hard to get the Fish Plant under way, and now everyone is complaining."

Andi nodded. "I'm interviewing her later. I'll find out what's going on."

Andi hesitated before she asked Hephzibah her next question.

"How do you feel about Hope Island being developed?"

Andi was curious because Hephzibah had spent her childhood years on the island. Greta, Hephzibah's mother, had left her abusive husband, Ed Brown, and taken her baby daughter to a women's commune on Hope Island. To Andi's mind, it was a bizarre decision, especially as Greta had left Harry, Hephzibah's older brother, with his drunken father. For years, Harry hadn't known his mother was only a short boat ride away. He only saw her a handful of times after that, and didn't even know she had died, until Hephzibah, a teenager by then, turned up at his door, not knowing where to go.

Harry, not a man to hold a grudge, looked after his sister, and they were very close.

Hephzibah talked little about her childhood. Andi was curious about the commune and how the women survived. But the commune seemed to be a taboo subject for a town that thrived on gossip.

Jim Peters had explained it as best he could. There were no women's rights or laws about domestic abuse. There was nobody to call or complain to if your husband came home drunk and hit you. Coffin Cove was a tough place to be. Some women turned to the Church, but the clergy were all "hellfire and brimstone", and women were natural sinners who needed to be "disciplined". Hope Island was the best refuge they could find, and at least there was safety in numbers. "Mostly," he'd added darkly.

Andi had mentally filed away the information, intending someday to dig a little deeper and write an article about Hope Island. The rumours about a development on Hope Island had piqued her interest once again.

Hephzibah took her time to answer Andi's question.

"You know, I think I've made peace with my past," she said eventually. "I was mad at my mother for many years, for subjecting me to such an . . . unusual childhood. I didn't feel normal. I had very little education and if it wasn't for Harry, I'd be on the streets. I did not know how to behave in regular society. But I understand why I was there, I guess. Now, I think it's time to move on. Hope Island is very beautiful. People should have a chance to appreciate it."

Not for the first time, Andi marvelled at her friend's wisdom.

"I'll know more when I interview the mayor," she said. "I should get to the office to prepare—"

"You should spend your time *investigating* our mayor," a voice said behind them. "Not interviewing her! Businesses are suffering enough in this town, without more expense for the taxpayers."

Peggy Wilson, the subject of their earlier conversation, was standing by the counter.

"I've lost bookings since all that nasty business. I need support from my mayor, not another development to compete against my business. It was better when Dennis was in charge."

Peggy Wilson revelled in gossip, and when there wasn't any, she wasn't above creating chaos purely for her own entertainment, Andi thought.

Peggy ran the Wilson Motel. For decades, it had been the only place for visitors to stay. Peggy's motel was clean and tidy but hadn't moved with the times. She didn't provide Wi-Fi, or in-room coffee, or any of the other little conveniences that tourists expected. She'd stayed in business because she was the only show in town. But that was set to change with all the recent developments. No wonder Peggy was angry. Someone else who was uncertain about the future. Andi felt a little sorry for Peggy but had to push back a little.

"You can hardly blame the poor woman for all those murders. And I seem to remember you complaining about Dennis Havers back in the day."

Hephzibah snorted and got up, taking the empty mugs with her.

Andi sighed inwardly as Peggy ignored Hephzibah and sat down in the vacated chair opposite her. Andi really didn't have the energy for Peggy today. She glanced at Hephzibah, hoping her friend would save her. But Hephzibah avoided making eye contact with Andi, and instead busied herself with rearranging the baked goods in the display counter.

"Well, Dennis was at least experienced. That woman doesn't know what she's doing. Look at the fish plant development. What a waste of money. Dennis knew how to get things done."

"Dennis Havers didn't do anything about the fish plant all the time he was in office," Andi said. "It was empty and falling down for years."

Andi didn't want to say what she really thought of Dennis Havers. He'd not been a good mayor for the citizens of Coffin Cove, preferring to use his power to line his own pockets. But he'd been the victim of a brutal murder along with his entire family, and since then, Dennis's failings as mayor seemed to have been buried with him. *Mustn't speak ill of the dead*, Andi thought.

Peggy was still talking, apparently not hearing anything Andi had said.

"Have you seen the new museum? What do we want with a museum? And that Dagg girl has got a dinosaur exhibit planned, of all things? What do bloody dinosaurs have to do with Coffin Cove? Nothing, that's what."

Andi heard a stifled giggle from Hephzibah.

"I believe Katie Dagg is organizing an exhibition called 'Coffin Cove Through the Ages', starting with the time dinosaurs roamed the earth." *And they haven't entirely left yet*, Andi added silently. "Peggy, kids love dinosaurs. The exhibition will bring families to town."

Peggy glared. "I suppose she'll be doing a bunch of Indian shows, too. Did you know the Indians have got some kind of deal with the developer on Hope Island? Some kind of back-room deal, I bet. How are we all supposed to compete with that?"

Andi took a sharp intake of breath.

"That's enough of that kind of talk, Peggy," Hephzibah snapped.

Peggy wasn't listening.

"Anyways, I heard the Indians are blocking that development. The contractor says they all stopped working because they found a pile of old bones. So I suppose us business owners and taxpayers will foot the bill for that too . . ."

"What are you talking about, Peggy?" Andi asked.

But Peggy was still talking. "And it's not just me worried about all this," she was saying. "Cheryl says the pub is struggling too and Walter is very worried indeed. Cheryl says he's hardly slept since all that terrible business, and now they're finding it hard to make ends meet. They're renting out your old apartment again. Cheryl says another journalist is moving in. I suppose the *Gazette* is the only business making any money these days. Murder must be good for Jim's bottom line too, eh?"

"A journalist?" Andi was still grappling with Peggy's unashamed casual racism, and any sympathy she had for the woman had evaporated. She got up from the table. "It's the first I've heard of it, Peggy. You must be mistaken."

"That's what Cheryl told me," Peggy said. "But that's by the by. What I want you and Jim to do is a thorough investigation into our mayor and the terrible job she's doing."

Andi opened her mouth to argue with Peggy but thought better of it. What was the use? She said instead, "You know, Peggy, that's a good idea. I'll run it past Jim when I get to the office. And I have an appointment with the mayor later today, so I will ask her about the 'pile of bones' and those back-room deals."

That seemed to do the trick. Andi made a dash for the door before Peggy had time to say any more. Hephzibah called after her.

"Here." She handed Andi another coffee in a to-go cup. "She's impossible. But you should know a few of the business owners are forming an association and intend to do what they can to stop the mayor's plans."

"Hmm. Good to know. Did you join?"

Hephzibah laughed. "No, I've been on these committees before. Every meeting turns into squabbles about who should be Chair, and who should buy the coffee. I haven't got time for all that. Are you home for dinner tonight?"

Andi smiled at her friend. "Tonight, yes. But tomorrow night, Harry's cooking for me."

Hephzibah clapped her hands. "Excellent. You and Harry should take a few days away somewhere."

Andi rolled her eyes. "Stop playing Cupid. I'm late."

Hephzibah had made no secret that she'd love her brother Harry and Andi to become a couple. Andi wasn't sure how she felt about that. Sure, she really liked Harry, and was attracted to him, despite their age difference. Harry was about ten years older than her. He was divorced and had a grown-up daughter who'd moved away, but that wasn't the problem. It was just that Harry really loved living in Coffin Cove. Andi couldn't see Harry leaving the place. And she wasn't sure she wanted to stay. Not for ever, anyway.

Andi shook her head, amused at Hephzibah's persistent attempts to get her and Harry together. She didn't have a good track record where men were concerned.

CHAPTER THREE

Andi pushed open the office door and walked to her desk.

"Carpetbagger," Jim Peters said.

"Pardon?" Andi dumped her bag on her chair, and took a swig of coffee, before perching on the side of her desk and waiting for her boss to explain himself.

Jim was completely engrossed in the news program, which was displayed on a large flatscreen TV fixed on the office wall. He didn't appear to have heard Andi. This wasn't unusual. Jim could tune out the rest of the world when he was focused on something. Andi sipped her coffee and settled at her desk, flipping through the pile of paperwork that never seemed to disappear.

Andi had a brand-new desk and chair, as cash flow at the *Coffin Cove Gazette* had improved. Jim had been generous with the business chequebook lately. He'd also ordered new filing cabinets, a photocopier and printer, and he'd bought himself a laptop and the TV.

She didn't begrudge Jim his recent spending spree. The *Gazette* had struggled for many years, and Jim had propped up the financially ailing newspaper with his savings. More than once, he'd wavered and nearly sold out to a large media conglomerate like most of the independent newspapers on Vancouver Island. But somehow, the *Gazette* had survived.

Looking round the *Gazette*'s updated office, Andi could see why Peggy had insinuated that they had benefited from murder. It was true that Andi's articles had substantially increased circulation, even in Nanaimo and other Vancouver Island towns. Advertising revenue was up, and their online presence had boomed. It was a sad fact. Tragedy and scandals were good for the newspaper business.

In the corner of the office, Andi spied another new desk and chair. It was piled high with cardboard boxes. They all had dates scrawled on the side in black marker, but it wasn't Jim's handwriting.

"Hey, Jim," Andi called across the office. "You're glued to that thing," she teased. "Are you getting any work done, or just watching daytime TV?"

Jim swung round in his chair and grinned at her. "Just keeping up to date with current affairs."

"What's up with all those boxes?"

"Just clearing out, I guess. It's all Dad's stuff."

Jim's father had started the *Coffin Cove Gazette*. Jim had left his career to help run the paper when his father was diagnosed with dementia. He'd taken over as owner and proprietor when his father died.

Andi suddenly remembered something Peggy Wilson had said earlier at the café. She'd mentioned a new reporter. Andi frowned as she looked at the new desk again. Was Jim making room for a new member of staff? Why hadn't he said anything?

"Jim—"

"Damn carpetbagger!" He was looking at the TV again. He grabbed the remote from his desk and turned the volume up.

"OK, that's the second time you've said that. What on earth are you watching?"

He pointed to the screen. The anchor of a Vancouver news program was interviewing a windswept, laughing couple as they stood on the lawn outside the Legislature Building in Victoria. They were both casually dressed and, although they looked like they were both in their sixties, by their tans and trim appearance it looked like they spent a lot of time outside. A typical West Coast couple, Andi thought.

"That's Michael Halwell, heir apparent to the current prime minister, and his socialite wife, Elizabeth. She was a wild one, back in the day. For the life of me, I can't remember what exactly the big scandal was, something to do with a wild night with a rock band."

There was something about Elizabeth Halwell which rang a bell in Andi's mind, but she couldn't recall. She must have seen her in the media before, maybe the scandal Jim mentioned.

"She's definitely good-looking, but she doesn't look like a rock chick. Why are we interested?" Andi asked.

"Didn't you hear what I said? That guy is widely tipped to be our prime minister next year. It'll be a big upset if he is."

"Great. Another old white guy. Exactly what the country needs."

Jim laughed. "Such a cynical attitude."

"So what did you mean by 'carpetbagger'?"

"Oh, it's a phrase used to describe a politician who runs for election in an area they don't have any local connection. Michael Halwell is running for the Nanaimo–Ladysmith Riding in the special by-election in a few months, and he's busily kissing babies to prepare for next year's general election."

"Now who's being cynical?" Andi pulled a face at Jim.

"Oh, you're right. At least if we get high-profile representation at the federal level, we might get more attention for Western issues. Historically, Ottawa hasn't given a shit about anything west of the Rockies. They even used to announce the winner of federal elections before the West had finished casting their votes."

"Really? I didn't know you were still a political junkie."

"I'm not, really. But one reason we operate like the Wild West out here, is because they have left us to our own devices. And small towns like Coffin Cove struggle. Especially now we've lost most of our fishing and forestry jobs."

"Mrs Halwell doesn't look as though she'll enjoy living in the Wild West," Andi commented.

Jim snorted. "Mrs Halwell's family is a political dynasty. She's the daughter of an ambassador, but I don't remember which one. She knows exactly what she needs to do to get her husband into office."

"Behind every successful man—"

"Is an ambitious, smart woman," Jim finished.

Andi studied the Halwell couple on the screen. Michael Halwell was a well-built man with an amiable smile. His greying hair gave away his age, but he exuded energy. As the reporter asked questions, Michael Halwell deferred to his wife, smiling at her as she answered.

Mrs Halwell leaned into her husband, slipping her hand under his arm and turning her head attentively towards him when he was speaking. They looked like a devoted couple.

Michael Halwell was talking about economic growth in western Canada.

"... *and Elizabeth and I are looking forward to exploring the small coastal communities of British Columbia, and asking the hard-working folk, the backbone of our economic success of the past, exactly what they need from us. I am here to serve ...*"

Jim turned it down again. "Same old, same old."

Andi nodded. This couple was well-heeled, not displaying ostentatious wealth, but they had the relaxed aura of people who didn't have to worry about paying their next hydro bill. Andi didn't give them much chance with the struggling electorate in Coffin Cove. She steered the conversation to current events in the area. "Talking about our elected leaders, our mayor is coming under fire at the moment."

Jim sighed. "I'm not surprised. The entire town was behind her and the Fish Plant. But a development on Hope Island? There's a lot of history — not good history — there.

Plus, all this change could mean competition for Peggy's motel."

Andi nodded. "That's exactly what Peggy said. She also said the contractors had found a pile of old bones. Did you hear anything about that?"

"I did," Jim said, to Andi's surprise. He usually told her everything. "But they could be part of the archaeological dig."

Andi hadn't heard about that either. "What dig?"

"There used to be an ancient settlement out there. Before they build anything, Three Cedars band wants to make sure no burial sites are disturbed."

"So Peggy was right?"

Jim smiled. "For once, yes. And she's right about the town needing an economic boost. But the mayor has to find a way to bring everyone along, not just force it on them."

Andi sat at her desk and flipped open her laptop. "I have the perfect opportunity to mention that to our mayor. I'm interviewing her in a short while. I'll get an update and comment on the archaeological dig. And I'll be able to tell her that Coffin Cove businesspeople are organizing themselves and have formed a business association."

Andi was pleased to see the surprise on Jim's face. Finally, she'd got a local "scoop" ahead of her boss.

"Interesting," Jim said. "And how did you find that out?"

"Peggy Wilson. At Hephzibah's this morning. She was complaining, and insisting we do an exposé on our corrupt mayor." Andi rolled her eyes.

Jim groaned.

Andi continued, "Peggy has got everyone riled up about it, and they intend to take their protest to the mayor, and force her to stop the Hope Island development. Before it begins. And another thing, Peggy said — Mayor Thompson has made some kind of deal with the First Nations. She wasn't polite."

Jim leaned back in his chair and flexed his shoulders and arms. "Nothing like involving First Nations to bring out the pitchfork brigade in this community." He shook his head. "That's the problem with this town. Everyone wants things to change, but everything has to remain the same. And that includes all the old prejudices."

"And nothing brings Coffin Cove together like a common enemy," Andi added. "I feel sorry for the mayor."

Jim nodded. "Me too. That lady has been through a lot. Still, she's tough and smarter than Peggy. I'm not writing her off yet."

Andi gathered up a notebook and her phone and headed for the door. "See you later."

Jim was already watching the TV again. It wasn't until Andi had walked to City Hall that she remembered she hadn't asked Jim about this new reporter.

CHAPTER FOUR

Andi smiled at the receptionist at City Hall and confirmed her appointment with the mayor, before sitting on a plush new seat in the foyer. She finished her coffee and made a few notes while she waited.

"I'm here to see the mayor," a voice said.

Andi looked up to see a tall woman with long dark hair standing at the reception desk.

"Do you have an appointment?"

"I do. My name is Ruth Cloutier."

"I don't see you in the book." The receptionist sounded irritated and pursed her lips. Her demeanour was almost combative.

Andi paid attention to the visitor. Ruth Cloutier was turned away from Andi, so she could only see her profile. She was a beautiful — and angry — woman.

"I *made* an appointment," Ruth Cloutier said. Her voice was calm, but spots of colour were forming on her face.

"Did you come in or phone? The problem is, the mayor already has an appointment, and she's booked out for the next few hours." The receptionist nodded in Andi's direction.

"Oh, my meeting won't take all that time," Andi said brightly. "I have no problem waiting for the mayor, if there's been a double booking."

"There hasn't been a double—" the receptionist argued, but Ruth Cloutier ignored her and walked over to Andi.

"Thank you." She sat stiffly beside Andi and stared at the receptionist, who banged files around, showing her displeasure.

Andi held out her hand. "Andi Silvers. I'm a journalist with the *Coffin Cove Gazette*."

Ruth Cloutier introduced herself and shook Andi's hand. "I'm a lawyer working for Lhihw Xpey First Nation," she said, her voice carrying a hint more warmth than before.

Everything about her exuded professionalism, Andi thought. She was dressed in a navy business suit, and her long dark hair was pinned back from her face. She was wearing drop earrings made from tiny colourful beads in an intricate native design.

Andi wondered about the rude attitude Ruth Cloutier had just encountered from the receptionist. Surely it wasn't because this smart lawyer was native? But then Andi remembered Peggy Wilson's words from earlier. Twice in one day, Andi had witnessed undisguised bigotry and hostility in Coffin Cove. She glanced down at her faded jeans and scuffed boots and compared herself to Ruth's immaculate presentation and realized that Ruth had two daily obstacles to face in her career — she was a woman *and* native. Ruth needed to be on the top of her game all the time. And still she encountered a level of ignorance and disrespect that Andi had never experienced.

The mayor's voice interrupted Andi's thoughts.

"Andi. And Ruth. This is perfect. I need to talk to you both." Mayor Jade Thompson threw a withering look at her receptionist. "I apologize for the mix-up. I was expecting you both."

The receptionist looked away. Not even a blush, Andi observed.

The women followed Jade down the corridor to the mayor's office. There had been many changes since Jade had been appointed, but there was obviously still a hangover of staff and attitudes from the previous mayor. Andi remembered when Dennis Havers was the most powerful elected official in town. The mayor's office and council had been there merely to prop up his financial empire. Service to the community was an afterthought.

Andi checked herself. Dennis Havers and his family were the recent murder victims. Nobody, not even a corrupt mayor, deserved such a brutal end. And anyway, it wasn't Andi's job to compare mayors. It was her job to hold the current officeholder's feet to the fire. And she was intrigued that Ruth Cloutier was invited to this meeting. Maybe Mayor Thompson had an announcement to share.

"Come in." Jade Thompson stood back to allow Ruth and Andi into her office, then sat down behind her desk. Her smile was warm, and Andi felt a genuine connection with this lady. In other circumstances, Andi believed she and Jade could have been friends. They had a lot in common. They were both women in careers while this community, until recently, had only valued men. But Andi knew Jade would never be completely open and honest with her. Andi didn't mind. It went with her territory. Most people had a mistrust of reporters.

Ruth Cloutier sat alongside Andi. She had relaxed a little, Andi thought. Jade and Ruth must have worked together for a while. Andi got the feeling that the two other women knew exactly what this meeting was all about.

Andi didn't have to wait long. Jade didn't waste time with pleasantries.

"Lhihw Xpey First Nation and the city of Coffin Cove have signed a memorandum of understanding to develop Hope Island," Jade said, using the proper native name of the local First Nations band. "Lhihw Xpey First Nation will build a small resort and a Hul'qui'minum language centre, and will operate cultural tours and wellness retreats. The arrangement is of mutual benefit; Lhihw Xpey First Nation will be able to further cultural understanding, and the city will gain some direct revenue *without* having to invest tax dollars." She looked directly at Andi to further emphasize her point. Andi guessed the mayor must have already felt some heat about this new project.

"And, of course, there is the indirect boost to the economy from tourist dollars, if we have another historical attraction nearby," Andi said.

"Exactly." Jade nodded. "Ruth is working on this project for Lhihw Xpey First Nation," she continued, "and everything was going well until we . . . encountered an obstacle. Ruth, maybe you could explain to Andi?"

"Hang on," Andi interjected. "Before we go any further, is this on the record?" She waved her notebook.

Jade exchanged glances with Ruth Cloutier. "Yes."

"We believe ancestors of Lhihw Xpey First Nation are buried on Hope Island," Ruth Cloutier began. "We hired archaeologists to investigate several areas where we can see middens — you know what middens are?" She looked at Andi.

"No, not really."

"They are heaps of shells, artefacts, bones — any kind of ancient debris, really — and they almost always point to evidence of a settlement and a burial area. As we suspected, this was the case on Hope Island. This is exciting, of course, and we can plan for the developments on areas of the island which do not affect sites of cultural significance. However, a short while ago, during the removal of the old lighthouse and cottage, contractors found *other* human remains."

Andi noticed Ruth's hesitancy. "I heard rumours," she said. "Is it another burial site?" she asked, making notes.

"We're not sure," Jade said hurriedly. "But because of the . . . *position* of the remains, I felt it prudent to call the coroner's office."

Andi put her pen down. "OK. *When* exactly did the contractors find human remains, and *where* exactly were they found?"

"A couple of weeks ago. And under the floorboards of the caretaker's cottage."

Andi was so surprised, she laughed. "You're kidding me, right?"

Neither of the other two women said anything.

"How on earth did you keep this quiet?" Andi demanded. "And why? The public has a right—"

"Yes, yes, we know." Jade waved her hand. "I decided it was best to keep the discovery under wraps to start with. At least until we knew what we were dealing with."

"And do you know? Do you know who the remains belong to? Or how long they've been there? And how did they get to be under the floorboards?"

Andi was beginning to understand the implications of the discovery, and the mayor's reasons for wanting to keep it hushed-up.

"Is there evidence of foul play, Mayor?"

Jade sighed. "We just don't know yet. Andi, I know you are annoyed, but Coffin Cove has been through an awful time. You know that better than most people. Business has suffered this summer because of the murders, and there's already opposition to this partnership and development. I thought it better to wait and have all the facts, rather than cause a stir in the town about nothing. It might be nothing," she added hopefully.

Andi doubted that this discovery would end up being "nothing" and wondered how much of this decision was about protecting Jade Thompson's career. "This information is now on the record, Mayor. I have to write a report about this."

"I know. I was hoping you could approach it sympathetically and without sensationalizing it?" Jade asked.

"It's the *Gazette*, Mayor, not a tabloid. We don't 'sensationalize' anything," Andi snapped. She was not in the business of writing puff pieces. And however much she admired Jade, she would write the article she wanted to write.

"How does this affect the development?" Andi asked Ruth, who had been sitting silently.

"Until we know anything for sure about the remains, the development is on hold," Ruth said.

"Are the remains aboriginal?" Andi asked.

"Again, we don't know." Ruth sounded annoyed. "I understand there used to be a commune on the island. They could be connected to that. And there is a man living on the island today who was a draft dodger or something. Who knows who else lived there? We just don't know until the coroner's report is complete. I believe they are running lab tests at the moment. I want to know as much as anyone."

Ruth's voice was raised. It surprised Andi. Sure, it was inconvenient for the project to have stalled, but Ruth seemed emotional, and for a moment, her professional guard had dropped.

"I'd like to go out to Hope Island," Andi said. "Then I'll write an article after I have comments from the coroner."

Jade nodded. "Maybe you could go with Ruth and meet the archaeologist?"

The mayor's phone rang. Jade frowned at it, then answered.

"What is it?" A look of annoyance crossed her face.

"Tell them 'No comment'," the mayor snapped and hung up the receiver.

Jade was visibly angry. "The local TV station wants a comment about the discovery of human remains on Hope Island," she said. "Coffin Cove will be back in the spotlight for all the wrong reasons. It's exactly what I've been trying to avoid."

"Maybe I can help," Andi said. "I can run an in-depth article about the history of the island and the new collaboration with Three Cedars band. I'll focus on the new, positive future for the island, while preserving the First Nations heritage. Something serious, to show Coffin Cove has moved on from all the ugliness of the past."

Jade nodded. "I like it. You and Ruth set up a visit to the island, and I'll put together a press conference."

After discussing the details, Andi's interview with the mayor was over. Ruth stayed seated while Jade showed Andi out. As she opened the door, Jade said, "When does the new reporter start? I'm glad the *Gazette* is expanding. Good news for Jim. Maybe he's thinking about retiring?"

"Uh, I'm not sure," Andi lied. She left before Jade could ask anything else.

What was going on? Peggy had said the same thing about another reporter. Was she the last person to know about the new hire? Then another thought crossed Andi's mind. Had she got so detached from work that Jim needed to replace her?

As Andi walked back to the office, she turned this over in her mind. Should she be worried about her job?

CHAPTER FIVE

Virgil Bell was restless and couldn't get back to sleep. This was a regular occurrence — at least, it had been for the last few weeks. He'd been dreaming, he thought. He lay warm under the covers, not wanting to move, but unable to shake a feeling of unease. Had he forgotten to do something? He never used to fret like this. He'd been woken fully from his fitful doze by the flash and fizz of purple-and-green lights illuminating his one-room cabin. He watched the display from his bed, but in the end, he grunted and rolled over.

Mother Nature would not be ignored. Virgil pulled himself upright, wincing with the effort, and swung his legs over the side of his narrow cot.

It was still warm in the cabin. The wood stove glowed in the corner, and Virgil hesitated for a moment, contemplating the comfort of his sleeping bag, but then he pulled on the clothes he'd left folded on the chair next to his bed. He glanced at his clock. Four in the morning. It didn't feel like he had slept at all. He grabbed his jacket, pulled on his work boots, and headed outside before the light display ended.

He gasped involuntarily as he opened the door. The temperature had plummeted, and the cold hit his chest. This was something else that had changed. The cold never used to bother him. But now, the frozen air penetrated his lungs and wrapped around his old bones. He didn't move back inside, though. He loved this powerful theatre in the sky. A reminder to be humble, to remember the insignificance and pettiness of humanity.

Virgil lifted his hand upwards to the heavens. Sometimes, the electricity from the light display was so thick in the air, Virgil imagined he could grasp it in his hand and capture some of that raw energy. He wished he could. Every day now, his body reminded him of his seventy years on this earth.

It was almost time to leave Indian River and head back to Whitehorse. Virgil had been planning the shutdown for weeks. If the sharp chill in the air didn't persuade him, then the arrival of the aurora borealis always signified the finale of the season. He was down to the last few weeks at the gold-claim site.

Virgil sighed. He was conflicted. He wanted to press on and keep the machines working longer to extract just a few more ounces of gold. But he knew if he ignored all the warning signs — the nightly light display and the film of frost on the machinery at the start of most days now — then one morning, he'd be punished with snow, freezing temperatures and unpassable roads. Up here in the Yukon, you were only afforded one warning. And Virgil knew this was it. He was too old to risk being trapped up here for months. Not only that: the crew was restless. They'd been working eighteen-hour shifts throughout the summer, and they wanted to go home.

Virgil turned and went inside. He made coffee on the stove and shook out the sleeping bag. He ate a bowl of porridge, as he always did, and spent a few minutes checking his emails. The sleek laptop was the only nod to modern technology in his cabin. It always amused Virgil when he opened the lid and signed in. Who would think this old dog could have learned new tricks? There was a brief message from Janice. She wasn't one to gush. The message read simply: *See you for Thanksgiving dinner. I've missed you.*

Virgil smiled and sent a short reply. He'd missed her, too. He closed his laptop after checking the price of gold. Not bad this season. Then, after stacking the wood stove with logs to keep the place warm all day, he pulled on an extra layer of clothing and headed back outside. He walked the mile to the worksite, carrying his toolkit. It was still dark.

There was no sign of movement from any of the four trailers that housed his crew. Virgil snorted to himself. Hungover, all of them. He'd granted them two days off before the final push to the end of the season. He'd driven them into town, as that was the only guarantee they'd all come back to finish their work. He didn't mind. It kept the crew happy. They'd whooped and hollered as they'd piled into a truck and left a plume of dust behind them as they'd blasted along the dirt roads into Dawson City.

In the early years Virgil had lived in a trailer alongside the crew, but he had tired quickly of the camp drama and inevitable petty squabbles that broke out when men lived on top of one another. It wasn't Virgil's job to deal with all that bullshit. He wasn't their mother. They had to blow off steam, Virgil knew that. And most of them drank hard and indulged in a hot tub party at the Downtown Hotel, and some even paid for sex. He didn't mind sleeping in a hotel bed for a night, either.

It was a hard life, working a claim. Virgil remembered collapsing on his mattress on his trailer, mosquito-ravaged and exhausted. His first season, he had often fallen asleep immediately in his filthy overalls, then woken the next morning to the stench of dried sweat and bug spray.

Some men only lasted one season. Some begged for a ride out before the season was half over. But Virgil had been working with this crew for years now, and they were all experienced.

He'd dropped them off at a bar in Dawson City and had checked into a quieter motel a block away. Virgil had settled himself in the motel room with a beer and called Janice. She'd been pleased to hear from him and they'd chatted about work they planned to do on their log cabin when he got home. Janice had a daughter from her first marriage, and Julie was expecting her first baby. Virgil had smiled as Janice had talked excitedly about names and her plans for knitting baby outfits and shopping with Julie. After a while, they had ended their phone call, and he had settled back on the bed to watch some TV.

Virgil had flicked through the channels, trying to find something on TV to pass an hour. Finally, he'd found a news program reporting from Vancouver, and he'd watched and then listened as his eyelids got heavy. Then, just as he was slipping into a comfortable slumber, he had heard something that made his eyes snap open. He'd sat up and turned up the volume.

Footage showing a coastline he knew very well was on the screen. He had listened carefully until the end of the segment, hardly able to believe his eyes and ears. He'd pressed the button on the remote control and lain back on the bed, hearing only his breathing and muffled noises from the street.

How was this possible? Images from his past, things he'd thought he'd left behind, flooded into his mind. He'd clenched his fists tight, got up from the bed and paced the room. After a while, he had calmed down and taken some deep breaths.

Wide awake, Virgil had sat on the edge of the bed in the motel room and assessed his situation. He'd been born into a religious family, and although it had been years since he'd attended church, he was still a God-fearing man. Was this some kind of divine retribution? Young people these days called it karma. Whatever it was, God had decided that Virgil must make amends for his terrible choices all those years ago, before he could live out his last days of peace and happiness with Janice.

In the early hours of that morning, Virgil had found writing paper in the bedside drawer. It was embossed with the hotel's address, but he had scratched that out and used an address in Dawson City of an old friend and business associate. He had written three letters, making them as brief as possible. Then he'd lain back and managed a couple of hours of sleep. He'd set the wheels in motion. He had felt calmer, decisive. A situation that had seemed insurmountable the night before was now manageable. It was true, he thought, God only sent a man the burdens and trouble he could manage.

But it had weighed on his mind as he'd driven the crew home, and it was another reason he had slept so little last night.

Virgil knew a light would come on in the cookshack in half an hour, and no matter how badly their heads hurt, all the crew would be back at work on time.

The days were shorter now. The leaves on the few trees left on the pockmarked landscape were turning from bright yellow to a deep gold. After a long summer when the sun hadn't set until midnight, now the daylight hours receded as fall approached. Soon, the darkness would last until mid-morning and return a few hours later. He and his crew needed to work fast.

Virgil had been mining gold for nearly five decades, three of them as a gold-claim owner. The tiny cabin with the wood stove, cot, chair and camping stove had been his home during the season. He left every fall to wait out the harsh winter in Whitehorse, and returned every spring to grind away with his faithful crew, until the earth gave up its treasures. He was always excited to see those tiny nuggets and shavings of yellow appear as if by magic from the mud and grime.

Except it wasn't magic. Gold mining was not a romantic adventure. From the gold-rush days of old to present times, the Klondike rewarded planning and preparation, not risky gambles.

Gold mining had been good to Virgil. He'd made steady profits, enough to smooth out the boom-and-bust years, and he'd paid his crew well. But he was nearing the end. The constant ache in his hands and knees had elevated to burning pain, and the doctor in Whitehorse had warned him he was on his last stretch.

"Make sure next season's a good one, Virgil," the doctor had told him last year. "Your arthritis isn't getting any better, and you can't take stronger painkillers, not with all that heavy machinery."

Virgil had nodded and agreed, not wanting to argue with his old friend. This season had been good, but it wouldn't be his last. One more year. He had a plan.

Virgil owned seventy gold claims along the Indian River. He only mined half of them, but that was OK. He planned to sell the rest. It would be a turnkey operation for someone. Then he and Janice could enjoy their retirement and never worry about money.

Yes, gold had been good to him.

Finally, Virgil heard the murmur of men's voices in the distance and the glint of high-vis jackets appeared in the morning gloom. All of them, Virgil noted, pleased he had lost no one to the lure of a warm bed and throbbing hangover. He'd told them if they didn't appear for the last couple of days, they'd lose their bonus. His crew knew him well enough to believe it wasn't an idle threat.

Soon the ground rumbled and vibrated as the bulldozers and excavators ripped and teared at the dirt, the giant metal monsters wheeling and spinning and dumping cascades of earth, perfectly timed to keep the sluicer constantly spewing.

Virgil never stopped for a lunch break. There was always something to do, and now they were in a race with the weather. He and the crew worked until the sun dipped below the scarred land and the cold again penetrated Virgil's layers of clothing. His hands were stiffening up. He needed to call it a day soon. As the grey light darkened and clouds lowered, he waved for the crew to finish.

They were quiet as they headed back to the cookshack. The previous night had caught up with them. Virgil guessed lights would be out early that night.

By the time he got back to the cabin, the clouds had cleared. Maybe he'd get another light display later. After stoking up the wood stove, he emptied a jar of elk stew into

47

a pot and heated it on his camping stove. He ate it, washed the pot and his bowl, then stretched out on his sleeping bag. He reached out a hand to click off the bedside lamp, and instantly moonlight flooded the cabin.

Virgil turned on his side and closed his eyes. He needed to rest, but images of the past crowded into his mind. Finally, he lay in the dark, looking through the window, waiting for the aurora borealis to entertain him for another night.

CHAPTER SIX

"What the hell!" Walter swore. "Not again."

He was staring at the garbage scattered around the dumpsters at the back of the Fat Chicken pub, his establishment.

Someone had been rummaging through the bags of trash. Walter was certain it wasn't a hungry bear. They were smart animals, but even they couldn't manipulate the latch with a paw. No, the scavenger was definitely human.

What the hell was this town coming to? He'd asked Sergeant Matt Beaufort to investigate, but he was too busy. Or didn't care.

"Maybe it's someone looking for food," Cheryl said, from behind him. "They must be hungry."

"Hmmph," Walter grunted. He didn't feel as charitable as his wife, but that was because he had to clean up, not her. Instantly, he regretted even thinking this about Cheryl. She did her fair share. More, usually.

Walter took a deep breath. It wasn't the debris making him grumpy. His nerves were still affected by the violent death of a neighbour a few months before. Andi Silvers had discovered her mutilated body at this very spot. Walter still saw the bloody scene when he closed his eyes at night. His gaze left the strewn garbage, and he stared for a moment at the stairs leading to the apartment above the pub. Andi had never returned to live there. She needed a fresh start, she'd told Walter. He didn't blame her, but he missed the monthly rent payment.

Walter felt Cheryl squeeze his shoulder, and it brought him back to the present. Not for the first time, he sighed with relief that his wife had been spared the sight of the murdered body. He shuddered.

"Come on, I'll help you clear it up," Cheryl said.

Walter nodded, and the two of them carefully shovelled up the bigger pieces of garbage and then swept around the parking lot and the apartment stairs.

Cheryl tossed the last shovelful back into the dumpsters. "Walter," she said, "we need to decide about the apartment."

Walter noted the firm tone in her voice.

"I know," he said at last. He leaned on the shovel and looked at her. He'd been avoiding this conversation for too long.

"We need the money," Cheryl said simply. "The pub had a reasonable summer, but now the tourists have gone . . ." She trailed off and sighed before starting again. "The thing is, Walter, you know we still have a long way to go before we're out of debt. And if we ever want to retire, we need to do something now. This apartment is just sitting here empty." Cheryl looked at Walter. "We have to move on. It was horrible, what happened, but it wasn't our fault."

"I know." Walter said. "But every time I walk out here, I see . . . I see . . ." He choked on his words, unable to stop a wave of emotion.

"Oh, Walter." Cheryl dropped her broom and hurried over to hug her husband.

That made Walter feel worse, and he rested his head on Cheryl's shoulder, wishing he could stop his tears. *Damn it*, he thought. *This has to stop*.

"You're right," he said at last, in as normal a voice as he could muster. "It's all cleaned out and ready to rent. I've just been putting it off. I don't know why. But we'll find someone." *Someone who doesn't know what happened here*, he thought.

Cheryl stood back and smiled at him. "Thank you." She kissed him. "I had an inquiry from a gentleman. He's coming in to have a look in a couple of hours. Another reporter, isn't that funny? I suppose he's working for Jim. This place will be perfect for him. It will be good to have someone new in here. I'll have a walk round and make sure it's as clean as you say." She nudged Walter, teasing him.

He accepted it with a smile. Cheryl had it all worked out. It made Walter feel both comforted and guilty at the same time. Poor Cheryl. She'd shouldered the burden of his grumpy moods and the increase in work. After the murders in Coffin Cove, there had been a slight increase in tourism. People — horrible people — came to the town and tried "sightseeing" at the crime scenes.

Walter shook his head in disgust. What was wrong with people? Maybe it was one of those sick bastards rummaging in his garbage. Maybe having someone living in the apartment would help.

He thought about what Cheryl had said. Another reporter? The *Gazette* must be doing OK. Some consolation for Jim and Andi. They just got that office done up, too. New computers and everything. The *Gazette* was the only business thriving at the moment.

Cheryl interrupted his thoughts. "Are we finished? We need to get back to the bar."

"Right." Walter looked around. "Yes. We're done here." He kissed his wife. "Thanks. For renting out the apartment, I mean. And . . . well, everything really." He stopped, not wanting to let his emotions get the better of him again.

Cheryl waved her hand. "You old softie. Come on, let's go in. We'll have thirsty customers waiting for us."

"Yes. Now the only problem I have is stopping the little toerags who keep messing with the garbage." Walter fiddled with the catch on the dumpster. "I'll have to chain this up."

51

"Cameras," Cheryl said suddenly. "Why don't we put camera- and motion-lights out here? It would make us all feel more secure, right?"

"Yes. You're right, I'll do some research. And you know what?" A thought occurred to him. "Peggy Wilson was talking to me earlier about forming a Coffin Cove business association. You know, a group of us working together to improve things. We might get some proper security, clean up around here a bit."

Cheryl said nothing but gave Walter a troubled look.

"What? You don't think it's a good idea?"

"I do. But Peggy Wilson has already been grumbling to me. She is a troublemaker, Walter, you know that. She's all riled up about this new proposal about a resort on Hope Island, and Mayor Thompson working with Three Cedars band. They're going to build some kind of cultural centre out there, she says."

"You're kidding me!" Walter felt some of his anger return. "We all had to pay more in taxes for the fish plant development. The mayor's going to spend all that on the Indians?"

Cheryl looked at him, a shocked expression on her face. "Walter! What's wrong with you? We're all part of the same community, all of us equal! We're not going back to the bad old days."

Walter felt a pang of shame. He wasn't like Peggy. He didn't discriminate or have any hatred towards native people. Not like decades ago, when the pub that used to occupy the site of the Fat Chicken had had a separate entrance marked "*Indians Only*".

Still, he was struggling, damn it! All the tax breaks the natives got, and now all the money being spent on a development? The businesses in town needed that money. What the hell did Cheryl expect? It was she who was always nagging to get them out of debt!

Walter glared at his wife and flung his broom down. "It's time we thought about ourselves. Peggy's calling a meeting of this new association and I said she could have it here. I'm tired of being fucking poor!"

He lowered his head and refused to look at Cheryl as he stepped back into the pub. He expected her to call after him, but his wife was silent.

* * *

Cheryl opened the door to the apartment. She was relieved she had aired it out earlier and cleaned. She wished she had persuaded Walter to paint when Andi left, but it wasn't bad.

She stood back and allowed the prospective tenant to step in.

"It's sparse," she said, "But I'm sure we can find more furniture if—"

The man smiled and waved his hand. "This is perfect. I'll take it for a month to begin with."

"Fantastic!" Cheryl beamed at him. He was handsome, she thought. Tall and a little stooped. He had grey hair, but plenty of it, and a charming smile. Cheryl felt she might have met him somewhere before, but when he filled in the rental agreement, she didn't recognize his name.

"You said you're a reporter?"

The man signed his name with a flourish and smiled. "I am indeed."

"Are you working with the *Gazette*? It's a funny coincidence, but Andi Silvers, the last reporter Jim hired, she had this apartment before you."

"Andi Silvers?" The man hesitated just long enough for Cheryl to notice. "I've read some of her work. She's very good."

He handed her the rental agreement and a cheque and thanked her before he left.

Cheryl returned to the bar and gave Walter the form and the cheque, forgetting how annoyed she'd been earlier.

Walter smiled. "Good job," he said, while he tucked the cheque into the banking bag. He studied the form. "So he's working with Jim?"

Cheryl frowned. She hadn't realized until that moment, but the man hadn't answered her question.

CHAPTER SEVEN

Andi walked straight past the *Coffin Cove Gazette* office and headed towards the Fat Chicken. Tonight she would allow herself a glass of wine. Harry had promised to cook, and given his specialty was seafood, Andi intended to purchase the best bottle of white wine the Fat Chicken offered. It had been an interesting day. Andi was looking forward to telling Harry all about her interview with Jade Thompson and Ruth Cloutier.

When she got to the entrance of the pub, she studiously avoided looking at the parking lot and the set of stairs leading to her old apartment. She wasn't ready to face any ghosts. It would take many more hours in Hephzibah's healing garden before she was ready for that.

Walter was alone behind the bar, rubbing at pint glasses with a grubby rag, which Andi was sure was depositing more dirt than it was removing. He wasn't in the mood for conversation either, merely grunting in her direction and then wordlessly turning his back on her to fetch the bottle of wine.

He dumped it on the bar in front of Andi. She considered asking him for a cold one but decided against it. "Something wrong, Walter? You seem out of sorts."

He sighed deeply. "Look around you. What's missing?"

"I'm not sure. Have you been robbed?"

"No. What's missing are all my bloody customers! How am I supposed to run a business with no customers?"

"Oh. I'm sorry, Walter." Andi wasn't sure what to say.

"It's not your fault. It's that woman. She got all our hopes up, and now she's pouring our taxpayers' money into some scheme with the natives."

Not again. Andi took a deep breath. "Walter, I'm not sure you have all your facts straight. I've just been interviewing the mayor and I can tell you—"

Walter waved his hand. "Don't bother, Andi. I know what I'm talking about. And it's not just Hope Island, it's the Fish Plant too. There'll be some damn trendy bistro in there, and what'll that do to my business? Eh?"

Andi opened her mouth to answer, but it was too late. Walter was fully committed to his tirade and didn't allow her to speak.

"Oh, it's OK for you and Jim. Everyone's seen the new office, and now there's a new reporter. I can't even afford a relief barman so I can have a night off with my wife. Ever since you wrote those articles and gave Coffin Cove a bad name, our business has been going downhill!"

Shocked at Walter's outburst, Andi grabbed her bottle of wine, turned her back, and marched out. What the hell was Walter talking about? Didn't he remember the slaughtered body in his parking lot? Maybe *that* had put people off, or maybe people preferred drinking their beer out of clean glasses . . .

She blinked back tears. What was going on in this town?

By the time Andi got to Government Dock, the sun had slipped behind the cliffs, and the sky had turned silver. The air was chilly now, a reminder that October was already here, despite the deceptively warm daylight hours. A glow from the galley illuminated the deck of the *Pipe Dream*, and Andi could smell another wonderful meal under creation in the kitchen. She could also hear off-key singing, and she smiled, despite her mind in turmoil over Walter's harsh words.

"Thank goodness you chose fishing as a career," she said, standing at the galley door.

Harry Brown turned away from the frying pan on the stove. His face was deadpan, but Andi knew him now. She saw the telltale twinkle in those blue eyes.

He waved a spatula at her. "What do you mean?"

"If you had chosen singing as a career, you'd be sleeping under a bridge." Andi laughed.

"Oh, I thought you were glad I was a fisherman, because now you get access to all this great seafood," Harry shot back.

He was retired now, but still went sportfishing, and always had an abundant supply of fresh seafood. He was a tall, well-built man, intimidating to those who didn't know him. He had a serious face, and it was hard to read him, especially when he grew a beard in the winter. Andi recognized the similarities between Harry and Hephzibah. But while his sister chatted freely, Harry was a man of few words.

She still wasn't sure if they were in a relationship. She'd stayed on the boat with him several times, and he'd been gentle and loving, but had never made any demands on her. Yet he wasn't a man for casual relationships.

"God, no," Hephzibah had said when Andi had asked if there were many women in Harry's life. "Not since his wife. That was a disaster of epic proportions." For once, she had not been forthcoming with the details.

Andi knew all about disastrous relationships and didn't hold it against Harry. For now, she was happy to accept things the way they were.

"That wine in your hand?" Harry asked.

"Yes, but it's not cold."

Harry took the bottle from her and put it in the fridge. "We have a few minutes before the salmon is ready. Why don't you tell me what's bothering you? It's written all over your face."

He led her back out to the deck and pulled two canvas chairs together. Andi sat down, and Harry settled himself and turned his chair to face Andi directly. In between Harry checking on their meal, Andi told him all about her day, starting with Peggy Wilson and ending with Walter's angry rant.

When she finished, Harry disappeared into the galley and came out with two plates of grilled salmon and sautéed vegetables. "I caught the salmon," he said, "and you and Hephzibah are responsible for the veg."

They both ate, sitting in the half-light, listening to the waves splash against the moored boats. Andi felt the stress of the day retreat into insignificance. Somehow, the complications of her life diminished when she was gently rocked by the ocean, sitting opposite Harry's calming presence.

Harry sat silent for a moment after clearing away their plates. "I know Walter's going through a tough time. It's been hard, financially, for years. But after the murders . . ." His voice trailed off, and he reached over and took Andi's hand. "He shouldn't have taken it out on you."

"Oh, that doesn't matter." Andi had already got over her initial reaction. "But it's the first time I've noticed such hostility towards Three Cedars band. I know the town is a bit redneck—" she rolled her eyes — "but Peggy and Walter? They were nasty. Racist, even."

Harry got up and walked into the galley. "Oh, that attitude's always been here. It's not as on display as it used to be." He emerged with the bottle of wine and topped up Andi's glass. "It wasn't so long ago there was a separate entrance for the 'Indians' at the local pub, and businesses refused to employ native people. And if they did, they paid them far less than white employees."

"There are laws against that kind of thing now, thankfully," Andi said.

"Sure. But there are lots of ways to get around those laws, and the bigoted attitudes of people can't be legislated away. Have you ever seen a native bartender at the Fat Chicken? Or a native housekeeper working for Peggy?" Harry narrowed his eyes at Andi. "I don't see any native employees at the *Gazette* either."

"That has nothing to do with racism. That's solely because, until recently, the *Gazette* could hardly afford me. Well, actually—" Andi remembered something else from her day — "a couple of people keep mentioning a new reporter in town. But Jim hasn't said anything. Not to me, anyway."

"I haven't heard anything." Harry kept his gaze on Andi until she finally confessed.

"OK, I'm worried he might fire me," she said at last. "No, I'm serious," she said, seeing Harry start to smile. "I haven't been on top of my game for a while. Not since . . . not since . . ." She choked back sudden tears. "Sorry, I've drunk too much wine," she muttered, wiping her hand across her face.

"I don't think Jim is going to fire you," Harry said. "Since you started at the *Gazette*, the newspaper has increased its circulation. It's doing well."

"Maybe Peggy and Walter are right. We've made money from murder." Andi sniffed.

"You don't believe that, surely? You investigated tragic murders and brought to light some nasty secrets this town has been hiding for decades. Things are changing here in Coffin Cove, especially now Jade Thompson's the mayor, and some people are feeling insecure. Walter's a friend of mine, but he benefited from the last mayor's shady deals more than once, and Peggy? It's about time she got some competition. Don't give up, Andi. The town needs more people like you and Jade."

Andi was surprised at the forceful way Harry spoke. "Thank you, I'll talk to Jim tomorrow and—"

Her phone interrupted her.

"That's Jim now." She tapped the screen. "Jim, we were just talking about you." She pressed the loudspeaker button.

"Was it all good?" Jim's voice asked. "No, don't tell me. Did Harry cook you another seafood dinner? It's about time you invited me."

"You're welcome anytime, man," Harry said.

"Sorry to interrupt your evening, Andi, but I heard something on the wire that I think you should cover."

"Oh?" Andi felt a spark of anticipation as she smiled at Jim's old-fashioned newspaper jargon. "Actually, I have some interesting information too." She told him about the human remains on Hope Island. "I'm going out there with Ruth and the archaeologist."

Jim was silent for a moment. "Sounds good, but can you put that off for a bit? I have something else for you. Out on the West Coast, a gas station on the edge of the Pacific Rim, a cashier has been shot and killed."

"What?" Andi was paying full attention now. "Any more details?"

"Not much, but it's strange. Looks like a robbery on the surface, but apparently nothing was taken. Shooter rushed in, shot the cashier and left."

"OK, but this is out of our area."

"Yeah, I know, but we're expanding, Andi. Besides, I thought you could do with a day out of town. I had a beer with Walter earlier. He's feeling bad about sounding off at you."

"Oh, well . . . it doesn't matter." Andi's mind was already on her new assignment. "I'll head out tomorrow morning. See what I can find out."

"One other thing," Jim said, stopping her from disconnecting the call. "Homicide has been called in. I hear your friend Inspector Vega is no longer on the team. Is there a story there?"

"I don't know." Andi was acutely aware that Harry could hear the conversation. "I haven't heard from him for months."

"Hmm, OK. Get Harry to drive you tomorrow. It's warm here, but you never know what the weather'll be like over Sutton Pass."

Harry nodded his agreement.

"Call me when you get back."

They finished their conversation, and Andi turned off her phone.

"Is that OK?" she asked Harry. "Can you drive me tomorrow?"

"No problem," he said. "The story sounds important. We should get an early start, so you want to stay here tonight?"

Andi got up and kissed Harry. "I was hoping you would say that."

CHAPTER EIGHT

The sun was an orange smear between the dark grey ocean and the morning sky when Harry woke Andi. He was holding a cup of coffee.

She took it gratefully. Harry was used to early mornings from his commercial fishing days. He loved to watch the sunrise. The experience was an acquired taste for Andi.

They were walking down the dock to Harry's truck as a blaze of sunshine illuminated the cliff face. The watery blue sky promised yet another glorious fall day.

"It'll be different weather on the west side of the island," Harry had told Andi before they stepped off the *Pipe Dream*. "Bring a rain jacket."

They dropped into Hephzibah's Café, and she handed them two of her new breakfast sandwiches. She waved away Andi's cash. "Market research, no charge," she said.

They took the only road from Coffin Cove to the Island Highway, and after an hour of driving north, Harry turned west on Highway 4. Another hour and they passed through Port Alberni, a mill town in the middle of Vancouver Island. They crossed the Stamp River and spied a black bear fishing for salmon and then headed towards Sutton Pass on the winding remote road that led to the westernmost point of Vancouver Island and Canada itself.

Clouds shrouded the summit of Sutton Pass, and soon they were driving through drizzle. Andi glanced at the dashboard and saw the outside temperature had dropped over ten degrees. "I'm glad you're driving," she said, "I'd be nervous on this narrow highway."

"I'm glad to be here." Harry did not take his eyes off the road but smiled. "I'll get to see my intrepid journalist girlfriend in action."

His tone was light, but Andi caught the significance of his words. *Girlfriend.*

"You certainly will," she said, just as casually, but couldn't help grinning.

It had been a long time since Andi had been in a relationship. Andi and Inspector Andrew Vega had become close during the murder inquiry earlier in the year. He had been the senior officer from the Integrated Homicide Investigation Team sent to Coffin Cove to lead the murder investigations. Andi had to admit, if their circumstances had been different, their brief moments of intimacy may have developed into something more. But neither of them had seen a way forward for a relationship. Their chosen careers were pitted against each other. Andi knew she would always dig for a story, and because of that, Andrew would always have secrets. He'd said he trusted her, but it had seemed unworkable.

They had put none of that into words. They had just stopped contacting each other. If they had wanted a relationship badly enough, Andi thought, they would have worked harder at overcoming the obstacles.

Instead, Andi had found herself drawn to Harry, and with no conscious effort, they were now . . . a couple?

Andi studied Harry's profile as he drove, wondering what he thought about their relationship. He was a quiet man, not given to talking about his feelings. Calling her his "girlfriend" was the nearest he'd come to declaring his feelings for her. Suddenly Andi realized she was happy with the way things were. It was comfortable. Why complicate everything by overthinking?

The road descended, and they drove past rocky creeks with glacial water roaring over rocks. Twice, Harry slowed the truck to allow a black bear to cross.

"It's definitely remote out here." Andi checked her phone and found there was no cell service.

"Yep. Makes Coffin Cove seem like a crowded metropolis, right?"

An hour later and Andi's phone started buzzing. Jim had texted an update on the shooting. There was also a text from Mayor Jade Thompson.

"Jade's organized a public hearing on the Hope Island development on the Tuesday after Thanksgiving."

"A chance for the mob to rage at her?" Harry sounded half-serious, although he had a grin on his face.

Andi sighed. "I hope you're wrong about that. Hey, talking about mobs — that must be the crime scene."

"It's the only gas station out here. Must be the one."

They had arrived at the first major intersection on the west coast of Vancouver Island. The Pacific Rim Highway was signposted left and right. Andi had been there once before and knew that turning right would eventually take them to Tofino, a remote fishing town which had become famous in the seventies for being a gathering place for hippies, backpackers and surfers. These days, upmarket hotels and spas had replaced the hostels, and the provincial Parks and Rec department prohibited camping on the wild, windswept beaches. Turn left, and they would be in Ucluelet, a smaller village that still welcomed the West Coast commercial fishing fleet. A sign welcomed them to the Pacific Rim National Park and pointed to the tourist information centre. Police cruisers blocked the entrance to the gas station, and a group of people had gathered in front of the uniformed officers.

Harry parked the truck behind a low grey building, which Andi assumed was the Visitors' Centre.

"OK, what now?" Harry asked.

"I make a nuisance of myself until someone tells me what's going on to get rid of me. Or they throw me off the site. Either is possible."

"Sounds fair," Harry said. "I'll tag along in case you need . . . Well, I can hold your notebook or something."

They both hurried towards the crowd.

"Andi Silvers, what a pleasant surprise." The voice sounded as if the surprise was anything but pleasant. Andi turned round to see a sturdy woman with brown hair pulled back into a ponytail. She was wearing sunglasses, and it took a moment for Andi to recognize her because the glasses covered most of her face. Andi read the plastic identity card pinned to the woman's suit jacket.

"Sergeant Fowler, nice to see you again," she said, as sweetly as she could manage.

"Actually, it's *Inspector* Fowler now." Diane Fowler pushed her sunglasses back. "So what are you doing here? The *Gazette* expanding, or did you get fired again?"

Andi ignored Inspector Fowler's sarcastic remarks. "Just doing my job, Inspector, just like you."

"Not like me at all, Ms Silvers. I'm afraid your trip is a waste of time for the *Gazette*. The local TV station has already made an appearance, and we'll be issuing a press statement soon. You could have got all that information from Facebook."

Andi and Inspector Fowler had clashed during the last murder investigation. She had disapproved of Vega bringing Andi into his confidence, and although she'd helped Andi out of a dangerous situation, Diane Fowler had made it clear she didn't like or trust Andi.

Andi decided she'd get more information if she tried to cooperate. "I'll stay out of your way, Inspector. I'm just here to get an update on the situation and, of course, I'll wait for the official press release."

Diane Fowler pursed her lips but didn't argue. "Just stay behind the tape, please."

"Of course." Andi looked around. The gas pumps and convenience store were cordoned off. Crime-scene investigators dressed in white overalls and masks were kneeling on the floor of the store. A TV crew was setting up at the corner of the parking lot, and uniformed officers were attempting to keep a small crowd of curious onlookers at the edge of the parking lot.

Harry had disappeared. Andi took a picture with her cell phone and looked around for someone to talk to. She had no intention of waiting for the press release.

Inspector Fowler was busy with the crime scene crew. The BC coroner's vehicle was parked in front of the gas pumps, blocking the view of the convenience store. It would be hours before they released any information.

Andi walked back towards the parking lot and found Harry sitting on the steps in front of the Visitors' Centre. He was patting the shoulder of a thin teenage boy, and an elderly lady was handing them each a cup of tea.

Harry looked up and waved for Andi to join them. "Andi, this is Ryan. He works at the gas station and saw everything that happened." Harry patted the boy's shoulder again. "Drink your tea, son. You'll feel better."

The boy was pale, and his eyes were red-rimmed. His hands shook as he sipped his tea. He was wearing a T-shirt that was several sizes too big for him and jogging pants. Both items had the price tag still attached.

The elderly lady eyed Andi. "The poor boy had to give his clothes to the police. All covered with blood. Are you a reporter?"

"Yes, I'm Andi Silvers from the *Coffin Cove Gazette*."

"Hmm. Well, don't bother Ryan too much. He's had a terrible shock, and he's been here all night. The police wouldn't let him go home and wouldn't let me call his dad." She shook her head. "It's a terrible business. Poor Joyce. I can't believe it."

Andi nodded. "I'm so sorry. Did you know Joyce well?"

"Everyone did. Joyce has run the gas station for years. She took over from her father. She'd worked there since she was a girl. Everyone liked her. She was a gentle soul." The lady had a catch in her voice.

"Why don't you close up here?" Harry said. "Go home and have a cup of tea yourself. Would you like me to drive you?"

"Thank you, but no. My husband is coming to get me, but I didn't want to leave young Ryan here all by himself."

Andi sat beside Ryan. "Is there someone at home? Can we give you a ride?"

Ryan nodded but looked unsure. "My dad will be home later. He's a fisherman. He probably doesn't know about any of this."

"What's your dad's name, son?" Harry asked. "Or his boat's name? I used to be a fisherman too."

"His name is Pete Randall. His boat is the *Pacific Son*."

"Big aluminium seiner?" Harry nodded. "I know the boat."

Ryan looked more at ease.

"Are you finished with the police?" Andi asked. "You've already talked to Inspector Fowler?"

Ryan nodded again.

"OK then, let's get you home."

Ryan slid into the back seat of the truck. He directed Harry to turn left towards the small town of Ucluelet.

As he drove, Harry chatted with Ryan about fishing and living on the West Coast. The teenager warmed to Harry, and by the time they pulled up outside a small rancher with a neat front garden, they'd learned that Ryan and his dad had lived together since his mother left, the job at the gas station was his first, and he'd really liked Joyce Mayfield, the owner and the unfortunate victim of the shooting.

Harry turned round in his seat to look at Ryan. "My girlfriend here is a reporter for the *Coffin Cove Gazette*. I know she wants to ask you some questions, but only if you're OK with that. You should know that Andi understands some of what you're feeling right now. Did you hear about the murder cases in Coffin Cove earlier this year?"

Ryan nodded, his eyes widening.

"Andi found one of the victims. She also helped with the police investigation."

Ryan looked at Andi. "I'll answer your questions," he said. "But I don't want you to use my name. What if he comes back for me?"

In a second, Andi was back in that dark place just after she'd found the murder victim. She remembered the fear.

"I know how you feel. I promise I won't use your name, and you can only tell me what you feel comfortable with, OK?"

"OK then. Come in. Dad will be back soon."

Ryan led them into his home. The front door opened into a sparsely furnished living room. It was chilly, so Harry stacked logs in the wood stove in the corner, and said to Ryan, "Sit there, near the stove. You've had a shock and you're shivering. I'll make you something to eat. Where's the kitchen?"

"I'm not hungry," Ryan protested, but Harry ignored him and disappeared. In a minute, Andi could hear cupboard doors opening.

"Don't worry," she said to Ryan, "he'll make you a sandwich. I know you don't feel like it, but you must try to eat something."

"OK."

Andi perched in a chair opposite the boy. He looked so small and fragile. Andi wanted to hug him.

"Look, Ryan, it doesn't matter about answering questions. We just want you to be OK."

Tears were streaming down his face. "I can't believe she's gone! I tried to stop the bleeding, and then I had to call 911, so I left her to get my cell phone . . . What if I'd stayed with her? She might not have died!" Ryan's voice had risen, and he looked wild-eyed.

"Ryan, this is not your fault," Andi said. "You did everything you could."

"I wasn't even supposed to be there. Joyce called me in to do the late shift because she wanted to sort out some inventory. And she knows I always take more hours. But the man — he must have thought she was on her own, 'cos he ran in wearing a ski mask thing, and pointed the gun at me, but before I could do anything, he shouted her name—"

"He called her name, Ryan? Are you sure?" Andi couldn't help questioning him.

"Yeah, I had my hands up and everything, and I said, 'Take the cash, man,' just like Joyce always said — she said, 'Don't be a hero if we get robbed, just give 'em everything they want' — and he just looks at me and shouts 'Joyce' and she came running out the back room, and he just swings the gun round and *boom*! He fires, and she goes down and I scream, and then he's gone and I'm on the floor — and there's blood everywhere — so much blood . . ."

Ryan covered his face with his hands and started to cry.

"It's OK, son." Harry came into the room with a plate of toast. "Here, eat this."

"Th-thanks." Ryan wiped his face with his hands. Harry disappeared again and came back with a roll of paper towel and handed it to the boy. He wiped his face and blew his nose noisily.

"Ryan, I know the man was wearing a mask, but do you think you recognized the man's voice? Or anything about his clothes or body shape?" Andi asked. She waited as Ryan chewed on a piece of toast.

He shook his head vigorously. "No. And I didn't see his vehicle, but I'm sure it was a diesel truck because I heard it pull up."

"Was there anyone who didn't like Joyce?" Andi asked. "Was she having any trouble with anyone? Someone in her family, maybe? It sounds as if the man knew her."

"No, everyone really liked Joyce. She was nice to everyone, even the rude customers. And she lives on her own. She doesn't have . . . *didn't* have a family. Her father owned the gas station, but he died before I was born."

"What about the gun?" Harry asked. "Do you remember what type of gun it was?"

"It wasn't a rifle," Ryan said. "I know those guns, 'cos my dad hunts. It was a handgun."

"Hang on." Harry pulled out his phone. He tapped on the screen and then held it out to Ryan. "Was it this one?"

"Nope. It wasn't a Glock. I know what they look like."

"What about this?"

It took three tries before Ryan nodded.

"Yes. I'm sure it was that one."

"Well done," Harry said. "This could really help. We'll make sure the police get this information."

Just then, they heard footsteps outside and the door burst open. An older version of Ryan rushed in.

"Ryan! Are you all right? Did I hear right? There's been a shooting?"

"Dad!" Ryan said and burst into tears again.

"Come here." Ryan's father went over to his son and pulled him into his arms.

"Thank God you're all right."

They hugged, and then Ryan's father looked up. "You brought him home? Thank you, do I know you?"

Harry nodded. "We've met before. Fishing. I own the *Pipe Dream*. Harry Brown."

"Right. Thanks for looking after my boy. Both of you. Do you know what happened?"

Andi explained.

"That's terrible! Do they have the person who did this?"

"Not yet. Ryan here has been really helpful, and I am sure the police will want to speak to him again." Andi got up. "Ryan, we'll be going now. You have been really brave. I know it's hard at the moment, but believe me, it gets easier with time."

Ryan looked better. He thanked them both and his father stood up and shook their hands. "Thanks again," he said. "What a horrible thing to happen. I can hardly believe it. We're a small community, nothing like this has happened before."

Harry and Andi walked to the door.

"Wait a moment," Ryan said suddenly. "There was something weird the other day." He stood up and rushed out of the room. A moment later he arrived back, looking excited.

"A man came in a couple of days ago — Wednesday, I think, and he talked to Joyce. I couldn't hear anything, but they were talking for about twenty minutes and Joyce was upset when he left."

"Were they arguing?" Andi asked. "And did you know him, or had you seen him before?"

"They weren't arguing, I don't think. I had to serve someone else, but I heard Joyce saying something about not wanting to get involved. I think that's what she said."

"Did she tell you who it was? Or what it was about?"

"No, she wouldn't say anything, but he left a business card with me. He came up to the counter and handed it to me, and said to give it to Joyce. And I meant to, but I forgot and just shoved it in my pocket. I was going to give it to her yesterday, but I'd changed my jeans and it was still in the pocket."

"So you got a good look at him?" Andi asked. "Do you think it could be the same man?"

"No, this guy was way taller. But he could have been doing a recce for someone else, right?" Ryan looked excited.

"Do you still have his details?" Harry asked.

Ryan held out a crumpled card. "Will you give it to the police for me?"

Harry shook his head. "Better it comes from you, and maybe we shouldn't touch it."

Ryan looked horrified. "Shit . . . sorry, because of fingerprints?"

"Don't worry, Ryan," Andi said. "Just give it to the police. They will want to talk to you again and take a formal statement. You can describe this man and give them the card. But if this man was connected with the shooting, I don't think he'd leave a business card."

Ryan looked disappointed.

"Here, let me take a picture." Harry pulled out his phone. "We can tell the inspector. She can look into it. You never know, right? And we can send her the information about the gun too. Great job, Ryan. I bet Joyce would be proud."

"Thank you," Ryan whispered, tearing up again.

His father gave Ryan's shoulder a squeeze. "These folks need to be on their way now. We'll wait for the police. You'll be all right, son."

Andi and Harry walked out to the truck and got in. Harry started the engine.

"We pass the gas station on the way back," he said. "Do you want to stop and talk to Fowler?"

Andi sighed. "No. But I should forward those pictures. I'll call the local detachment and get an email address or something."

She made the call. In minutes, she was scribbling down an email address for the investigation team.

"Are you going to write up anything Ryan told us?"

Andi shook her head. "No. I'll be patient and wait for the press release. If I printed something he said, it would just piss off Fowler. I'll email the pictures and let her interview Ryan again."

"Wow," Harry said. "Is this a brand-new, responsible Andi Silvers?"

Andi laughed. "Not at all. I just felt for that boy. I know what it's like . . . He just doesn't need the extra drama of seeing his name in print. Not yet, anyway."

Harry took a hand off the steering wheel and squeezed her leg. "Straight home, then?"

"Home," Andi agreed. "But give me your phone. I should send those pictures before we lose cell-phone service."

Harry passed it over and Andi scrolled through his pictures. Then she stopped, looking at the phone in horror. "Is this the business card?" She held the phone up for Harry to see.

"Yep. Do you think that guy might be involved? It was weird, him coming in before and upsetting Joyce. Andi?"

Andi couldn't stop staring at the phone.

"Andi? Do you think he's involved?" Harry repeated.

"No," Andi said finally, hardly able to get the word out.

"Why not?" Harry slowed the truck and pulled over. "What's wrong?"

Andi pointed at the phone. "This business card. The name on it?"

"Bob Hinton," Harry read. "Do you know who that is?"

"Yes," Andi said. "Bob Hinton is my father."

CHAPTER NINE

"Why would your father want to interview Joyce Mayfield?"

"I have no idea," Andi answered.

She really didn't. Andi wasn't sure what to think or feel.

The rest of the journey home from the West Coast was quiet. Harry, maybe sensing Andi needed time to collect her thoughts, didn't bombard her with questions. Andi was grateful.

That evening, Hephzibah baked a steak pie with veggies from the garden and Harry stayed for dinner. Hephzibah chatted about her day in the café until Harry finally asked the question that Andi had been asking herself.

"You've never talked about your father," Hephzibah said. "I didn't know he was a journalist too."

"He was quite famous in his day," Andi answered. "He interviewed the rich and famous, politicians, celebrities . . . until he was fired over an article he published about — oh!" Something was in the back of her mind, but she couldn't quite grasp it.

"What?" Hephzibah asked. "What's wrong?"

"Nothing. I don't know. Anyway, he was fired, and then he started drinking heavily. My parents divorced and I haven't seen him much since Mum's funeral."

"Why do you call him Bob? Oh, sorry, that's personal." Hephzibah caught herself.

Andi smiled. "It's OK. He wanted me to call him Bob. He was . . . eccentric? Arrogant? Both, I think. He didn't really plan on having kids, at least, that's what my mother told me. When they met, they were both really focused on their careers, so when I came along, Bob was resentful of the energy and money it took to be a parent. My mother was a talented artist, she could have been great, I think, but Dad — Bob — didn't want anyone else to get any attention, and he certainly would not compromise his career to help look after me." Andi sighed. "I tried hard to please him. He was furious when I said I wanted to be a journalist. The sad thing is, I wanted to be like him."

Andi lapsed into silence. She tried to push thoughts of her family, and her father in particular, to the back of her mind.

"So, what is Bob doing here?" Harry asked his question again.

"I really can't think of any reason he'd even be out West," Andi said. "He used to say that nothing interesting happened out West, it was all hippies and loggers, and nobody in Ottawa gave a shit."

Harry grunted. "He's not wrong about that. The Feds don't really care much about us out here, and they do not know what we do. The last minister for fisheries and oceans couldn't identify a salmon. He made the mistake of visiting a fish processing plant in Steveston and they asked him to identify different species of fish. He couldn't do it. We never saw him again."

Andi laughed, and asked Hephzibah for more steak pie, hoping to divert the conversation away from her father.

After dinner, Harry drove his truck back to the dock. Andi was sleepy, but she wanted to get her article drafted while the information was fresh in her mind.

"Drop me here," she said when they got to Main Street. "I'll go to the office for an hour or so and then walk back to the boat when I'm done."

"I might be in bed already." Harry yawned. "Don't work too hard."

Andi wandered down the street towards the office. It was quiet, apart from the faint hum of chatter from the Fat Chicken every time the door swung open.

Andi avoided the pub. She didn't want to see Walter. It bothered her that anyone would think she welcomed tragedy, so she had something to write about. *Profiting from murder.* She knew first-hand how a violent death affected everyone involved. It was like dropping a stone in a still pond. There were ripples of destruction long after the first splash.

On the other hand, holding back information or making the truth more palatable didn't serve anyone. Andi thought about Ryan. She hoped the boy was all right. It had taken her a long time to be able to close her eyes and not see the mutilated body of the murder victim she had discovered. Andi couldn't imagine the trauma of witnessing a fatal shooting.

But there were details about this shooting that made no sense to Andi. It wasn't a robbery, unless a vehicle had distracted the shooter outside before he'd had a chance to take anything. But the shooter wasn't flustered or in a panic, according to Ryan. He'd had the opportunity to shoot Ryan but had taken his time to call for Joyce and wait for her to appear before killing her in cold blood.

And then there was her father's card. Andi didn't believe in coincidences. There was something more to this shooting, and she was determined to investigate further.

Andi was buried deep in thought, planning her article, when voices startled her.

Light from an open door illuminated the street. It was the office door, and two men were standing in the doorway. Andi could hear laughter and recognized Jim's voice. What was he doing here? The other man was in shadow, but something was familiar about his outline.

Something made Andi hold back. What was Jim up to? She wished he would tell her.

The two men shook hands, and Jim turned to switch off the light and lock the office door. The other man moved away and, for a second, his face was in the light.

Dad! What the hell are you doing here? Andi thought. *And how does Jim fit into all of this?*

CHAPTER TEN

A waitress hovered over Inspector Andrew Vega as he scanned the laminated menu one more time. "Ready to order?"

"The Billy Burger," he said unenthusiastically, "and a coffee. Black, please."

"Fries or salad?"

"Salad . . . No, fries." Vega changed his mind. What was the point of a salad when he was already coating his arteries with fat from the burger? Plus, the salad at Billy's Diner was probably a couple of limp lettuce leaves and dried-out cucumber slices. So fries it would be. Vega sighed. Not for the first time, he was regretting this impulsive trip.

The waitress made no acknowledgment of his change of mind, just scribbled on her notepad and turned away.

Vega had seen the faded sign for Billy's Diner a few kilometres before the turn-off. He'd been driving for five hours today, and the last two days he'd been on the road at dawn and hadn't stopped until dusk. He hadn't much idea about where he was going, but he'd never explored the north of the province before, and so he'd programmed "the Yukon" into his GPS and thrown warm clothes into the truck, as well as chains and safety equipment if the weather turned bad. He was prepared, even if the road trip was last minute. This far north, it could snow in the fall. That was the extent of his research. Other than throwing a couple of granola bars on the passenger seat, Inspector Andrew Vega, Master of All that was Orderly, was winging it.

He'd enjoyed the first two days of driving. Leaving the city in his rear-view mirror, he'd felt a sense of freedom, and the weight of work easing from his shoulders. He'd stopped when he felt like it, responding to his growling stomach. On planned road trips, Vega usually had carefully packed coolers full of the healthy food options he favoured. This time, he didn't care. He pulled off the road when he saw the neon lights for a motel and fell into bed, barely noticing the cheap sheets and thin towels.

It was three days in now and his eyes were tired.

He'd taken the exit and parked in front of a wooden, low-slung building. A large sepia poster depicting a cowboy announced that Billy's Diner had been operating since 1870, but the style of construction suggested 1970. Inside, the smell of stale grease hung in the air, and for a moment Vega had been tempted to change his mind and keep driving until he reached Whitehorse, but before he could back out a waitress was already looking at him expectantly.

"Just for one, please," he'd said, and the waitress had led him to a booth.

Vega pulled out his phone and checked his messages. Nothing. There was cell-phone service, and the ringer was on. He held it for a moment, contemplating making a call, then changed his mind. This wasn't the place. He slipped the phone back in his pocket and glanced around the diner. Most of the tables and booths were filled with older couples or men dressed in overalls. A TV played soundlessly in the corner, a rerun of a baseball game. Nobody paid it any attention. There was the low hum of conversation, interrupted only by the clang and clatter of the kitchen.

Andrew Vega was suddenly lonely. Nothing about this trip was planned. He rarely took vacation time, and when he did, his excursions were meticulously researched. When he'd opened his mouth and requested the time off, he'd been as surprised as Superintendent Sinclair. She'd looked at him steadily for a moment, and before he could retract his words, she'd said quietly, "Andrew, that's a good idea. Take some time to recharge."

And then it was too late. Another two weeks away from work. He'd cursed himself. It wasn't the outcome from this meeting he'd intended. Three months before, they had suspended him from his position at the Integrated Homicide Investigative Team, pending an investigation into his last case. Inspector Vega, it was alleged, had broken with protocol and failed to follow procedure. He'd also disregarded an order from a senior officer. On the other hand, Vega's actions had undoubtedly saved lives, so he was expecting to be reinstated, albeit with a slap on the wrist. But one officer had been shot, and the suspect had died too.

Sinclair had been direct. "I would have done the same thing," she'd said. "But there are consequences for your actions, that's just how it works."

Vega thought Sinclair had sent him in because she knew he wouldn't hesitate to do the right thing, even if it meant breaking the rules and damaging his career prospects. At least, he hoped that was the reason, and not because she'd needed a fall guy for when things went wrong. When he'd asked for leave, he'd expected her to say no, and explain the department needed him back. But she hadn't, and it was her calm agreement for him to be away even longer that had rattled him. He knew he wasn't indispensable. No one was. But he felt out in the cold, and it was taking a toll.

He'd been childish, he thought. Demanding a holiday instead of jumping straight back in. All he'd done was put the team under more strain. And here he was, in the back of beyond, wishing his phone would ring, and Sinclair would call him back and cancel his leave.

It wasn't just a phone call from Sinclair he was attempting to conjure up, if he was being completely honest with himself. He was hoping to hear from Andi Silvers. She was a damned interfering reporter who made a habit of impeding his investigations. She was sarcastic, stubborn, frustrating, and she'd got right under his skin. And he couldn't stop thinking about her. It would have been a relationship doomed to failure from the start. She was a journalist — an investigative journalist — and he would never be able to talk about his work.

Both he and Andi were committed to their careers. Neither of them was very good at compartmentalizing their lives. It had been a good thing to abandon hopes of a future together. Besides, that probably wasn't even an option now. They hadn't spoken in a while. Should he have called? How did these things work?

"Your burger." The waitress interrupted his thoughts when she set a plate down in front of him.

"Oh, thanks. Looks delicious."

It really is, Vega thought. He ate hungrily, finishing all the fries. The waitress topped up his coffee and took his empty plate. Vega refused dessert, but sat there, his hands cupped around the mug of coffee, wondering what to do next.

Outside, the October sun was dipping lower in the sky. Vega tried to feel enthusiastic about his trip. What was the use of obsessing about Andi? Might as well make the most of this vacation. When was the last time he took time off? He'd never visited the Yukon before. He'd make the most of this and do some exploring. Get his head straight, and he'd be ready to dive back in.

Vega beckoned to the waitress again. "You know, I've changed my mind. I'll have a piece of that apple pie." He smiled. "And is there somewhere to stay around here? A hotel or something?"

"You'd do better to drive on another few miles and stay at Whitehorse," the waitress said, smiling back. "Not many places to stay around here. But be careful. It's getting cold. Roads might be icy."

Before Vega could ask her any more, her attention was caught by a couple waiting to be seated. She settled them in the booth next to his and went to fetch his apple pie.

"Much to do in Whitehorse?" he asked as she set it down in front of him.

"If they've had a fall of snow, you could go dog sledding, it's—"

Raised voices from the adjoining booth drowned out her next words.

The waitress rolled her eyes and mouthed "*Sorry*" at Vega, before walking over to the booth and asking loudly if they would like coffee.

Vega focused on his apple pie. But it was impossible not to hear the argument between a man and a woman who Vega assumed was his wife or partner. The angry voices got louder as soon as the waitress left their table. They seemed to be arguing about domestic chores.

Vega ate faster. Time was getting on and he felt uncomfortable being an unintended audience for the warring couple. He stood up and felt in his pocket for his wallet. As he did so, Vega took a quick look. He couldn't help it, he supposed. Being nosy was all part of the job.

He couldn't see the man's face — he had his back to Vega — but the woman had a thin, pinched face, with deep lines around her mouth. It was impossible to tell her age. Her brown hair was pulled back into a ponytail, and she had small dark eyes that darted back and forth, as if she were looking for a way to escape. She was dressed in a heavy sweater and jeans. As she nervously fiddled with a frayed cuff, Vega caught sight of telltale scabs on her forearm.

It made sense then. The man was angry with her. She was trying to make excuses for something Vega heard, but he knew the story. The woman reminded him of the pale, ghostly figures that wandered the streets of East Vancouver, many of them homeless and most of them addicted to something. The man's frustrated reaction was familiar too. Vega had met many weary relatives of drug addicts at their wits' end, their patience and compassion beaten down in the face of this insidious disease.

Vega walked past them and saw the man had clenched his fists. He hesitated, and the man seemed to sense Vega looking at him. He glanced up and met Vega's eye, then relaxed his hands.

The man was older than the woman. Maybe he was her father? Drugs ravaged human bodies, and it was possible this woman was considerably younger than she appeared.

The woman leaned across the table and muttered something to the man. He sat back in his chair as the waitress delivered two cups of coffee.

Vega moved on. It wasn't his business. Besides, he was on vacation. He stood by the till.

"I'll be with you in a moment, sir," the waitress called.

Vega paid his bill and left a generous tip in exchange for a hotel recommendation in Whitehorse. Minutes later, he was on the road, hoping to reach his destination before the gloomy light faded into pitch black.

* * *

The waitress had earned her tip. The hotel facade was dated, but Vega was pleasantly surprised to see the room was spotless, although it also needed updating. He watched some TV, and leafed through the brochures, making a mental note of places that looked interesting.

He took a shower, drying himself with a threadbare towel, and lay on the bed. Maybe this trip was a good idea after all.

It had started to snow when Vega arrived in Whitehorse. By the time he had checked in, the flakes were coming down thick and fast, and sticking. Vega wasn't used to snow. Not like this. The wet flurries on the West Coast soon turned to slush, usually after causing chaos, and it was only on the ski slopes of the mountains that Vega had experienced a snowfall of more than a few inches. He felt a childish excitement. What did it matter? He was here on holiday, and why not play in the snow for a few days?

The clerk at the front desk had handed Vega a pile of brochures and maps.

"Lots to do here," he'd said cheerfully. "And if the forecast is right, you can go dog sledding."

Vega propped his head up with a pillow and flicked through the brochures, making plans in his mind. The clerk had reminded him it was Thanksgiving weekend, so his plans for recreation might have to wait a day or two. Most tourist places would be closed. But he had a few pointers for tomorrow.

"Fireweed Bookstore," the clerk had told him. "They have a coffee shop. They'll be open for breakfast, too. Have you got plans for Thanksgiving dinner?"

Vega hadn't even thought about it.

"Here." The young man had handed him a leaflet. "It's for the Klondike. Best food in town, and Julie, the chef, always does a superb Thanksgiving turkey. Reasonable price, too."

Vega had thanked him and stuffed the leaflet in his pocket.

"And another thing, sir, you'll need some suitable footwear."

"Oh?" Vega had looked down at his hiking boots. They had seen better days.

The manager had handed him another brochure. "These guys will rent you some boots. Much better for walking in the snow. And if you need proper gloves and a jacket, they can fit you out with those too."

Vega made a mental note to get better prepared. It seemed there would be plenty to keep him occupied over the next few days. Just what he needed, he thought as he drifted off to sleep. Putting fifteen hundred kilometres between him and work would do him the world of good.

CHAPTER ELEVEN

"Hey, Buddy, what's up, boy?"

Janice bent down to scratch behind the dog's ears. She was rewarded with a gentle headbutt and a whine, before he stood again fixated by the closed door, the ominous rumble of his growl echoing around the log cabin's vaulted ceiling.

"Is it a bear?" She checked out of the window but saw nothing except the gravel driveway and her truck. That meant nothing, of course. Just because she couldn't see any wildlife, wolves, bears and coyotes were still out there, obscured by the dense bush surrounding her homestead. Usually, they avoided any place inhabited by humans, unless they were hungry or sick.

Janice knew what Virgil would say. "*Get that gun out and keep it loaded by the door.*"

It was the last but one thing he always said to her when he left every spring. Then he'd kiss her and say, "Love you, girl," before getting in the truck and driving away as Buddy chased him, barking wildly until the truck disappeared down the rutted track out to the Alaskan Highway.

Janice never got her gun out. She'd lived out here in her family's log cabin, in the shadow of Grey Mountain, for almost her entire life. She was used to the wildlife.

She stood for a moment, scanning the perimeter of her property, looking for the slightest movement. Nothing. The tall firs that edged the paddock could hide a bear, and she'd never see it.

A gust of wind caught the wooden door of the barn, banging it shut, making Janice jump and Buddy bark.

"Just the wind, silly," she said, more to herself than the dog.

She grabbed a jacket from a peg, shoved her feet into gum boots and opened the front door. Buddy ran out, barking, towards the barn. Janice followed him. She pulled open the barn door, scraping it across the gravel and stood in the doorway.

"Look, nothing here." Just the old tractor covered in a tarp and a heap of Virgil's tools in the corner.

She pushed the door closed. The latch was hanging from one rusty nail, so Janice hauled a couple of logs from the woodpile and leaned them up against the door to stop it rattling in the wind.

Buddy had lost interest and was chasing leaves in the driveway. Janice smiled. It was easy to get spooked by the wind out here.

She stood for a moment, watching the clouds scuttle across the sky. It was getting colder. An ominous band of dark grey was gathering around the mountain. A dump of snow was entirely possible, and then the Yukon might be in the grip of winter weather for six months or more. Janice whistled to the dog and started back inside.

"Keep guard there, Buddy," she said. She left the elderly terrier whining with his nose pressed against the glass and went back to the warmth of her kitchen.

It was her favourite place in the house. She sat at the table with her hand around a mug of tea, breathing in the sweet aroma of her baking, just as she had done when her grandmother was alive.

The cabin was quiet, just the odd creak or groan from the wooden logs as they expanded and contracted with the changes in temperature. Janice found these familiar noises comforting, as if the generations of her family who had lived here before her were reminding her they were still there, keeping a watchful eye.

This home held so many happy memories. Janice's own childhood, and then Julie growing up. Janice's daughter had spent endless hours watching her mother bake. Janice was sure it was the reason Julie loved running the Klondike restaurant in town.

Janice had started the restaurant after Julie's father had died in a logging accident. He'd had no insurance, but his logging colleagues and local families had put their hands in their pockets and made sure Janice had enough money to survive those first terrible years after she lost her husband. She had used some of that money to invest in the Klondike, and by constant hard work and sheer force of will, she had made a success of it.

But now she was in her sixties and retired. Julie had been running the restaurant for five years and was getting ready to welcome her first child into the world.

Janice smiled. In three months, she would be a grandmother. A new chapter of her life. And who would have thought at her age she would have found romantic love again?

The wind whistled and pulled her out of her thoughts. Despite her many blessings, today she felt unsettled and anxious. She was as jumpy as Buddy. It wasn't the wind. What was she worried about? She couldn't put her finger on it. But something didn't feel right.

Virgil would be home the day after next. It was always a transition, for both of them, to share space with another human being after being alone for months. It took her a while to get used to a warm body in bed with her, and the sound of his breathing.

And this time, well, it was going to be different. Virgil had emailed to say he was only staying for a few days before he had some family business to sort out.

Virgil had a sister, and he occasionally wrote to her. Janice wondered if he wrote about her. Them. Whether he told his sister about the life they had together, living as man and wife for years and the way he treated Julie as if she were his own daughter. They'd been together so long, Janice couldn't imagine Virgil with a past, relatives she'd never met and friends she'd never know.

Maybe this was what was bothering her. Was she jealous? She didn't think so. But she wondered why he didn't suggest she go with him to visit his mysterious sister.

I need to see my lawyer, he'd emailed, *and there are some things I need to fix from my past. When I get home, I'll tell you all about it.*

I only have one year left up here on the claim. Then I'll be home for good.

I love you. V.

Janice had read and reread the email. Virgil loved her. She knew that. But he wasn't a man who readily declared his feelings.

She chastised herself. *Fancy being bothered because a man tells you he loves you! You're behaving like a teenager.*

As for Virgil's past, well, they'd got together when they were both long in the tooth. Of course he had a past. She did too. Virgil had told her the important stuff, she was sure.

Last spring, before Virgil left for the claim, they'd sat on the back deck, huddled under a blanket and breathing the cool, fresh air.

"Marry me," Virgil had said so quietly, Janice wasn't sure she'd heard him correctly.

"What? Why?"

A part of her, the young girl in her, had felt a surge of emotion, but looking at Virgil's serious face, she had been more worried than excited.

"Why?" she had asked again. "Aren't we OK as we are?"

"Yes. But I want you to be secure. If anything happens to me."

"What's going to happen to you?" Janice had kept her tone light. "You're a tough old goat. You'll live for ever." She had nudged him, but he hadn't laughed.

"I want to live my days out with you and the kids. I need to know you will all be OK. If I'm here or not."

He had bowed his head and whispered, "I want to marry you. I want to sell the claims and live the rest of my life with you here. Or anywhere you want to be."

When he had looked at Janice again, she'd seen tears in his eyes.

"Of course I'll marry you," she'd said.

Now Janice rubbed her hand absently on the surface of the wooden table, as if drawing reassurance from the memories of her grandmother and mother giving out advice with tea and cake, as she did these days for Julie.

Maybe I just don't like change, she thought. Her relationship with Virgil was easy and familiar. Safe. Maybe she just didn't want anything to spoil that.

"Ridiculous." Janice said the word out loud and stood up. She'd get on with planning her Thanksgiving meal and stop this silly fretting. Julie had promised her a pumpkin pie and she planned to pick it up tomorrow when she did her last grocery shopping before Virgil got home. She pulled a notebook and her grandmother's recipe book from a drawer and settled down to make her list.

Two hours later and it was dark. Janice finished cleaning up in the kitchen and looked around for something to do next. She wasn't hungry, and it was too early to go to bed. She thought about emailing Virgil, but decided against it. What would she say that couldn't wait until he was home? Besides, he'd be busy closing down the claim. Then he had to stay over in Dawson City to meet his buyer and make sure he paid the crew before he drove home.

Virgil had worked so hard all these years. Janice knew he made a good profit working his claims. He shared little about his business but didn't hide it either. He kept his accounting records in the small bedroom, which used to be Julie's. He even used Julie's old desk. His files were neatly stacked on a bookshelf, and Janice left all his unopened mail in a box for

Virgil to read when he got home. It never occurred to her to snoop.

Eager to distract herself, Janice went upstairs and hauled the eiderdown off their bed. She picked up her book from the bedside table and went downstairs into the living room. They didn't have a TV, just an old-fashioned record player and a collection of vinyl records. Instead of tossing and turning alone in bed, she'd build a cozy fire, and read and cuddle with Buddy.

She was relieved to see there were plenty of logs and kindling beside the fireplace. The wind had died down a little, but black clouds hung low, threatening snow or maybe a thunderstorm.

Janice didn't close the blinds. She loved to watch storms as they reverberated around the valley, crashing off the mountainside and lighting up the Yukon River.

She built a fire in the grate, and soon the small room was warm and snug. Janice poured herself a glass of wine and curled up on the sofa, Buddy's head resting on her thigh. She flicked through her book but set it down after a while, content to gaze at the flickering firelight. Her thoughts wandered between Virgil and Julie, and her grandchild on the way. Before long, her eyelids drooped, and she drifted into slumber.

Janice woke when she felt Buddy stiffen beside her. The dog jumped off the sofa and ran towards the front door. She sat up.

The fire had died down to glowing embers and Janice shivered. Outside, it was pitch black.

Buddy whined and stood trembling in the hallway, ignoring Janice when she called his name.

A bear?

Then she heard a scraping sound outside, like somebody or something scuffing across the porch. Buddy was in a frenzy now, alternating between a rumbling growl and loud barking.

Damn it. Virgil was right. She needed the gun. If a bear was up on the porch . . . Well, she'd heard stories before about sick and hungry bears breaking into houses.

Janice hauled herself off the sofa, groaning as she stretched out her stiff limbs. The gun cabinet was in the dining room, beyond the kitchen. She only used her dining room for special occasions. At the moment, the table was covered with all her canning jars.

Where was the gun cabinet key? She thought she remembered putting it in the drawer with all the fancy silver cutlery that had belonged to her grandmother. Virgil would be annoyed with her when she told him. But she imagined him laughing when she told him how spooked she'd become by a racoon scuffling on the porch.

But for some reason, Janice knew it wasn't a raccoon. She stood for a second in the hallway, a chill descending on her, despite the blanket around her shoulders.

Buddy was barking frantically now. Janice needed to move.

Get the gun. Get the gun. Get the gun.

The phrase went around in her head as she saw the iron door handle move. Why hadn't she locked the door?

"*Because I never lock the door,*" she'd laughed to Virgil.

Get the gun. Get the gun.

She forced her legs to move, as the door swung open, and Buddy launched himself at the blackness.

Janice ran.

Behind her, she heard a crack and then another. Buddy was whining and growling. Janice kept moving. A man's voice cursed.

Another crack. Buddy went silent.

No time to worry about her loyal protector. *Get the gun.*

Janice thumped her thigh against the kitchen table, and it halted her momentarily. She heard heavy breathing behind her, but she knew if she looked back, it would slow her down.

She heard a click, and she ducked instinctively. Another crack, and a bullet whooshed past her head. Then she felt a burn in her thigh and she stumbled. She put a hand to her leg and felt warm wetness. She kept moving, grabbing at the kitchen counter to keep herself upright.

Finally, she was in the dining room. She yanked at the cutlery drawer and dropped to her knees as knives, forks and spoons scattered on the floor, along with the precious key.

She rummaged clumsily. There it was. Her fingers clasped around the key, but she felt a human presence near her.

She kept her head down and scuttled on all fours towards the gun cabinet. Another bullet ricocheted off the mahogany dining table, and canning jars crashed to the floor.

She pulled herself up, her hands shaking as she tried to get the tiny key in the padlock.

No time. She heard another click, and she turned, her hands up in the air, to confront her attacker.

"Plea—"

Janice dropped to the floor. Fiery pain rushed through her seconds after she heard the last crack of the gun.

CHAPTER TWELVE

There were still traces of the aurora borealis in the dark sky when Virgil rose in the morning of his departure. An hour after his last bowl of porridge at the cabin, the truck was packed, and he'd locked his cabin door and secured the windows with boards. It wasn't thieves he was worried about — not the human kind anyway. He didn't want to get back in the spring and find bears had used his home for a hibernation den.

The sun was still under the horizon, but the pitch black had faded to metallic grey when Virgil's lone truck cast shadows over the track as he drove away. The crew had left the previous day.

Virgil turned up the heater. The first part of the journey was on rutted roads, and as the truck jolted and bounced over the hardening ground, he knew for certain he only had a year left in him. This life was hard on an aging body. And he missed Janice too much.

After two hours of concentrated driving, swerving to avoid treacherous potholes, Virgil sighed with relief as he saw the sign for the Alaskan Highway. He turned towards Dawson City. He needed to meet his buyer, and then he could head towards Whitehorse and be home before dark.

* * *

"Virgil. What you got for me, boy?"

Clarence always called Virgil "boy", even though Virgil was sure they were about the same age.

Clarence was a small man with dark skin. Virgil thought Clarence was part native but had never asked. He didn't care. Clarence always gave him a good price for his gold.

"I got this for you." Virgil took out three large glass jars from his duffel bag and set them on the counter.

Clarence operated out of his tiny house in Dawson City, and he'd converted his living room into a makeshift office. He always sat alone behind his wooden counter, and spent his days, as far as Virgil could tell, watching soap operas on the small TV he had perched in the corner. He didn't seem bothered about security, although Virgil had once seen a large, tattooed man carrying a shotgun under his arm through an open door to a room behind the office. "My nephew," Clarence had said casually.

Clarence poured the gold on to his scales. He always took his time, making sure he emptied all the gold out of Virgil's container, using a soft, clean brush to get the tiniest flakes out. Every small fleck of gold made a difference to Virgil's profit margin. It was why Virgil liked dealing with Clarence. The man was honest.

"Good season, boy," Clarence commented as the digital scale registered the number Virgil had expected. He wrote an amount on a piece of paper and slid it across to Virgil.

Solemnly, Virgil picked it up and nodded. Then Clarence reached into a drawer under his desk and started to fill Virgil's duffel bag with stacks of cash, bound into neat bundles. He zipped up the bag and passed it to Virgil. "Wait, I have something else for you."

Virgil waited. He had no need to count the cash in his bag. He knew it would be all there.

Clarence handed him an envelope. Virgil recognized the writing immediately. It was his sister's. He tore it open and read the contents. Virgil smiled. He knew he could rely on Clara. She was looking forward to seeing him. He hoped she would still be happy to see him when he told her everything.

"Good news?" Clarence was watching him.

Virgil nodded. "Yes. From my sister."

"See you next year, boy."

Virgil rarely wasted time with small talk, and he never shared his plans with anyone, but this time, he hesitated.

"Next season is the last, Clarence. I'm selling up."

Clarence raised his eyebrows. "You got a buyer?"

"Not yet. But I will."

"What'll you do?"

"This and that."

Clarence touched his forehead as if saluting Virgil.

"Good luck, boy."

* * *

"At last," Virgil said as he passed the welcome sign for Whitehorse. The sky had become overcast with low, dark clouds that threatened snow.

He stopped to fuel the truck one more time before he got home. At this time of year, a wise man made sure his truck was always gassed up. When the weather turned really bad, there was often a fuel shortage.

Virgil exchanged a few friendly words with the cashier who welcomed him home, and then he was back in the truck for the last few kilometres. His back and neck were aching. He thought of a hot bath, followed by a whiskey in front of the fire, holding Janice's hand.

Sentimental old fool. But he didn't care. Only one more year and he and Janice would spend all their waking hours together.

He had a fleeting worry that being together continuously might spoil the good thing they had going. He had mentioned this to Janice last time he was home.

"Don't be silly, old man," she'd said. "We'll rub along fine. As long as you keep out from under my feet," she'd added with a wink.

Virgil smiled. He wanted to be under her feet for the rest of his days.

He slowed the truck and made a right turn off the highway. Trees bent low over the muddy trail, obscuring Virgil's view, but he could see a heavy vehicle had been up here recently. Branches were snapped off, and there were fresh ruts in the trail. Virgil hoped Janice didn't have visitors. He wanted her all to himself.

He was glad to see the driveway was empty except for Janice's truck. He parked right outside the door and slid out of the driver's seat, groaning as his stiff body unfolded.

"Hey!" he shouted.

Usually, when his truck came up the driveway, Buddy would bark his head off and bounce up and down on the back of the sofa by the window.

It was quiet.

Virgil shrugged and walked up the porch to the front door. It was slightly open. Virgil smiled. Janice must be in the kitchen.

"Hey, it's me!" He almost laughed at the stupidity of the statement. Of course it was him.

He stopped in the hallway. It all looked the same. Faded rug on the floor, a jumble of footwear in the corner, and a heap of waterproof jackets, hats and scarves slung over a chair. "Untidy and chaotic," he often grumbled to Janice, who always ignored him.

He opened his mouth to call again, and something stopped him. He'd felt like this before when he was out hunting once. He had been bent over the dead body of an elk when all the hairs on his neck had stood up. He'd slowly turned to face a grizzly bear snapping its jaw and pawing the ground.

Virgil felt the same rush of adrenalin, and it was as if his senses had suddenly awakened. He sniffed the air. Woodsmoke.

To his right was the door to their comfy living room with an open fire. He briefly recalled looking forward to curling up with Janice in front of it. He dismissed the thought. No time for that now. On the left was the door to Janice's study. Ahead was the winding wooden staircase to the upper floor. The only other door on this floor was to the kitchen, out back.

He went right and pushed open the living-room door. Nobody here. But he could see that Janice had been in here recently. A book was opened and turned upside down on the table, and a blanket was bunched up on the couch. It was cold. There had been a fire in the grate. That explained the woodsmoke smell, but all that remained was a pile of ash. Virgil picked up the poker and scratched around in the grate. Not even a glowing ember. The fire had gone out hours, maybe even a day, ago.

Virgil looked slowly around the room, stifling the feeling of panic with calm logic. Janice wasn't here. Her truck was still outside. She could have left in someone else's truck — maybe the same one that had left the ruts in the track — and she must have left in a hurry. Even Janice locked the door when she left. She must have taken Buddy with her. Maybe the dog was sick? Maybe she'd gone with the vet to town?

Virgil started to relax. "Too much time on your own," he muttered, and he looked at the fire again. He should get that started, warm the place up. He turned to walk out of the room but stiffened. He'd heard something. A voice?

"Janice?"

His voice echoed as if he were in a cave.

Virgil strained to hear that sound again. Could it be the house creaking? No. There it was again.

Someone crying? No. Not crying. Not *human* crying, anyway.

It was coming from the kitchen. Virgil walked fast, broke into a run. He burst open the kitchen door.

No, no, no . . .

He sank to his knees. There was Buddy, lying on his side in a pool of blood, whimpering.

"What happened, Buddy? What's happened here?" Virgil hugged the dog to his chest and felt the tiny heartbeat fade into nothing. *Too late.*

He gazed into the dog's wide brown eyes and saw the life drain away. He ran his hands over the matted fur and felt broken bones — and something else. A gaping, bloody hole on the side of the dog's chest. Virgil was sure it was a gunshot wound. The bullet hadn't gone in, but it had done enough damage.

Virgil knew his dog. Buddy would have put up a fight if Janice was in danger.

No time to grieve for his loyal friend. He had to look for Janice. She wasn't in the kitchen, which he now realized was in chaos. Cupboard doors were flung open, and a chair lay overturned.

One thing Virgil was sure of, if there had been an intruder, Janice would have run for her gun. She kept it loaded, but it was locked in the cabinet. Virgil had been on at her for years about this.

"Loaded gun's no use locked up," he'd warned her.

But she wouldn't leave the gun out.

"More accidents with a loaded gun left lying about," she'd said. "The dogs will warn me if there's a bear about. I'll have plenty of time to get the gun."

But a bear had not threatened her. For the first time, Virgil saw the smears of blood across the kitchen floor, and what looked like bloody handprints on the open cabinet door.

It was as though a person had grabbed doors and furniture before collapsing to the ground. Virgil followed the tracks of blood with his eyes and then placed the body of the dead dog gently on the floor. He could feel panic rising from the pit of his stomach, and his breath came in quick gasps as he tried to process the scene in front of him.

Someone had killed his dog. Maybe Janice had fled. Or she could be hiding in the house. There was another alternative, but he shoved that from his thoughts.

Although his compulsion was to run through the house screaming for Janice, he was aware this was a bad idea. He might put her in danger. For all he knew, the person who did this could also be in the house. He clenched his fists and mentally pushed aside his emotions.

No time for feelings. This was a hunt.

Virgil stood and backed slowly out of the kitchen. He moved to the front door and only ran when he got to the porch. Janice's house stood in a clearing. It would be easy for a gunman to hide in the treeline, with clear sight of the front of the house.

Virgil flung open the door of his truck. He always kept his rifle under the back seat, but he had all his stuff piled on top. He rummaged frantically.

Shit. He was a sitting duck. And Janice. The emotion he'd quelled came rushing up through his body. He wanted to weep.

He heard a movement behind him.

"Show yourself! What do you want? What's going on here?" He ducked behind the truck door, his words echoing around the clearing. Nothing stirred. He listened for a crack of a frozen branch, or the crunch of footsteps, but none came.

"I've got a gun," he bellowed, bluffing.

Fuck this, he thought. He had to get to Janice. He turned to run back towards the cabin.

Before he could move more than a few steps, he felt somebody rush up behind him. He couldn't be sure, but he thought he smelled sweat just before he heard a loud *pop*, and the frozen ground came rushing up to meet him.

CHAPTER THIRTEEN

Beth Stanton woke to the sound of her cell phone vibrating and skidding across her bedside table. It took a second for her to shake off the fog of sleep and focus on the screen.

Trina. Her little sister.

Damn.

Beth held the phone until the buzzing finally stopped. Then it buzzed once more, indicating the caller had left a message.

She put the phone down. She didn't want to listen to the message. Trina had just started to call Beth in the middle of the night again. Beth had hoped this time Trina had straightened out her chaotic life, but these calls meant the last six months of stability were over.

Beth groaned when she saw the time. 4.30 a.m. The alarm was set for 6.00 a.m. No point trying to get back to sleep now.

She swung her legs out of the bed and sat up. In a few minutes, she was under a shower, letting the piping-hot water pound her body. It wasn't until she was pouring her second cup of coffee, she noticed the light blinking on her phone.

Two messages. And the most recent one was from the detachment.

She swore as she put her phone to her ear, skipped Trina's message and listened to the low mumble of Sergeant Levine.

No time for more coffee. PC Beth Stanton grabbed her phone, her duty belt and warrant card, and bundled up in a thick jacket, gloves and hat.

Would she ever get used to living up here? Beth had arrived in spring, while there was still snow on the ground. The summer had been pleasant enough, except for the black flies and the midnight sun, but the warm weather had departed abruptly in late September, giving way to freezing temperatures and thick morning frosts.

Not that Beth disliked it here in the Yukon. In other circumstances, it would have been an adventure. But she'd taken the posting to get away from the family drama. Unfortunately, the drama had followed her. Even though Beth had found her sister a great job in a high-end Vancouver nursing home, her sister had quit after a few weeks and had arrived in Whitehorse with the new "love of her life". And now Beth was grappling with a new job and a new community, plus a sister who thought it was Beth's job to pick up the pieces every time she shattered her life.

Beth tried to feel compassion for Trina. Addiction was a disease, not a personal failing. But when would Beth ever be free to live her life without worrying — and paying — for her sister? Trina seemed incapable of helping herself.

She glanced at the blinking light on her phone again and shoved it in her pocket. Whatever it was this time, Trina would have to wait until the end of her shift.

"Snow tonight for sure," Sergeant Norman Levine had called after Beth as she finished her shift the previous evening. "Drive carefully tomorrow."

He was right, Beth saw with dismay when she opened her door. It was still snowing, and a stiff wind was whipping up banks of snow in front of her driveway. She had to hurry. Sergeant Levine's voice had been uncharacteristically urgent. His message had requested Beth's presence "*as soon as you can make it.*"

Sergeant Levine was waiting for Beth. She could see his dark figure inside the glass door of the detachment. She parked the truck, thankful it had started with no problems, and it had only taken her a few minutes to clear the snow from the windscreen. The snow ploughs had already been out, and the roads were deserted at this time in the morning.

Levine was pacing up and down as Beth entered, stamping the snow off her boots. She nodded to the constable on night duty, and then looked expectantly at her sergeant.

"Sorry to call you in early," he said.

"No problem," Beth answered. She'd only known the sergeant a short while, but she knew he didn't encroach on his staff's personal time lightly.

"Thing is, well . . . it's probably nothing, just Julie fretting over nothing."

Levine was talking about his wife. They were newly-weds, with a baby on the way. Julie owned the best restaurant in Whitehorse, the Klondike, and she had taken Beth under her wing. Julie had helped Beth find her apartment when she'd first arrived. She was a practical, down-to-earth girl, not given to worrying about nothing.

"What's the problem?"

"Janice, Julie's mother. She hasn't been answering her phone. Julie thought nothing of it at first, but it's been going on for a couple of days. Janice was expecting Virgil for Thanksgiving dinner and had arranged to pick up a pumpkin pie from the restaurant, but she didn't show. Julie can't get through to Virgil's cell phone either."

Beth had met Janice too. She was an older version of Julie, a friendly woman with an easy smile, and the same practical nature. She lived on the outskirts of Whitehorse. Virgil was her companion, of sorts. He was a gold miner, with multiple claims somewhere north of town, and during the spring and summer, he was away. He always came back in the fall around Thanksgiving and lived with Janice during the winter. It was a strange arrangement, but Julie seemed happy for her mother.

"It works for them," she'd explained to Beth. "He's a strange old coot, but he cares for Mum, and makes her happy. And I'm fond of him."

"Maybe Virgil had an accident? Or broke down? And Janice went to help?"

"Yes, it's possible." Levine rubbed his face. "I said the same to Julie. But it's not like Janice to go off on her own without calling Julie or me. And it doesn't explain why the phone line was working yesterday morning, then went dead."

"Let's head out there." Beth grinned at her sergeant. "But you drive. I'm not used to all this white stuff."

It was still dark when they turned on to the narrow track leading to Janice's log cabin. Beth checked the time. It was seven thirty and wouldn't be light for another few hours. The sergeant had told Beth it would take a while to adjust to the dark of a Yukon winter.

"It's important you get outside when it's light. If you embrace the winters, learn to play in the snow, then you'll love living up here. It's the people who hunker down inside getting depressed about the dark who don't do well in the Yukon."

Beth had listened to his advice, but she was struggling to follow it. For her, the blanket of darkness, which only lifted into grey light for a few hours in the middle of the day, seemed threatening and ominous. She tried to stay in the city limits on her days off, attracted to the cozy twinkle of lights in the bookstore and coffee shop. She couldn't imagine living out in the remote wilderness like Janice.

"Damn."

Sergeant Levine stopped the truck. The beam from the headlight lit up a large cabin in a clearing. Two trucks were parked in front. The driver's side door on one was wide open.

"No lights on at all. And usually Buddy would be barking up a storm."

Levine clicked on the light in the truck. Beth could see his normally calm face was twisted in fear.

"There's something wrong here," he said in a low voice. "I have a bad feeling about this, Beth. Let's take it slowly."

He reached behind him and grabbed a flashlight from the back seat. Beth saw him touch his gun, and she checked hers, hoping she wouldn't have to use it.

She opened the truck door and felt a blast of cold air. Snow was falling again. Beth's boots sank into the blanket of snow already there. It was quiet. Beth followed Sergeant Levine, using his tracks to keep from stumbling. Levine stopped by the first truck. The snow was too high to see the license plate. Levine shone his flashlight in the open door.

"Virgil's truck. Don't touch anything."

Beth stuck her head in. She could see a large duffel bag, cardboard boxes and a toolbox on the back seat. Snow had blown in the open door and partially covered a jacket on the passenger seat.

"Doesn't look like he unpacked."

"No. Look, the cabin door is open." Levine was already moving.

Beth could hear the urgency in his voice, and she put out her gloved hand and tapped his arm. "Slowly, remember? Is that Janice's truck?"

Levine nodded. "Think so. Let's check out the cabin."

A wooden porch ran along the front of the cabin. Beth shook the snow off her boots as Levine pushed the front door open wider.

"Janice? Virgil? Anyone home?" His voice echoed back. "OK, let's go in."

Beth nodded. Her heart was beating faster. Despite the layers she was wearing, she shivered.

They stood in a foyer. Levine felt his hand along the wall and flicked a switch. Light suddenly filled the space. Beth blinked for a second.

She had been here once before. Julie had brought her out to introduce her to Janice. Beth remembered a small dog barking and wagging himself in two as she stood in exactly the same place as now. Janice had rushed out to grab him, scolding him and laughing. There had been outdoor clothes piled on a chair, sounds of country music coming from the back of the house, and the smell of baking mixed with woodsmoke.

Now the cabin was silent. Even with the lights on, the place felt abandoned.

Beth steeled herself to focus. Now was the time to apply training, not daydream. She looked up and around, standing still. If there was anyone here, they might hear the creak of floorboards or the rustle of movement.

Nothing.

To the right was an open door to a living room. In the shadows, Beth could see the outline of a couch and chairs arranged in front of an open hearth. There were no glowing embers in the grate.

Levine nudged Beth and nodded his head. To the left was a short corridor with a door at the end. The door was open, but Beth couldn't see through. She remembered it was the kitchen.

"Prints."

Beth looked at the floor. On the polished board, there were the distinct dark marks of a boot.

"Shit." Beth moved closer and crouched to get a closer look. "I think this is blood, Sergeant."

The footprints led out from the kitchen.

Levine pulled out his gun. Beth followed suit, and they both moved swiftly down the corridor. Levine pushed open the door, and Beth fumbled around for the switch.

The sergeant gasped as light flooded the room.

At first Beth thought she was looking at a mophead or a pile of rags submerged in a pool of blood. Then, as her eyes became accustomed to the light, she saw it was the body of a small dog. Janice's dog. Buddy.

"Look." Levine was pointing beyond the bloodied body of the dog. "Go back to the truck, Beth. Phone for help. Tell them to approach with sirens off. We don't know what's gone on here. Then come back but be careful. Don't touch anything and watch where you step. Oh, and Beth? Use the private channel. I don't want Julie hearing this."

Beth was impressed with her sergeant's calmness. This was his mother-in-law's home, yet there wasn't a trace of panic in his voice.

"What are you going to do?"

"See those marks on the floor? They look like drag marks." Levine had lowered his voice. "I need to find Janice and Virgil. I'll be careful, I promise."

The sergeant pulled out his gun. "Go!"

Beth carefully retraced her steps back to the front door. She ran to the truck, grabbed the radio and relayed the information to the night constable. There was a brief hesitation at the other end of the line before the radio crackled and the constable confirmed two police cruisers and ambulances were on the way.

Beth took a deep breath of the cold air and turned to go back into the cabin. The pitch dark was fading to charcoal, and she turned off the flashlight. It was still eerily quiet, and the crunching of her feet in the snow sounded especially loud as she moved back to the house. She knew she should be careful. Whoever had been here and killed the dog might be hiding somewhere close. Yet there were only Virgil's and Janice's trucks in the driveway.

Her cell phone vibrated in her pocket and she pulled it out. Might be the detachment.

"Damn it, Trina," Beth muttered and shoved her phone back in. She had to focus.

Before she could move another step, Levine threw open the front door and rushed out. Even in the dim light, Beth could see his face was pale and his eyes were red. He sagged against the door of their cruiser.

"You found Janice?"

He nodded. He grabbed Beth's arm as she started to move again.

"Don't. You can't help her. And it's best to leave the crime scene as it is."

"Is it bad?" Beth felt stupid as soon as the words came out of her mouth. Of course it was bad.

Levine answered her anyway. "As bad as I've ever seen. She was shot. She's been dead a while, but the cabin is freezing, so it will be hard to tell when it happened. Must be a couple of days, because that's when Julie . . . Oh dear God, Julie—"

"Don't think about that now," Beth said, seeing his face fill with panic. "Did you find Virgil? We should get back in there and find him."

"You're right." Levine straightened, visibly attempting to pull himself together.

The sky had turned a light silver, and there was a faint glow of orange on the horizon. Beth looked carefully around her. The snow had obliterated any tracks except their own, in and out of the cabin.

"Virgil must be here, unless he left on foot," Beth said, half to herself. "He must have thought something was wrong, because it looked like he got out of his truck in a hurry." She waded through the snow again and this time made her way around the truck to the other side.

"Dear God! Sergeant!"

Beth stumbled over a mound in the snow. As she fell to her knees, her hand brushed away some snow to reveal a piece of blue material.

"What is it?" Levine was behind her.

"I think I've found Virgil." Beth couldn't stop her voice from shaking.

They both scraped away the snow.

"He's been shot too."

Beth heard Levine, but his voice seemed to come from far away. She was looking closely at the deathly white face of Virgil Bell. Maybe . . . did she really see that?

In a second, she pulled her gloves off.

"What the hell are you doing?"

Beth ignored Levine and felt around on Virgil's neck.

"I've got a pulse," she shouted. "Get blankets! Jesus Christ. Virgil's alive!"

CHAPTER FOURTEEN

Someone handed Beth a cup of tea. She was glad to hold on to it. It was warm in the detachment, but she couldn't stop shivering.

It was noon. The sun was as high in the sky as it was going to get, and the clouds had receded. Thanksgiving Day. Random thoughts kept popping into her mind, and Beth wondered if she were in shock.

She'd seen dead bodies before. Too many. She wasn't desensitized. Every death affected her. But there was something different about finding a person so near to the edge.

A few minutes after she had found Virgil, the site was suddenly full of lights and noise. Paramedics had taken over the sergeant's and Beth's attempt to warm the man with blankets.

He was indeed alive, but barely. Hypothermia, frostbite and a gunshot wound, the paramedics told Beth. If they had found him any later, well, there would have been two murders to investigate.

Time had passed in a blur. A crime scene investigation team had arrived. Janice's body would not be removed for hours. There were photographs to be taken, fibres and fingerprints to be found, the entire cabin to be searched.

Beth and Levine had followed protocol. She wished she had found Janice instead of the sergeant. It was so hard to do this job when you were personally involved.

Beth felt a hand on her shoulder. Levine stood there, still pale, but he looked his usual calm self.

"Thanks for everything, Beth. You were professional. Saved Virgil's life."

"Will he make it?"

Levine shook his head. "Just a slight chance. Who knows how long he was out there? Even a healthy person doesn't stand much chance in these conditions, but with a gunshot wound too . . . It's a miracle he was still alive when we found him."

"He might be the only one who can tell us what happened to Janice."

Levine's face clouded.

"It's the first question Julie will ask."

"Does she know yet?"

"No. I've finished up here for the time being. I've asked to be the one to tell her."

"I'm so sorry, Sergeant."

"Beth?"

She looked up at her sergeant and friend.

"Of course I will." She knew without him saying anything that he wanted her to go with him to tell Julie. It was a terrible part of their job, delivering the worst news anyone could have. He could have asked any constable to go with him, but Beth knew he was thinking about Julie. It would be better for her to have familiar faces around her. And under the sergeant's controlled exterior, Beth knew he was grieving too.

Silently, she got into the truck beside him. He drove out of the parking lot and turned right, towards the downtown area.

"We're not going to your home?"

"No. Julie will be at the restaurant. She has a full house for Thanksgiving. I can't put off telling her until she gets home. This is a small town. Word of Janice's death will be all over in an hour. She can't find out from anyone but me. It's going to be hard enough as it is. For both of us."

"Right."

Beth knew what it was like in a small community. Rumours spread like wildfire. Already phones would be ringing, and it wouldn't be long before the entire town knew about Janice's murder. Thinking about phone calls reminded Beth again about the calls she'd received from Trina. Perhaps she should call Trina back later and see what she needed. Beth sighed. Trina knew her too well. All she had to do was persist, and Beth's anger and irritation would eventually dissipate.

"OK. We're here." Levine sat in the truck for a moment, and Beth saw his hands were still gripping the steering wheel.

"Come on," she said gently. "Let's do this."

* * *

The Klondike was a small restaurant on the corner of Main Street overlooking the Yukon River. In the summer, tourists lined up outside to get a salmon dinner and then milled around on the riverbanks, taking in the historical site of the SS *Klondike*, one of the sternwheelers that had taken supplies from Whitehorse to Dawson City in bygone eras.

There was nobody on the streets today.

Beth shivered. It had got colder. The sun had retreated behind heavy clouds that threatened another dump of snow.

Levine pushed open the restaurant door and stamped snow off his boots in the foyer. Beth followed suit. When he pushed open the inner door, a rush of warm air and hum of activity greeted them. Beth could hear the clanking of pans and raised voices coming from the kitchen at the back. The restaurant was small, only having enough room for thirty customers at a time. Julie had planned two shifts for Thanksgiving dinner, finishing up with a small gathering of staff and family. Beth had been included, and the way Sergeant Levine and his wife had welcomed her into their community touched her.

But now, Beth was dreading this moment.

Faces turned towards Levine and Beth as they squeezed past the tables to the back of the restaurant. A few people called out a greeting to the sergeant, but his face was set hard, and he ignored them all.

The kitchen door swung open, and Julie burst through it, carrying a tray piled high with crockery. Her face was flushed and she manoeuvred awkwardly. The baby wasn't due for another month, but Julie was enormous. She'd insisted on working right to the last minute.

"Norm!" Julie smiled and put the crockery on a table. "Did you get hold of Mum? I've got her pumpkin pie here . . . Oh, hi, Beth . . . Oh . . ."

Her voice trailed off.

"Julie, honey, I need to tell you—"

"Norm? What's wrong? What's happened?" Julie's voice got small.

"Julie, sit down," Beth cut in. She could see the sergeant was fighting to stay calm.

"Beth, tell me." Julie's voice was flat. She sat on a chair.

Beth squatted beside her and took her hand. "Julie, something terrible has happened," she said gently. "Your mum is dead. She was murdered. I'm so very sorry."

For a moment, Julie stared at Beth. "No, no, that can't be right. Norm? Norm? That's not right, is it?"

Tears were streaming down his face at Julie's frantic words. The news seemed to sink in, and Julie started weeping as Levine gathered her in his arms.

Beth stood helplessly.

There was a shocked murmur from the customers in the restaurant, and some of Julie's staff came out to see what was going on.

Levine still held his wife tight. Beth tapped him on the shoulder.

"Take her home, Sergeant. I'll close the restaurant."

Julie struggled out of Levine's arms. "No, no, I can't do that. I have customers."

"They can manage without you, Julie. You're going home. I'm sorry, but we will have to talk to you soon."

Beth saw understanding in Levine's eyes. Through all the grief of losing Janice, both he and Julie would have to endure a full murder inquiry. And Julie would have to be told about Virgil. But at the moment, Beth knew the best place for Julie was at home with her husband.

Levine bundled Julie into a coat and scarf. She was shaking. They both walked slowly out of the restaurant.

Beth turned to one of Julie's waitresses who was standing beside her. "Can you and the rest of the staff manage Thanksgiving dinner today? Without Julie?"

The white-faced girl nodded. "We know what to do. What happened to Janice? Can you tell us?"

Beth was aware of the hush in the restaurant. Janice had owned the Klondike before her daughter. Everyone knew her, and most people knew Virgil. Sombre faces looked at Beth as she struggled to stay professional.

"All I can tell you at present, is that a terrible tragedy has happened, and Sergeant and Julie Levine are directly affected. I am sure someone at the detachment will release a statement soon. I'm sorry."

"Is Janice dead?" someone asked.

Beth hesitated. She wasn't sure what to say.

"Come on, Janice must be dead. Otherwise, you wouldn't be here. Was it an accident?"

Beth backed towards the entrance. "I really can't—"

"Excuse me." A man stood up, blocking her path.

"Sir, I've said all I can. You'll have to wait. Please excuse me," Beth snapped. The last thing she wanted was the sergeant and the super angry because she'd leaked sensitive information. For all she knew, the murderer could be sitting in the restaurant right now, watching the fallout from his or her actions.

"It's OK, Constable." The man held out an open wallet.

Beth was confused. "Inspector Vega? IHIT?" How on earth had an inspector from the famed Integrated Homicide

Investigative Team shown up right now? How could he possibly . . .?

"I'm on vacation, Constable," the man said.

She felt like an idiot and blushed. "Sorry, sir, it's been a long day."

"I understand. You handled the situation very well. The young lady who just left with the sergeant? Are they related?"

"Yes, sir. Husband and wife. And the victim . . ." Beth bit her lip. Even if this man was an inspector, he wasn't with the Whitehorse detachment, and she could imagine what her super would say if she'd been running her mouth off with an officer from out of town.

"No problem, Constable. Follow procedure. Now, I'd like to talk to your super, if I may? Could you give me a ride to the detachment?"

"We'll have to walk, I'm afraid, sir. My sergeant took the cruiser to take his wife home. But it's only a few blocks."

"OK then. It's Constable . . . ?"

"Stanton, sir. Beth Stanton."

The inspector had a firm handshake, and Beth took the opportunity to really look at him. Taller than her. Olive skin. He might have a Middle Eastern heritage? Good-looking for sure, and maybe not too much older than her. The problem with the RCMP was that there was still an old-fashioned attitude about women. But Inspector Vega seemed friendly enough and hadn't pulled rank and insist she tell him all about Janice, so Beth was grateful for that.

They walked together in the icy cold to the detachment, where Beth's colleagues were waiting in a sombre mood.

"Come in, Inspector." Chief Superintendent Carter welcomed him into his office. "I'm afraid we've just had a murder that will shake our community to the core."

Thinking of Julie and Norman Levine, Beth silently agreed.

* * *

112

Andrew Vega was nervous as he waited for Superintendent Sinclair's secretary to connect his phone call.

"Vega? Tell me what's going on."

He heard Sharon Sinclair's measured voice and relaxed a little. He had done nothing wrong. In fact, he'd followed protocol to the letter.

"Ma'am, as you'll be aware now, there's been a murder here in Whitehorse, and as I was here on vacation, I offered my help as long as it's cleared with you, of course."

"I see." If Sinclair was surprised at his choice of holiday destination, she made no comment. Nor did she ask how Vega had got involved.

She asked a few abrupt questions about the murder and then said, "IHIT can't release any more resources. The Yukon isn't part of our jurisdiction, but the chief has said they could do with your expertise, so I'll allow it. But Vega?"

"Yes, ma'am?"

"You're a guest. Don't tread on toes. And keep me informed, please."

She ended the call. Vega looked at the blank screen of his phone, and for the first time in several weeks, felt relieved. He was back at work where he belonged.

CHAPTER FIFTEEN

Jim was tired and dusty. He was moving all his father's boxes of archived documents from his office into his living room. He'd spent all day Sunday piling up his truck and transporting them to his home.

He'd been planning to grab a pizza and enjoy a bottle or two of cold beer the previous evening, when he'd been interrupted by Bob Hinton.

Jim knew all about the man. Hinton had reported on domestic politics in Ottawa while Jim had been a war correspondent. He had veered off into "celebrity journalism", which was far more lucrative, but then had got involved in some kind of scandal and disappeared off the scene. It was sheer chance their paths hadn't crossed before, Jim thought.

Jim had welcomed a break from moving boxes and had enjoyed his chat with Bob. It was a professional courtesy for visiting journalists to make their presence known with the local guys, and Bob had explained he was on the island pursuing a lead for an old investigation.

"Just a story I should have written decades ago," was all he'd said, before revealing that Andi Silvers was his daughter. Jim was first surprised, and then he could see the similarity. Andi had the same dogged determination when she was on the scent of a good story. Hinton had been the same when he was younger. Jim recalled some of the political scandals Hinton had uncovered. At least one government had lost an election as a result of his reporting. Jim had always believed Andi could produce work of similar significance.

He wondered why Andi had never mentioned her father. Then he realized Andi had never spoken about her family at all.

Hinton had asked Jim not to say anything to Andi about his stay in Coffin Cove.

"We're estranged," he'd explained. "I'd prefer to break that news myself."

Jim had reluctantly agreed. He didn't like keeping secrets, and just lately he'd been keeping some from Andi himself. As a result, he'd avoided the office and kept out of Andi's way. He knew she was beginning to suspect something, and soon, he would have to face her.

Jim walked into his kitchen, opened the fridge, and popped open a beer. He returned to his living room and gazed at the pile of boxes. Deep down he had to acknowledge a truth — he was still a bit resentful about the years he'd spent running the *Coffin Cove Gazette* instead of pursuing his own dreams. He'd been envious of Bob.

Jim sat in an armchair and wondered whether he'd kept the *Gazette* going out of sheer guilt. Jim's father had wanted him to work at the *Gazette* from the beginning. But Jim had left Coffin Cove after his marriage split up. He had wanted nothing more to do with this town. He'd wanted to spread his wings and travel the world. He'd had a great career. But after Jim's mother died, his father's health had failed and Jim came back to help. He'd intended to leave again once his father died. But he hadn't. He'd kept the *Gazette* running because it had been his father's dream.

Now Jim couldn't make the same mistake again. Life was too short. He had dreams too and if he didn't start working on them soon, either the *Gazette* would suck his dwindling savings up, or he would be too old.

Andi would be annoyed, but she'd get over it. She'd soon bounce back. And she'd done splendid work while she was in Coffin Cove. The community respected her. Jim hoped he'd been able to teach her a few things.

He finished his beer and checked the time. Clara Bell had invited him to Thanksgiving dinner. The fierce elderly woman had told him she would have an early dinner with Jim and then take the leftovers to Ed Brown later that evening.

"That drunk old fool is too proud to eat with his family," she'd said when she'd invited Jim. "So I make sure he has somethin' in his stomach apart from booze."

"You're a kind woman," Jim had said. "Looking after all us strays and lame ducks."

"Don't be late," she'd snapped, but she had smiled slightly, and Jim knew she had been pleased to be appreciated.

* * *

Clara Bell's place never changed, unless you looked carefully.

Jim was a regular visitor to her home, one of the few people she welcomed to her domain. There was an order of sorts to Clara's "collection" of objects. An assortment of fencing panels leaned against the woodshed. Piles of ropes, netting and old prawn traps were arranged around an old rowboat, and a tangle of rusty metal traps rested against ornate iron gates.

Not for the first time, Jim wondered at the effort it must have taken for Clara to get all this stuff to her small trailer at the end of the rutted, unmarked track off the main road in and out of Coffin Cove.

Jim drove past "Trigger", a plastic life-sized model of a horse standing guard at the entrance of Clara's property. It was five minutes to three. When he opened the truck door, he could hear the rumble of Clara's generator, and he unloaded three jerry cans of diesel — his Thanksgiving present to Clara.

"Set those down over there, James."

Jim grinned at the white-haired woman who had appeared at the door of the trailer. Clara never shortened his name. "Happy Thanksgiving."

"Dinner's nearly ready," she said in reply and disappeared inside.

Jim followed her. He noticed Clara had done some clearing out. Usually, cardboard boxes were piled almost to the ceiling, leaving narrow trails to other rooms, each of which was also full.

Clara was in her tiny kitchen, and she pointed to an alcove Jim had never noticed before. A table was laid for two. No boxes were in sight, and a window looked out to the back of Clara's property. The trailer was brighter and more welcoming than on Jim's previous visits. He wondered if she had made the effort on his account.

"Sit yourself down. Turkey needs to rest."

It was a command, and Jim obeyed. Clara Bell was not to be messed with. She could be prickly. She was a small woman, with her shock of white hair and dark, intelligent eyes. Jim watched her in the kitchen, hauling a large turkey out of her oven. She held herself upright, no sign of frailty.

She must be eighty at least, he thought. He had known Clara his whole life. His father had held Clara in high regard. "She's a wonderful woman," he had told Jim once, when Jim was chuckling about Clara's eccentric ways. "Clara nursed both her parents when they fell ill, without a word of complaint. She put her life on hold and got no help at all."

Clara talked little about herself. She didn't talk much at all. She wasn't a gossip. In fact, Jim had never known Clara to have much of an opinion about anyone but ask her a factual question about past events or who was related to whom, and Clara would know the answer.

She was well-suited to her part-time job at the museum, although her young boss, Katie Dagg, the senior curator at Coffin Cove Museum, had tried to coax her to be a little less fierce with the visitors.

"Done some clearing out, Clara?" Jim dared to ask.

"My brother is coming to visit. I was looking out some old documents."

"I see. How long is it since you've seen him?"

Jim knew Clara had a brother. He'd left Coffin Cove as a young man and had never been back as far as Jim was aware. Clara had never spoken of him, but Jim remembered his father saying the boy had gone north to try his hand at gold mining.

Clara was carving the turkey. Sunlight glinted off the blade as she expertly sliced meat on to a plate. She didn't answer Jim's question immediately, but as she set the plate on the table and went back to collect serving bowls of vegetables and mashed potato, she carefully slid a black-and-white photograph from under a pile of papers on the windowsill.

She gave it to Jim and sat opposite him.

"That's Virgil. He left here fifty-seven years ago. He's not much for writin' but he sent me that picture a few years back."

Jim looked at the picture, and Clara's dark eyes stared back at him. Virgil Bell was slightly built, like Clara, but the picture must have been taken when he was still in his thirties, because his hair had no hint of grey. He had his sleeves rolled up to reveal ropey muscles. The man wasn't smiling, and he wasn't looking straight at the camera, but somewhere beyond the person taking the picture. There was a sense of restlessness about this man.

"Someone broke his heart in Coffin Cove," Clara said matter-of-factly, "so he left. Food's gettin' cold. I'll say grace."

Jim bent his head while Clara spoke the blessing.

They ate in silence. Jim wanted to ask more about Virgil and his impending visit, but Clara would tell him in her own time, so he concentrated on his meal. It had been a long time since he'd enjoyed a roast dinner.

He waited until she was clearing the plates away to make room for dessert before he spoke again. "It'll be nice for you to see your brother after all these years."

"I reckon. But he's not coming just to see me." Clara put a pumpkin pie on the table.

"Looks delicious, Clara. You make that yourself?"

"That Katie Dagg made it for me." Her face broke into a rare smile.

Jim smiled too. Clara and Katie were firm friends after a rocky start to their relationship.

"I wanted to talk to you about Virgil."

Jim nodded. So there *was* an ulterior motive for this dinner. He smiled to himself. He didn't mind.

Clara was silent. It was rare she asked for help or shared a problem, and Jim guessed she was struggling.

"Tell me about your brother." He helped himself to another slice of pumpkin pie.

"He looked after me when we were little. We didn't have much, but we were happy, more or less. Virgil's older'n me, by a couple of years. He worked with Father on the boat. Coffin Cove was different then. Wasn't much for families. There was one school, but Mother taught me a bit at home. Virgil took me hunting, and sometimes, I would go on the boat and clean fish for 'em. But it all changed when he met Alice."

Clara stood up and went into the kitchen. She kept her back to Jim and banged dishes on the counter.

"Alice?" Jim prompted gently.

"Alice. The jezebel who broke his heart."

Clara turned round, and her eyes were watery and red. This was very unlike Clara. He'd never seen any display of emotion from her before.

"Before I tell you about Alice, you have to know more about Virgil."

Clara handed him another photograph. This one showed two young men on a boat, each holding up a salmon. They were both laughing, and it took a second for Jim to recognize Virgil Bell.

"Virgil looks a lot happier in this picture," Jim commented. "Who's the other lad?"

"That's Ralph Stewart."

The name rang a bell for Jim, but he couldn't place it.

"He was Virgil's best friend, right from when they were little. They did everything together. Ralph was like another brother. He was always at our house. And if we couldn't find Virgil, we knew he was with Ralph, getting up to no good."

Clara's voice had softened, and Jim wondered if she'd had more than sisterly affection for Ralph back then.

"When Virgil started working for Father on the boat, Ralph worked with him. They were going to buy a fish boat together. A whole fleet. They had it all planned out. And then it all went wrong. Because of Alice."

"They argued over a girl? That's not unusual. Had a few fights myself over a pretty face."

Clara didn't smile. "It was more'n that. It was betrayal. And my brother was never the same again." Clara's voice cracked a little, and Jim waited until she had composed herself and went on with her story.

"Alice was supposed to be an artist." Clara snorted. "Artist. I never saw no paintings. Con artist more like. She hung out in the bars looking for a man. She saw Virgil and thought he was a meal ticket. He fell in love, of course. Couldn't get enough of her. She was very pretty and charming. She soon had Virgil all soft over her. But she'd also caught Ralph's eye and Alice couldn't decide between the two of 'em. Ralph was just as soft as Virgil, and Alice liked that all right. She played each against the other, and no matter what I said, neither of them could see it."

There was hurt in Clara's voice.

"Well, before Virgil knew what was going on, Alice was pregnant, and Virgil wanted to marry her. He was convinced the baby was his. Wouldn't listen to anyone. 'My Alice wouldn't lie about that,' he said. Why not? She lied about everything else. My mother and father were furious. They didn't like her — didn't trust her — but what could they say? Virgil wanted to do the right thing by her." Clara sighed.

Jim prompted Clara to go on. "But it didn't last?"

"No. Trouble was, Alice wasn't happy. Didn't matter how hard Virgil worked, she still wanted this or that, or she wasn't happy with him being at sea. He didn't know what to do. One day, I looked in to see the baby, and found the poor little beggar all on his own in the crib. Alice had gone out somewhere. She did that a lot, so I spent more and more time with the baby. She started dropping him off at our house. I reckon she was seeing someone else — probably Ralph — but Virgil was still besotted and wouldn't have a word said against her."

"Their marriage caused a rift between Virgil and Ralph?"

Clara shook her head. "Not at first. I reckon Ralph was relieved. He wasn't the sort to get married, not then, anyways. He wanted to get rich. For a time, he and Virgil patched up their differences and were still working on buying that fish boat. But that went by the wayside when Virgil came home one day and found Ralph in bed with Alice. Virgil's own bed."

There was disgust in her voice. "Even then, he forgave her. Blamed Ralph at first." Clara sighed. "Then he blamed us when Alice left. Said we were too hard on her. He threatened Ralph too, said he would kill him. It all calmed down, but by then Alice was long gone, with all Virgil's money. Wouldn't have been so bad, but she took the baby too. That tore Virgil apart."

"Where did she go?"

"Nobody knows. Virgil went looking but couldn't find her. So he just upped and left. Didn't say a word to anyone. My mother and father never got over it. I didn't hear from Virgil for years, and then, out of the blue, he sent a letter. And that photo. But it was too late then. Mother and Father had passed away."

"And Alice?" Jim couldn't help it. This story intrigued him.

Clara shook her head. "She never came back."

"And what about Ralph?"

Clara gave a short, humourless laugh. "Ralph did all right. Owns half of the island now, I reckon."

The bell rang again for Jim. "Ralph Stewart — you mean Stewart Developments?"

Clara nodded. "That's right. The same selfish son of a bitch." She said it matter-of-factly, but it was a shock to hear Clara use coarse language.

Jim looked again at the photo. Now he recognized the other boy laughing at the camera as the famous Vancouver Island business tycoon who was born and raised in Coffin Cove. Ralph Stewart had always been candid about his humble beginnings and Jim remembered an interview Stewart had done with *Forbes* magazine where he attributed his work ethic to the grounding he got in the fishing and logging industry on the island.

Now Ralph Stewart was the sole owner and CEO of one of the largest privately owned companies in the whole of Canada.

"And Virgil's coming to Coffin Cove now," he said. "Why, Clara? Why, after all these years?"

Clara was silent for so long, Jim thought she hadn't heard.

"He's getting married again," she said finally. "But first, he has something to do. Something to tell me, he says."

"What's that?"

"I don't know. Here, I want you to read his letter." She retrieved an envelope from a drawer and handed it to Jim. The address was written in a spidery scrawl, and in the corner, the return address was Dawson City, Yukon.

Virgil wasn't much of a writer. It was just one page.

Jim read it and handed it back to Clara. She peered at it again, as if trying to decipher a hidden meaning she'd previously missed.

"He wasn't specific," Jim said. "He wants to get rid of a burden he's been carrying around all these years? Sounds like some sort of confession. Have you shown the letter to anyone else?"

Clara shook her head. "I've been wonderin' about showin' it to Ed Brown. He knew Virgil when they were young. He might know what Virgil means."

"It might just be he needs to make things good with you," Jim said. "He wasn't around when your parents passed, was he? He might just want to apologize, wipe the slate clean, now he's getting ready to retire and marry again."

"No. I don't think so," she replied.

"Do you have any idea what he means?"

To Jim's surprise, the old lady's eyes filled with tears.

Her voice dropped to a whisper. "I'm worried, James. You know that body they found?"

"Body?" For a moment, Jim was confused, then he realized what Clara meant. "You mean the human remains on Hope Island? What about them?"

A tear trickled down her cheek. "I'm worried it might be Alice. I'm worried . . . Virgil might have . . ." She couldn't finish. "Virgil had a bad temper, you see, and . . . there could have been an accident, and that's why he left all of a sudden and never came back."

Jim stopped himself from reacting. He could see Clara was deathly serious. Poor Clara. She must be worried sick. He couldn't laugh this off.

He took her hand. "Now, you listen to me. I've heard that they found the remains with scraps of native beadwork. Alice wasn't native, was she?"

Clara shook her head.

"I would put that worry away. I'll make some calls, see if I can get some information about the remains. But if I were you, I'd wait until Virgil arrives. I'm sure he just needs to reconnect with his sister."

Clara looked directly at Jim, as if checking he wasn't patronizing her. In the end she said, "I'm just a silly old woman." She wiped a tear away. "More pie, James?"

* * *

Jim left Clara's trailer an hour later. On the passenger seat beside him was the rest of the pumpkin pie.

When he got home, he made a call to a source on the mainland, who promised to get him some information.

As he ate another slice of pie, Jim wondered if it was ever possible to close the door on the past. When he unlocked his front door and stood in the living room, which was almost a shrine to his father, he knew it was time to try.

CHAPTER SIXTEEN

Grace Hurst, a competent-sounding lady, confirmed Ruth's information about the middens and the burial site discoveries.

"I think the remains found under the caretaker's cottage are far more recent," she confided to Andi, who had called to set up her visit to Hope Island. "Even if the remains were placed there before they built the cottage, the location makes no sense at all. They built the cottage on a rocky outcrop. I'll show you what I mean tomorrow."

Andi had arranged to go to the island with Joshua Moore. Harry had set it up for her, against Hephzibah's advice.

"I never really trusted him," she'd said. "He was always watching us. It felt . . . predatory. And nobody knows anything about him. Apparently, he just turned up one day, looking for work, back when all the mills were operational."

"But wasn't that common in those days?" Andi had asked. Coffin Cove's boom era had attracted men like Joshua. They were called "blow-ins", looking for cash-in-hand work, no questions asked. Most of them drifted away as quickly as they arrived, once the work dried up.

"Yes, but Joshua was different . . . I don't know, Andi. You'll have to judge for yourself. Just be careful, that's all."

When Andi first saw Joshua that morning at Coffin Cove dock, she instantly knew what Hephzibah had meant. Joshua reminded her of a cat. In one fluid movement, he jumped off his tiny boat and tied it up. As Andi introduced herself, he rested his head on one side and narrowed his dark eyes before looking her up and down. There was something about his faintly amused manner and controlled energy that made Andi feel like a trapped mouse awaiting its fate.

It was a bumpy ride out to Hope Island. Andi hung on to her camera and bag and tried not to end up on the floor. She attempted to strike up a conversation with Joshua and asked him about living on Hope Island as he steered his battered little aluminium speed boat. But he either couldn't hear her over the roar of the engine, or he chose to ignore her. Andi couldn't be sure which. She sat back on the small metal seat and concentrated on bracing herself against the roll of the boat on the choppy waves.

Finally, Joshua throttled back, and the engine noise dropped to a purr. Andi opened her mouth to say something, but saw that Joshua was peering out of the window, focusing on guiding the boat through a narrow rocky channel.

The entrance to Mercy Bay on the west side of Hope Island was treacherous and required a level of skill far above the average weekend boater. The tide was running out fast, and rocky crevices were visible below the surface of crystal-clear water. There were barely inches to spare as Joshua steered the boat deftly against the tide until they were clear of the shallows and idling towards a dock at the far end of the bay. Fifteen minutes later and the tide would have been too low, even for Joshua's boat.

As Joshua tied up, Andi stepped off the boat, and the wooden boards creaked beneath her feet. She grabbed hold of a rope railing and walked unsteadily to the end of the dock.

A set of stone steps led up a cliff to a grassy landing. Joshua climbed them without saying a word, and Andi followed. At the top, there was a trail, and Joshua started off walking at a fast pace, almost loping along.

As Joshua moved quickly along the trail, he talked. "The two problems about livin' in a commune are how to deal with the shit, and what to do with the dead bodies. Because all fucking hippies think about are their 'aura' and the way their energy aligns with the stars or fucking whatnot, but they forget two basic things about life: we shit and we die. And if you're gonna live in a commune, there's gotta be rules for where you shit, and what to do with the dead bodies."

"Pardon?" Andi was struggling to keep up with the man and wasn't sure if she had heard correctly. Then she realized he was answering the questions she'd shouted to him on the boat. *He* was *listening*, she thought.

"Fuckin' hippie women." Joshua seemed fond of that phrase, because he muttered it more than once.

"Huh," was all that Andi could manage in reply, as she struggled to keep pace with the wiry old man. His physical fitness would have put a much younger man to shame. He paused, and Andi caught up at last, stumbling over gnarled roots from ancient maple trees that shaded their path. This was the most he had said since he had picked her up from Coffin Cove that morning.

Her breath came in gasps, and Andi couldn't help but be overwhelmed by Joshua Moore's body odour. She hadn't noticed in the boat because of the ocean breeze. But now the smell made her eyes water. When was the last time he'd had a shower? Or washed his clothes? He was dressed in a strange assortment. It was as if when one item of clothing finally wore out, he just covered it over with a newer layer. Even up close, Andi found it impossible to guess Joshua's age. His face was dark mahogany, his skin creased and worn like polished leather. His hair was thick and white, pulled back in a ponytail, and matched his beard. He moved easily, no sign of aching joints.

After a few moments, Andi got her breathing under control. Joshua had his hand outstretched and was pointing like a tour guide. His face was impassive. Andi was glad she'd pulled on her hiking boots as she tentatively stepped off the pathway and peered through the dense undergrowth in the direction of Joshua's gesture.

Andi could see what looked like a bench. It was rotting and crumbling at the edges. As she moved closer, her nostrils confirmed her suspicions. A smell, far worse than Joshua's stale sweat, emanated from three holes in the bench, which straddled a pit. Even in the shadow of the trees, it was warm enough for large blowflies to hover in intense brown clouds above the makeshift latrine. One rested gently on Andi's cheek, and she brushed it away, repulsed.

The expression on Joshua's face hadn't changed. She tried her hardest not to give him the satisfaction of seeing how revolted she was, but she could feel the telltale beads of moisture on her forehead and upper lip.

Was he testing her for his own amusement? Having an inward chuckle at the city journalist horrified at such "rustic" living arrangements? Or was he genuinely trying to illustrate the raw realities of living on Hope Island?

Andi gave him the benefit of the doubt. For now.

Joshua didn't say any more until the trail opened up and Andi saw a bulldozer and an excavator parked in a clearing. A sturdy-looking woman with short grey hair was waiting by the parked machinery. Andi guessed this was Grace Hurst, whom she had arranged to meet.

She turned to Joshua to thank him, but he'd retreated into the trail and was observing from a distance. Andi felt some sympathy for him. He'd made the island his home, and shortly he'd have to move. The transition from living in isolation to living in Coffin Cove would not be easy.

"Andi, how are you?" Grace strode over and shook Andi's hand. "Ruth will be here in a short while. She's on the boat waiting for a call. Shall we get started?"

Andi nodded and started asking questions about Grace's qualifications and experience. She liked to get as much background as possible for her articles.

"Can you show me where the remains were found?" Andi asked.

Grace nodded to a crumbling stone structure. "That's the caretaker's cottage. We can look, but we can't go in."

The cottage was half-hidden by brambles. At one time, it had been shadowed by the lighthouse, but the contractor had done a thorough job of dismantling that structure.

As Andi's eyes adapted to the gloom, she could see through a hole in the side wall.

Grace pointed into the cottage. "That's where the foreman fell through the rotten floor and found the remains underneath."

Andi made out the cracked floorboard and the scuff marks in the dust and dirt.

"It's highly unlikely this is an ancient burial site," Grace said. "But the foreman found a piece of material decorated with beadwork along with the remains and made the connection."

Andi remembered the strange things Joshua had said on the trail. "Is it possible the remains are from the commune?"

Grace looked at her in surprise. "A hippie commune?"

Andi explained the history.

"It's possible," Grace said and shrugged. "We won't know for sure until we get the results from the lab. One thing's for sure, if the remains belong to a member of this commune, I suppose it will be the first time that a white person's grave has disrupted a native development."

Andi acknowledged the irony with a smile. It would be an interesting angle for her article.

Her phone buzzed. She excused herself and walked away. It was Jim.

"I have the report from the lab," he said. "About the remains."

"How did you get it?" Andi was amazed. "Grace hasn't heard anything yet."

"Friends in high places. Do you want to know this or not?" There was an edge to Jim's voice.

"Go on."

"The remains are female, adolescent or early twenties."

"OK." Andi held the phone between her shoulder and her ear, scribbling notes.

"That's not all," Jim said.

Andi waited. She had walked while she was listening and without noticing, she was back at the head of the trail.

"The remains are about forty to fifty years old. It's not an ancient burial site in the historical sense. And it wasn't a natural death."

"What does that mean?"

"It means this young woman was killed. Markings on her bones suggest she was stabbed."

"She was murdered."

Andi looked up to see Joshua standing in front of her. He must have heard her side of the conversation. He was staring at her. It was unnerving, so she turned to walk back. Grace was waving at her to join them. She had her phone in her hand.

Andi finished the conversation with Jim and walked back.

"Did you just hear?" Grace asked, clearly animated.

Andi nodded. "A young woman, unnatural death, possibly stabbed. And not ancient remains."

"Here's Ruth now. I wonder if she's heard."

Andi saw Ruth's tall figure hurrying towards them. When she got closer, Andi could see her face was pale. "Are you OK?"

Ruth nodded but said nothing.

"You've heard the news?" Grace asked.

"I have." Her voice was a whisper, and she sounded as if she was going to cry. Andi glanced at her in surprise. Why was she so emotional? She was about to ask, when a movement caught her eye.

Joshua had moved closer, as if he was eavesdropping. Andi wasn't bothered by anything Joshua might have heard — everyone would know soon enough — but she was transfixed by the look on his face. He was staring at Ruth Cloutier as if he had seen a ghost.

On an impulse, Andi held up her cell phone and took his picture.

CHAPTER SEVENTEEN

Beth parked her truck on Main Street. She needed a distraction. Her shift didn't start for an hour, so she walked along the street and stopped in at the coffee shop attached to the Fireweed Bookstore. She was glad to get in out of the cold. Overnight, the temperature had dropped further, and the impacted snow on the roads and sidewalks had turned to ice. Sand and grit had been deposited everywhere, and the winter wonderland of yesterday looked brown and grubby in the glow of the street lamps.

Beth waited for her coffee, her mind whirring. She had hardly slept at all the previous night. She couldn't get Julie and Norman out of her mind, let alone the frozen face of Virgil Bell.

As she fumbled for her truck keys with one hand, clutching the hot coffee in the other, someone grabbed her arm.

"Why haven't you returned my calls?"

Trina was standing beside Beth, her thin face twisted in anger.

"I really need to talk to you."

Beth's surprise at seeing Trina so early in the morning was immediately replaced with irritation. Couldn't Trina for once ask how *she* was doing? She opened the truck door and put her coffee inside before she turned to answer her sister.

"I've been busy, Trina. You've probably heard there's been a murder outside town. Actually, I can't talk now. I have to get to work. I'll call you this evening."

Trina's hand didn't leave Beth's arm. "I have to talk to you. It's about Archie. He needs some help."

"What's he done now?" Beth couldn't help herself. "More trouble?"

She'd only met Trina's new boyfriend once and had instantly disliked him. He was much older than Trina, and something about the way he'd held on to Trina's elbow and answered for her during their brief conversation had bothered her. He'd smiled at Beth and had said all the right things about helping Trina with her "compulsions", as he'd called her drug addiction, but Beth hadn't trusted him one bit.

Trina had been open about Archie's run-ins with the law but had maintained to Beth that he'd been unfairly persecuted. "He's a good man," she'd insisted. "You're brainwashed by your job."

Trina didn't answer Beth's question. Her grip on Beth's arm tightened. "I just need to talk to you — *now*!" She shouted the last word.

Beth pulled her arm away. "No. I'm going to work. Whatever it is will have to wait. Now, here's twenty bucks. Get yourself something to eat. You look like shit."

"You can't bribe me with money," Trina hissed at Beth, but grabbed the twenty-dollar bill Beth was waving at her.

"Why not? It's always worked in the past!" Beth turned her back on Trina and got in her truck.

"Constable!"

Damn it. Beth looked up to see Inspector Vega standing beside the truck. How long had he been there? Trina had melted away, having got what she really wanted, Beth supposed. She hoped Vega hadn't heard the exchange between her and her sister.

If he had, he didn't mention it. "How are you this morning, Constable?"

"Fine, sir," Beth replied, trying to sound calm and professional, but still agitated about Trina.

"Excellent." Vega smiled. "Is the coffee any good here?"

"Best in town, sir." Beth smiled back, again noticing Inspector Vega's good looks.

* * *

"Virgil Bell remains in a stable but critical condition." Vega began the morning briefing with the brief statement and waited for the buzz of conversation to die down and the team to take their seats.

He ran his eyes over his small team. All young and inexperienced. Sergeant Levine looked tired, but that was to be expected. Vega had hesitated about his involvement in the investigation because of his connection to the victims.

The chief had changed his mind. "It's a very small town, Inspector. Sergeant Levine has an excellent relationship with the community and probably has vital information, even if he doesn't know it yet."

Vega had agreed. He had recent experience working in tight-knit communities, he thought, remembering his last investigation in Coffin Cove. Local knowledge had been invaluable in solving the murders.

The others were keen and hyped-up about a major investigation. Vega understood. He remembered the initial surge of anticipation at the beginning of a complex case, a thrill even. He needed to harness that eagerness quickly. Vega knew from experience that if they didn't get some promising leads soon, the investigation would grind on, extinguishing any last flickers of enthusiasm.

Beth Stanton was interesting. She'd only been a RCMP member for a few years, but held great promise, according to her file. Her sergeant back in the Okanagan had been disappointed by her transfer to "M" Division in the Yukon but had noted she would benefit from the experience and "a fresh start". Vega wondered if that had anything to do with the woman he'd seen talking to Beth that morning. He'd seen Beth push money into her hands. The woman looked vaguely familiar to Vega, and she had all the telltale signs of a drug addict. Maybe he had just been reminded of someone in a past investigation.

He turned his attention to the briefing. The team of officers was looking at him expectantly. Sergeant Levine had already introduced Inspector Andrew Vega as a "consultant officer" from IHIT before Vega had joined the briefing. If there had been any grumbling, Vega hadn't heard it and he wasn't bothered, anyway. They all had a job to do, and with his leadership, they would all work as a team.

"OK, we'll start with what we know, then we'll do some brainstorming. No idea is too stupid. Well—" he paused — "some ideas are too stupid, obviously." There was a polite ripple of laughter from the room.

"We have one deceased victim, shot, and one victim in the hospital with a gunshot wound to the head. Could have been an interrupted robbery, but apart from evidence of the actual shooting, no other rooms are disturbed. Murder–suicide gone wrong? Possibly."

Vega grabbed a black marker and walked over to the whiteboard at the front of the room. He liked to display information visually. It helped him see the big picture and capture patterns. Someone had already pinned up a grainy picture of Janice and Virgil on the wall.

Vega drew a long horizontal line in the middle of the whiteboard. At the far end, he wrote "*Victims found*", with the date and time of the discoveries of the bodies.

"We're still waiting on the forensics, but we do have the start of a timeline for Virgil and Janice's movements. We've found emails from Virgil on Janice's computer. Who has those, please?"

Vega stepped aside and waved up a nervous-looking tech guy, who hurried to the front of the room, clutching a handful of papers.

"I've got a printout of Virgil's emails. The most recent ones give us an idea of Virgil's movements in the days before the murder. There's a copy for all of you, but basically, Virgil writes to Janice that he expects to be home for Thanksgiving. He says he's stopping to see Clarence as usual, and he thinks Janice will be pleased with the season's haul."

The young man broke off and looked around. "We've confirmed Clarence Bailey is a gold buyer in Dawson City. We're waiting for confirmation that Virgil stopped there and for how long. But we think he left the cabin on his claim in Indian River early on the day before Thanksgiving, and he should have arrived late in the afternoon, depending how long he spent with Clarence Bailey. The road was dry, and the weather was clear, so he shouldn't have been delayed at all."

"OK, good. Can we see if and when Janice read that email?"

"Oh, yes, sir. He sent it on the fourth, early in the morning, and Janice read it. She answered, saying that she was looking forward to seeing him."

"So Virgil wasn't specific about his plans. Do we know if Virgil always finished the season around Thanksgiving? Is that normal?"

"Yes, sir," an officer answered. "Thanksgiving is usually when the weather turns, give or take a few days. Most of the gold claims are shut down then."

"So, common knowledge?"

The officer nodded.

"Let's add what we know from Julie Levine," Vega continued. "Julie phoned her mother on the sixth in the afternoon but didn't get any answer. But she was alive — if it was really her answering the email — on the morning of the fourth. It also puts Virgil out of the picture as the shooter if his timeline checks out and he didn't leave Indian River until the morning of the seventh."

"And we don't know why Janice didn't answer her phone. She might just have missed the call," an officer interrupted.

"Exactly. We won't know much more until we get the forensic report. Are there any other emails?"

"One to Virgil's doctor in Whitehorse, making an appointment for the following week, and one to his lawyer also asking for an appointment."

"His lawyer? Does he say why?"

"No, sir."

"Is the lawyer local?"

"Ah, no, sir. Looks like he's in Vancouver."

"OK, follow up and see if they spoke at all. See if the lawyer knows what the appointment was about. Might be relevant."

Vega stopped scribbling and faced the room again. "We need background on Janice and Virgil. Now, I know most of you knew Janice well. We need as much background as possible. Dig into their finances. Was Virgil's business doing well? These gold claim guys can owe enormous debt on some of their machinery. Check into everyone on his crew and all his business associates."

Vega paced as he talked. This part of the investigation was about brainstorming all the leads and establishing facts. He knew how important it was for him and his team to keep an open mind and not settle on a particular theory. Everyone was a suspect in Janice's murder, including Virgil.

Vega brought the briefing to a close after assigning tasks and scheduling the next briefing for later that day. He wanted to go out to the crime scene again, now that the bodies had been removed and Forensics were finishing their work.

Vega looked around the briefing room. Constable Beth Stanton was reading through Virgil's emails with Sergeant Levine. Vega had tasked them with looking through all Janice's correspondence for the last few months. But it only needed one of them.

"Constable Stanton?"

Beth looked up. "Yes, sir?"

"You're with me. I want to go out to the crime scene. Ready?"

For the first time in weeks, Vega felt less unsettled. He realized suddenly that it had been a while since he'd thought about Andi Silvers.

CHAPTER EIGHTEEN

Beth filled her kettle and plugged it in. She wished she had something stronger to drink, but it was late, and she didn't feel like bundling up again just to go out and buy a bottle of wine. She was tired.

Tea would do fine. She'd even make a pot, the way her mum used to, when Beth was a teenager and needed to chat. Mum had always had something to eat for her. She'd make a grilled cheese sandwich for Beth and then sit on the other side of the table, listening to Beth's teenage problems, nodding wisely and offering advice. Beth wished she had someone to talk to now. Especially after today.

Beth swirled hot water around the teapot to warm it up and then spooned in some loose tea. She filled it with hot water and carried the pot and a mug into her tiny living room. As an afterthought, she went back to the kitchen and found the end of a loaf of bread. No cheese, but toast and jam would do tonight.

Beth left her tea and toast on the coffee table and fiddled with the propane stove in the corner of the room, then turned on a lamp. She let her tired body collapse on the couch, and she pulled a blanket around her until the stove had done its job and warmed the room. Not for the first time, she mentally thanked the sergeant and Julie Levine for steering her towards a modern, well-insulated apartment, even though the rent was much higher than the older buildings she'd first toured when she arrived in the Yukon. In a few minutes, Beth's shoulders relaxed in the warmth, and she snuggled under the blanket, sipping her tea.

Despite her tiredness and the coziness of the room, Beth's mind was active. Try as she might, the vision of Virgil's half-frozen body in the snow was fresh in her memory. Beth was thankful that Levine had spared her the scene of his slaughtered mother-in-law, but Beth's visit with Vega to Janice's house had been enough to feed her imagination. Not that she'd never seen gruesome scenes before — she'd attended accidental deaths and even homicides as a police officer. But the brutality of the attack on Janice was evident from the blood splatter and smears on the kitchen floor through to the back deck, where Janice's body was found.

Even Vega had been quiet.

"She put up a fight," he had said, pointing out bloodied handprints on walls and doorways.

"If she put up a fight," Beth had answered, "surely there would have been blood all over Virgil, if he was the killer? Sir."

Vega had nodded.

"You're right, Constable. It seems unlikely that Virgil was involved. Not directly, anyway. But at the start of an investigation, it's best to have all possibilities on the table. Even those we don't want to believe."

Beth poured herself another cup of tea. She wondered how Virgil was faring. Vega had insisted the hospital staff speak to nobody but himself, and they had left a police officer on duty outside Virgil's hospital room. Another constable was trying to trace a relative.

This must be awful for Julie and the sergeant. They must want this solved as quickly as possible, Beth thought to herself. Then another thought struck her, and she jerked upright. *Could Norman or Julie Levine be suspects?*

Most murders were committed by people close to the victim. Opportunity? Levine was a dedicated sergeant and worked long hours. It was unlikely he had the time during a shift to drive out to Janice's house, kill her, wound Virgil and then get back to the detachment without being missed. And Julie? She was always busy at the restaurant. A couple of hours' absence wouldn't have gone unnoticed. But if they had done it together? After hours?

Beth shook her head. She must be tired. This was just fantasy. What possible motive could the Levines have to murder Janice? The sergeant had always talked affectionately about his mother-in-law, and Janice had given the restaurant to Julie. Both of them seemed genuinely happy for Janice and Virgil.

What about Julie's father, Janice's ex-husband? Julie never mentioned him.

Beth realized Inspector Vega must be going through the same thought processes as herself, but he at least had the benefit of objectivity. For Beth, drawing up a list of murder suspects meant looking around at her own new friends and acquaintances in this little town. Probably why having a separate officer from IHIT was a good idea.

OK, enough with this. She had to relax for a while and then get some sleep. It was nine o'clock already, and she'd have to be up early. Vega had made it clear he expected the team to be working long hours on this investigation.

Beth looked around for a distraction. She needed to wind down before she went to bed, otherwise her mind would be in overdrive, preventing a refreshing night's sleep.

She didn't have a TV, mainly because she couldn't afford the cable, but she had a pile of books after spending so much of her free time in the Fireweed Bookstore. She figured she was saving money by not having any social life, and reading was her way of switching off after a stressful day. She'd always been an avid reader. Every spare moment she had when she was a child was spent with her nose in a book. Beth got off the couch and ran her finger down the stack of novels, looking for something light but absorbing. She loved to get lost in a story.

"My little bookworm," her mum had called her.

Trina had been completely different. Whereas Beth had loved nothing more than spending hours curled on the couch with a book, Trina had a restless energy and had needed constant attention to keep her out of trouble. Beth had often been dragged away from her beloved stories to entertain her attention-seeking sister.

It was then that Beth had felt the first stirrings of resentment towards her younger sibling. Trina had grown up expecting every whim to be indulged. When their mum died, Trina went completely off the rails. Always one to be attracted to drama, Trina had started experimenting with drugs and booze, and expected Beth to pick her up when things inevitably went wrong.

And never once said thank you, thought Beth.

Trina had mocked Beth for her choice of career. "*Thought you would be a librarian, not a copper.*"

After today, Beth wondered if a librarian's life would be preferable. When Beth had joined the RCMP, she'd been so determined to make a difference in people's lives. But she hadn't made one iota of difference in Trina's life. And it was hard to see how anyone, even the talented Inspector Vega, could bring any positivity to Julie's life after Janice's murder.

God, she was back to thinking about the case again.

Beth's phone buzzed. She put down her mug of tea and looked at the screen.

Trina.

For a second, Beth wondered if thinking about Trina had somehow manifested the call.

Silly. She recalled she'd promised Trina she would call. She'd instantly forgotten her promise. She had made it just to get rid of her, if she was honest.

As she held the phone in her hand, not wanting to answer, the buzzing stopped. A few moments later, there was a familiar ping, letting Beth know her sister had left a message.

Beth could imagine what it said. Trina wouldn't be inquiring after Beth's health or checking in to see how her day went. It would be nice if just one time—

Beth's phone buzzed again. She grabbed it and jabbed her finger at the screen.

"For God's sake—"

"Constable Stanton? Beth?" Beth recognized Inspector Vega's voice.

"Sorry, sir, I—"

"Apologies for disturbing your evening. Could you come to the hospital right away? There's been an incident. I know you are off-shift, but Sergeant Levine is looking after his wife and—"

"No problem at all, sir. I'll be there in ten."

"Make it five, Constable." The phone went dead.

* * *

Beth arrived at the hospital in six minutes. There was one cruiser in the parking lot, but no sirens or lights. The hotel reception was empty. A lone janitor was washing the floor and pointed to a corridor when Beth asked for directions to the Intensive Care Unit.

Beth followed the signs and found Inspector Vega talking to a doctor outside Virgil Bell's private room. They stopped talking as Beth approached. There were only the three of them in the corridor and Beth wondered why the uniformed officer stationed outside Virgil's door was nowhere to be seen.

"Ah, Constable Stanton, you made it."

There was a cool tone to Inspector Vega's voice. Beth was confused. Why had she been dragged out of the warmth of her apartment? What kind of incident had occurred here?

"Dr Goodall was concerned about certain individuals inquiring after Virgil's health. They were both quite insistent that they get an update on his condition and refused to leave a name."

"Oh?" The situation was no clearer to Beth. Couldn't this have waited until the briefing tomorrow?

"The individuals concerned were unaware of the security cameras. Ah, Constable, is the footage available for Constable Stanton to view?"

An officer Beth recognized from the detachment had appeared. "Yes, sir. She can view it in the office down the corridor. It's all ready to go."

"How is Virgil?" Beth asked. The doctor and Inspector Vega exchanged glances, but nobody answered her.

"Beth, I'd like you to see the video footage."

"Yes, sir." Beth was getting worried. This was weird. There was something Vega wasn't telling her.

She followed Dr Goodall and Inspector Vega into a small, windowless office, hardly bigger than a storage cupboard. Vega sat in front of the computer screen and moved the mouse. In a brief second, the screen came alive, and Beth could see a grainy view of the hospital lobby and a nurse sitting behind the reception desk. The time displayed in the corner of the screen was 16.49.

Vega stood and gestured for Beth to sit in front of the screen. He brushed past her, and Beth got a whiff of sweat. She glanced at Vega's face and saw the dark circles around his eyes, and shadows of facial hair forming. He must have been working for nearly sixteen hours.

"Start the video, please, Constable Stanton."

Beth clicked the mouse, and the image came alive. The nurse was clearing items on the desk and Beth guessed she was closing it down. The hospital didn't have a twenty-four-hour reception.

"Wait a moment," Vega said. "Here he is."

The nurse looked up as a man entered the lobby. His face was turned away from the camera, and he was wearing a baseball cap, but Beth could see a limp ponytail sticking out from under it. The images were black and white, so Beth couldn't tell the colour of his clothing, but he was wearing jeans, she thought, and some kind of puffer jacket.

The man leaned over the reception counter, his face near enough to the nurse for her to draw back. Beth leaned forward and could see there was a verbal exchange between the man and the nurse. Then, in a sudden aggressive move, the man smacked his hand on the top of the counter. The nurse flinched and reached for the phone on the desk. The man backed away from her, gesturing angrily, and then turned and walked out the entrance, as the nurse spoke into the phone.

A moment later, another figure entered the screen from behind the reception desk. As the figure came into view, Beth could see it was Dr Goodall.

Beth clicked the mouse, and the image froze.

"What did that man want, and do we know who it is?" she asked.

"We're working on his identity," Vega answered.

From behind him, Dr Goodall spoke for the first time. "The receptionist called me, as you can see. The man was insisting he was related to Virgil Bell and wanted to see him. When the nurse said it wasn't possible, he got angry. He left only when the nurse said she was calling me."

"But we've not traced any of Virgil's relatives yet?"

"That's correct. And nobody except for the hospital staff and our team is supposed to know where Virgil is, or even if he's alive. That information has been withheld from the public. Unfortunately, the nurse confirmed Virgil's whereabouts to that man." Vega's tone was curt. "Beth, continue watching, please."

Beth clicked the mouse. For a moment, she watched the nurse and Dr Goodall exchange words and then the uniformed officer appeared in the corner of the screen.

Beth heard Vega breathe heavily behind her, and then he leaned across her and took the mouse. A couple of clicks and the video was fast-forwarding, the black-and-white figures moving like cartoon characters on the screen.

"There," Vega said after a minute, his breath hot beside Beth's face. She could sense anger and frustration. She did not know why he'd summoned her but wasn't telling her what this was all about.

"Watch, please."

Beth looked at the screen. The time in the corner now read 20.55. The screen was darker, as there were only night lights in the reception now, and the desk was empty and unmanned.

The entrance door opened, and a figure entered the dimly lit foyer. It was hard to tell whether the figure was male or female, because of a bulky hoodie that was pulled over the figure's face. The figure moved quickly past the reception desk and hesitated, looking from left to right. Then they moved to the right towards the ICU, just as Beth had done a short while before.

"Wait," Vega said from behind.

As the seconds moved on, nothing happened in the reception area that Beth could see. Then, at 21.03, the hooded figure came racing back into the foyer and out the door.

"OK, stop the video there."

Beth twisted round in her chair and looked up at Vega. Before she could ask questions, he leaned past her again and clicked the mouse twice.

"This is outside in the parking lot."

The screen was much darker and grainier than the inside camera, but Beth could just make out the same figure standing outside the hospital entrance.

She could see now that the figure was likely female. The hood was off, and there were strands of long hair. The woman or girl seemed to be looking down at an object in her hand.

Beth moved her face nearer and squinted.

"Here, we can zoom in." Vega clicked the mouse over the figure, and it loomed up on the screen. There was a faint glow from the object in the woman's hand, and Beth guessed it was a phone.

Suddenly the figure stuffed the phone in a pocket, as if she were trying to hide it, and looked to the right of her. A bright light illuminated her face.

"Headlights," Vega stated. He was leaning forward beside Beth, both hands on the desk.

"There!" He grabbed the mouse again and paused the video.

In a split second, the woman had lifted her face and was looking straight at the camera.

Beth stared at the screen, knowing now why Vega had called her, and the reason for his brusque tone.

She was looking at the face of her sister, Trina.

CHAPTER NINETEEN

It was late afternoon and chilly enough for a jacket. Andi walked down to City Hall for the mayor's promised press conference about the Hope Island development. With the news about the human remains, Andi expected the presser to be an interesting one.

She found a space at the back of the conference room. She was early. She'd abandoned the office in frustration. Jim hadn't been there again and wasn't answering calls. Andi didn't know what to make of his strange behaviour.

From her vantage point, Andi could see Peggy Wilson and a group of Coffin Cove business owners. She assumed they were representing the new business association and wondered what questions they would have for the mayor. She could already hear Peggy's strident tones, and she guessed this meeting would be contentious.

Never a dull moment, she thought as she pulled out her notebook. She'd already jotted down some questions she wanted to ask.

The conference room was filling up and the noise level was rising as more people squeezed into the room. The staff had moved the tables and chairs for standing room only. At one end there was a makeshift stage, so the mayor and the

RCMP spokesperson, Andi assumed, could make an official statement and take questions.

Andi worked her way to the front, smiling and nodding at people she knew. Peggy Wilson looked in Andi's direction and then, deliberately, turned her back.

Right on time, Mayor Jade Thompson arrived with Sergeant Matt Beaufort and, to Andi's surprise, Inspector Diane Fowler. Chief George Timms followed them in and stood beside the mayor.

Inspector Fowler briefly locked eyes with Andi and frowned.

Andi sighed to herself. Nobody was happy to see her today.

One of the mayor's staff called for quiet, and the noise volume dropped.

The mayor was direct and to the point. "As most of you will have heard, human remains were found on Hope Island. Because of the position of the remains, they were determined not to be part of the ancient burial site recently surveyed by our provincial archaeologists."

She spent a few minutes explaining the work of Grace Hurst and her team, and how the remains had been found. Then she introduced Inspector Fowler.

"The human remains are those belonging to a young female, probably aged in her late teens or early twenties. This young lady did not die of natural causes. The remains have been on Hope Island for over forty years. Although this is a long time, if anyone has any information—"

A loud murmur rippled around the room. "Another murder? Is that what she means?" Andi heard someone say.

"What's that going to do for business?" Peggy Wilson shouted.

Inspector Fowler was still speaking, but a man raised his voice to interrupt.

"Inspector, about the female murder victim — was she aboriginal?"

Andi stood on tiptoe to see who had asked the question.

What the hell? Dad?

It had been five years since Andi had seen her father, apart from the quick glance outside the office a couple of evenings ago. As she watched her father speak, she was back at her mother's funeral. Andi had fought with her father. It had been a terrible day. Andi had given the eulogy, and Bob Hinton had wanted to stand up and say something. He was drunk. Andi could smell the alcohol as he'd lurched up the aisle.

Andi had waited for him after the mourners had left.

"Never come near me again," she'd said. "You're disgusting."

Five years, she thought, *and now you're here. What the hell do you want?*

Inspector Fowler was regarding Bob Hinton with the disdain she usually reserved for Andi and all reporters. "It's an ongoing investigation, and I'll update you when . . ." Fowler hesitated just long enough for Bob Hinton to finish.

"When you see fit, Inspector? I'd hoped we would have more transparency—"

"When I have more information," Inspector Fowler spat out, her face red with annoyance.

Why does he have to be so combative? Andi thought.

* * *

Bob Hinton moved in the crowd, and Andi could get a better look at her father. He'd aged. His hair, still thick and wavy, was greyer now. He was slightly stooped, and he'd lost weight. He bent down to speak with someone, and when he moved his head, Andi saw with surprise he was talking to Ruth Cloutier.

"So this development is cancelled? How much taxpayers' money has been wasted on this Indian stuff?" Peggy Wilson's angry voice distracted Andi.

Mayor Thompson stepped forward to answer, but Chief George held up his hand and looked directly at Peggy. "The development is not cancelled. It has been put on hold until we find out — until the *investigators* find out — what happened to this poor soul, and she and her family can be at peace. After that, Lhihw Xpey First Nation will continue their partnership with the city of Coffin Cove. I can assure you, ma'am, not a penny of taxpayers' money has been, or will be, wasted on 'Indian stuff'."

There was something in his calm, dignified voice that silenced Peggy Wilson.

Andi smiled to herself. It wasn't often that Peggy was lost for words. When she looked around, her father and Ruth Cloutier were gone.

* * *

"He wouldn't be here unless there was something in it for him," Andi tried to explain to Hephzibah later that evening as they sat at the kitchen table. "He's here to make a point. Everything I do doesn't measure up to his successes. He's still a superior journalist, and I'll always be second best."

Hephzibah was quiet. Andi was grateful for that. Nobody in her life understood her combative relationship with her father, which had caused her so much stress over the years. People liked Bob Hinton. He was personable and took an interest in people's lives. He had the gift of being able to make everyone feel important.

Except his family, Andi thought bitterly. *We were never important, just in the way of his career.*

"Did you find out what your father is doing here?" Hephzibah asked.

Andi shook her head and told Hephzibah about the question he had asked at the meeting. "He was with Ruth Cloutier," she said.

"Maybe he's working for Three Cedars? Like Ruth?"

Andi shook her head. "It doesn't sound like my father."

Hephzibah looked at Andi without speaking. The long pause made Andi squirm.

At last, Hephzibah spoke. "People change, Andi. Do you want to know why he's here? Or do you just want to complain about him?"

"Of course I want to know why he's here!"

"Then ask him, for goodness' sake! What are you afraid of?"

Andi stared at her friend. "Nothing."

"I heard your father's staying in your old apartment at the Fat Chicken," Hephzibah continued. "You could join Harry for a drink, and who knows? Your father might be in the bar."

"That's exactly where he'll be." Andi made no attempt to hide her irritation. If her father had rented an apartment, rather than a room at the Wilson Motel, he intended to stay for a while.

* * *

Andi opted to walk to the Fat Chicken. It was just after seven thirty, and it was nearly pitch black. She heard the hum of chatter and clink of glasses as she pulled open the door. Harry was sitting at the bar. He looked up as the door swung shut behind her, and he smiled and gestured for her to join him. She smiled back and slid on to the stool beside him.

"Just talking about you," Harry said. "Your father. He's impressed with your work at the *Gazette*."

"Is that right?" Andi said, a little more sharply than she intended.

"Really, Andi. You should give the guy a break."

"You're right."

"I am?"

Andi couldn't help laughing at Harry's raised eyebrows and mocking tone. "Statistically speaking, you have to be right occasionally, I suppose."

Andi waved off Walter, who was about to ask if she wanted a drink. "No thanks, I think I'll go see my father. I guess it's time to straighten a few things out."

"Er, Andi, it might not be the best time. Why don't you have coffee with him in the morning?" Harry's tone was anxious.

"You and Hephzibah have been nagging me to talk to Bob . . ." Andi noticed Harry colour up a little. "Oh, what is it? What's going on?"

"It's just . . . Well, your father was in here with the lady from Three Cedars, Ruth—"

"Cloutier." Andi finished for him, unable to stop the annoyance in her voice. "So?"

"So they seemed to be . . . Well, they sat together, and then left together." Harry looked sheepish. "Look, Andi, it's none of my business, but you might not want to go barging in, that's all."

"Nothing ever changes," Andi exploded. She got off the stool.

"Where are you going?"

"To see my loving father!"

She stormed out of the pub, ignoring Harry calling her name.

Her temper dissipated when she came to the foot of the stairs leading up to her old apartment. She hadn't been back here since the murder in the spring. She stood in the dark, her hand on the wooden railing, and fought off the feeling of nausea, which had risen from nowhere. Andi closed her eyes and tried not to think of that awful morning when she'd found the mutilated body at the bottom of the stairs, just about where she was standing now.

"Damn it," she muttered, and forced herself up the steps and banged on the door.

What was wrong with her father? Would his womanizing never stop? And Ruth Cloutier. She wasn't much older than Andi herself. God, it was embarrassing.

"Andrea!" Bob Hinton stood in the doorway, not a hint of embarrassment on his face. "What a surprise! Come in and join the party."

Andi stared at him for a moment. "Are you sure I'm not interrupting anything?"

If her father heard the sarcasm in her voice, he ignored it. "Not at all. In fact, it's good you're here."

Andi stepped into the apartment.

"How have you been?" Bob asked, "I was going to look you up tomorrow—"

"What's going on, Dad? Why . . ." Andi stopped. Ruth Cloutier was sitting in an armchair, holding a glass of wine.

"Andi, nice to see you again," Ruth said.

Andi ignored her. "What the hell is going on? You can't keep your hands to yourself, can you? And what the hell are you doing in Coffin Cove? Are you just here to embarrass me?"

"Andrea, stop right now." Her father's voice was low, but his face was flushed with anger.

"I should go." Ruth Cloutier got up, but Bob gestured at her to sit down again.

"No, Ruth. Please stay. My very rude daughter is about to leave."

"Damn right I am," Andi shouted and marched out of the apartment.

The door slammed behind her, and she stood in the night air, crying.

CHAPTER TWENTY

Ed Brown crushed his beer can with his fist and threw it at the garbage can, which was already overflowing. He'd eaten the rest of the Thanksgiving leftovers that Clara had bought for him the day before. The empty plate was on the porch beside him.

Clara had brought something else, too. Trouble.

At least, that's what he'd thought at first. Ed had read Virgil's letter and had handed it back to her with a shrug of his shoulders.

"Can't remember nuthin'," he'd said.

But he did remember. Every single detail. It had haunted him for years. And that nightmare had returned with a vengeance since those remains had been discovered on Hope Island.

Even amid horror, all those years ago, Ed had been quick to spot an opportunity. He'd hidden some items for years. They were tucked away, ready for the day when he could realize their worth. Now Virgil had decided to "unburden" himself — Ed snorted as he recalled Virgil's letter — he'd need these items. He called them his "insurance".

Ed had spent the day wondering how he would use his insurance. It might save his skin, prove his innocence, but surely there was a profit-making opportunity here? Earlier, he'd made a phone call to someone powerful, using the cell phone that Harry paid for. As he'd expected, the person had taken his call, undoubtedly knowing what it was all about. They'd negotiated, and they had promised to call him back the next day. Ed had hoped for a quicker answer to his offer, but he'd agreed to wait.

In the meantime, he'd have to talk to Joshua Moore. If the man wasn't on board, he could screw things up for Ed. Ed would have to cut him in. It was the cost of doing business.

Ed heaved himself from his chair, walked over to the crumbling woodshed and squeezed past the pile of stacked logs. At the back, under some sheets of rusty tin, he pulled out a metal box. Puffing with the exertion, Ed shuffled back past the logs and placed the metal box on the passenger seat of his pickup truck.

The truck started first time, for once, so he left it idling while he went back to the porch and grabbed the last six beers out of the large cooler he always kept beside his canvas chair. He found a smaller cooler in the junk pile, dumped some ice in it with the cans and put it in the back of the truck.

Then he thought for a moment and went back to get a bottle of whiskey. He put it in the cooler with the beer. He didn't intend to be out all night, but you never knew.

It took half an hour for Ed to drive into town. If he drove too fast down the rutted track from his trailer to the road, the jolting aggravated his back, and if he went over the speed limit, there was always the remote possibility that new constable in town would figure out Ed had lost his licence decades ago. As he drove through Coffin Cove, he passed the turn-off to Seaview Road and Hephzibah's house, and for a moment, imagined his daughter and son having Thanksgiving dinner the day before. He supposed that reporter girl had been there too.

He had an idea and pulled over. Ed had an uneasy feeling about Joshua. What if he didn't agree to the plan? He put his hand on the metal box. He had kept this insurance for decades, and now it might pay off. One thing he'd learned in his life was to trust no one. He laughed to himself. Hell, the last person anyone should trust was him.

That was it then. Having decided, he drove the truck past the Fat Chicken and smiled when he saw Harry's truck in the parking lot. Good. It was still early. Harry would be in there until closing time. Maybe the apple didn't fall too far from the tree after all.

Ed didn't give his children a second thought unless he needed something. It hadn't been his idea to have children anyway. That was all Greta.

Ed was always being nagged to have dinner with them. These days, Hephzibah invited him to everything. Birthdays, Christmas, Easter, even random invitations celebrating nothing significant.

Ed snorted. He didn't care if he was invited or not. He'd never go, because he couldn't drink without Hephzibah fussing over him, trying to get him to quit, and Harry would watch him in silence, with disgust in his eyes, the same way he'd done since he was a ten-year-old boy.

Fuck that. There was no way he was going to be made to feel guilty about the past. Greta was dead to him the day she left with his baby girl and ran off to be with a bunch of sluts, living like fucking hippies. He'd endured years of humiliation because of her.

He parked his pickup by the old fish plant. People were used to seeing it there. Not that anyone was around. It was getting darker, and the October nights were chilly.

He climbed out of the truck, hauling out the metal box and grabbing his flashlight from the back seat. He slammed the door shut and then opened the tailgate and dragged out the cooler and his tackle box. It would take two trips. Didn't matter. He was down here often enough. If anyone saw him, they wouldn't take any notice.

Ed saw a faint glow of light coming from the galley of the *Pipe Dream*, moored at the end of the nearest jetty. Harry always left a light on. The metal box was heavier than Ed remembered, but it only took a minute before he was standing on the deck of Harry's boat.

"Harry? You home?" he called, just in case.

No reply. Ed looked around the deck, searching for a hiding place. He cursed under his breath. Harry kept his boat neat and tidy, no piles of junk, and everything had its place. He was about to give up and take the box back to the truck when he remembered the hatch. Harry kept his prawn traps and other fishing gear in the hatch where he had used to store the salmon catch in icy slush before offloading them at the processing plant.

The hatch door was heavy, but Ed got it open. He shone his light into the bowels of the *Pipe Dream* and spied a ledge off to the side. Struggling to keep his balance, Ed slid the metal box into the darkness. He lowered the hatch door, trying not to let it bang.

He hopped off the boat and hurried back to the truck to pick up the cooler. He needed a beer now.

Ed was wheezing when he reached the other end of the dock. He peered into the gloom of the evening light to make out the name painted on the side of the small boat tied up in the usual spot. The *Vera May*.

Harry had bought the 1967 Tollycraft cruiser for Ed. He'd rebuilt the engine and fixed up the cabin with a stove and a little fridge. Harry paid the moorage too.

Ed didn't know why and didn't bother to question his son. He rarely used the boat for fishing, but it was useful to get over to Hope Island to meet Joshua.

Tonight, it was a particularly important meeting.

Ed climbed on board and felt around the ledge at the top of the cabin door for the keys. Harry checked on the boat regularly, made sure the tiny fridge was clean and the stove had propane. Ed knew without looking at the gauge on the dashboard that the boat was full of fuel. He dumped his cooler on the floor and went back out on the deck to untie the boat.

That done, he took one more glance around the quiet docks before he re-entered the cabin and turned the key in the ignition. Soon the *Vera May* was chugging slowly away from the dock.

* * *

Twenty minutes later, Ed was navigating the narrow channel at the entrance of Mercy Bay. The main dock was on the north-facing side of the island, but the developers were using it, and, since the discovery, the police were too. Few boaters wanted to risk the shallows at "No Mercy" Bay.

Ed had the boat lights on, and in the shadows, he could see the dark outline of someone waiting on the shore. He focused on avoiding the last rocky outcrops before chugging slowly up to the small wooden jetty where Joshua met him.

Joshua Moore was a strange man. He'd appeared on Hope Island from nowhere, it seemed, way back in the sixties. Everyone assumed he was a draft dodger. Not Ed. He knew an ex-con when he saw one.

Joshua had set himself up as the commune's unofficial caretaker and women's "protector". Ed had to laugh at that one. More like Joshua wanted a piece of pussy when he felt like it. Maybe he had even had Greta once or twice.

But Joshua was a smart one. Ed had to give him that. The commune was supposed to be a secret, a place for "abused" women to hide from their husbands. But everyone knew about it. Fishermen from up and down the coast used to laugh about it. Sometimes when they'd had a few in the old pub, they'd talk about going over to the island and giving those women what they really wanted.

Joshua had seen the opportunity, but he had needed Ed to make it happen. Plenty of cash to be made from pimping out those girls. Greta had tried to keep a lid on it, but some of those women were pros, anyway. They didn't know a different life.

Ed and Joshua had made good money until it all fell apart. Now they had a chance to make some more.

Ed tossed him a rope, but Joshua didn't tie it up. Instead, he climbed on to the boat. He was carrying a plastic fuel container.

"Take me back to town," he said. "I need gas and I have business there. We can talk on the way."

Ed hesitated. This wasn't his plan, and he opened his mouth to argue.

Joshua grabbed his arm. "Don't want to be seen with you on the island. The cops are still here. Forensic guys. I'll stay with you for a few days."

It was a statement, not a request, but again, Ed didn't argue.

Joshua waited until Ed was clear of the rocks and heading slowly back to Coffin Cove.

"Let's talk," Ed said, impatient to share his plan.

Joshua listened. The boat chugged on towards the lights of Coffin Cove. When the *Vera May* was tied to the dock, Ed reached into the cooler and brought out the bottle of whiskey.

They talked some more, and Ed kept topping up his glass. Joshua was agreeable to the plan but didn't believe Ed had already made the phone call.

"Here's the goddamn phone," Ed said, slurring his words, and reaching into his pocket. "They're gonna call back tomorrow. It's all set."

* * *

When Ed woke up, he was in darkness. He was disorientated, and he lay still, trying to remember where he was and why. He could taste stale whiskey in his mouth and his head hurt. Gradually, he recalled the boat trip and Joshua from the night before. Or was it still night-time now? He stretched his hand out and felt something sharp bite into his finger.

"What the . . .?" Then he remembered. He was lying in the bow of the *Vera* May, in among old fishing rods. The sharp object must have been the hook from a fishing lure.

He and Joshua had finished the whiskey, he remembered. He'd crawled on to a bunk and passed out.

Ed eased himself backwards out of the bow, taking care not to bang his already throbbing head. The boat was still in darkness. No way to tell what time it was. Joshua wasn't there. Ed could smell sweat and body odour from the night before and something else, something familiar.

He sat down heavily, holding his head. What had they been talking about last night? He vaguely remembered Joshua asking about Ed's insurance. He was certain he hadn't told him where it was. If there was cash to be made, Ed wasn't giving up the goods until he had the cash in his hand.

Ed needed air. He got up and pushed on the cabin door. It didn't move. Jammed? The wood got swollen sometimes. Ed tried again. *Damn.* He looked around the cabin for some tools — maybe he could take the hinges off.

Ed was sweating and felt sick. He couldn't see anything, but he noticed a galley window was open above the stove. Weird. He hadn't noticed that before. But if he had to, he could climb over the stove and squeeze out the window. That might be quicker than messing about with the stuck door. As he got near the stove, Ed sniffed. That familiar smell again. Rotten eggs. And he heard a hissing sound.

What the hell? Ed bent over to check the knobs. Why would anyone have turned on the stove?

At that moment, he felt a rush of air beside his head. He screeched as something white-hot scalded his cheek.

He stared down at a glow on the floor in horror — a glass bottle jammed with a burning rag.

Ed had a split second to process the significance of this before an explosion burst his eardrums and a ball of fire rolled up his body. His senses acknowledged the stench of his own melting flesh until his brain shut down in shock and pain.

CHAPTER TWENTY-ONE

The explosion almost shook Harry out of his bunk. It felt like a heavy impact on the side of the *Pipe Dream*, and then the boat was awash with orange light.

Propane, Harry thought as he scrambled to get on clothes and grabbed his fire extinguisher.

The light was the steel grey of just before dawn, and smoke was spiralling into the morning sky when Harry reached the deck. For a moment, he couldn't see where the explosion had come from. He hopped on to the dock and ran towards the smoke. He could hear shouts coming from the boardwalk. The explosion must have woken half the town.

A boat was on fire.

Harry ran down the dock until he could figure out where the burning boat was tied up.

"This way," someone shouted.

The smoke was getting thicker, and Harry started coughing. His eyes were stinging, but he could see the flames now. *Oh, God, no.*

The *Vera May*. Had his father left the stove on? Please God, he wasn't on the boat.

A second or two later and Harry was dousing the flames with the powder extinguisher. Several other men joined him.

Harry noticed with relief that the fire hadn't reached any other vessels. The heat was intense, and Harry could only get close for a moment at a time. Flames were consuming the wheelhouse, which was almost gone. Smoke billowed in his face, burning his eyes and throat, and making him choke. Over the loud crackle of flames, he heard a creaking sound.

Someone shouted, "Look out, it's sinking!"

The *Vera May* was still tied to the dock, and the rope was straining and slowly ripping a plank of wood away from it. Harry bent down and pulled the end of the rope, releasing the boat. The men moved back and regrouped to turn their extinguishers on the remaining part of the vessel that was still blazing before it was slowly consumed by the sea.

Someone had a powerful flashlight and the beam of light travelled back and forth across the water. *Looking for someone*, Harry realized.

He hoped his father was safely at home in bed.

"Did someone call 911?" Harry shouted and heard back an affirmative.

"Was anyone on board?" the man beside Harry asked.

Harry shook his head. "No idea," he croaked, his mouth and throat caked with soot.

In the distance, they heard sirens.

Several people were gathering at the boardwalk, and Harry hurried towards them, but as he got nearer, he couldn't see his father in the crowd. He had to call Ed. Make sure the unthinkable hadn't happened.

Harry ran back to the *Pipe Dream* and grabbed his cell phone. He tapped in Ed's number.

No answer. Straight to voicemail.

Don't panic, Harry told himself. *He always forgets to charge his phone.*

The sirens were louder now and there was more shouting. There was nothing he could do to help here. Briefly, he considered calling Hephzibah, then decided not to worry her. He'd drive up to his father's trailer and check on him. Put his mind at rest.

Harry snatched up his truck keys and hurried back down the dock. Still blinded by smoke, he bumped into someone.

"Sorry, man," he said, and then saw it was Joshua Moore. The man was holding a gas canister and watching the firefighters run down the dock. For a second, Harry was surprised to see him, but he dismissed the thought. "Hey, have you seen Dad?" he asked. "The fire was on the *Vera May*."

Joshua shrugged. "Sorry. Ed picked me up yesterday. He was going to give me a ride back to the island this morning. He said to meet him here. I got here early when I heard the noise—" he nodded towards the fire engines — "I needed some diesel." He held up the canister.

It was an odd thing to say, and even in the midst of his worry, Harry stared at him. "Right. I gotta get up to his place," Harry said, then stopped, his heart in his mouth. "Shit. That's his truck."

Harry swung back to speak to Joshua again, to ask where Ed was going meet him, but the man was gone, vanished into the smoke. There was something else odd about the meeting, but again, Harry pushed it away. He had to focus on finding his father.

Hope fading, Harry checked Ed's truck. There was no way to tell how long it had been parked. It was strange. Ed was never down here early. He always slept in. And Harry had never known him go out of his way to help Joshua — or anyone else, for that matter. Something was wrong.

"Harry!"

He turned to see his sister and Andi standing behind him.

"Harry, is it true? Is it the *Vera May*? Where's Dad?"

Harry shook his head. "Hep, it doesn't look good." His voice was croaky from the smoke, and his eyes were gritty, but he saw his sister's expression fade from confusion to horror, as she processed the significance of his words.

"No," she whispered.

Andi grabbed Hephzibah's hand. "I'll take her to the café," she said. "Why don't you find out for certain what's happened, OK?"

Harry nodded gratefully. "I'll drive up to Dad's place. Maybe he left the truck here because he'd been drinking. Clara might have given him a ride."

He didn't mention Joshua. He needed to think about what the man had said. Something didn't ring true.

CHAPTER TWENTY-TWO

Beth parked her SUV in the parking lot opposite the apartment building. Trina lived there with her new boyfriend, Archie. Together, they were the two most wanted people in Whitehorse.

Beth hadn't visited Trina here. Trina had given her the address and Beth had driven past once or twice, partly out of concern for her sister, and partly from curiosity, but she hadn't stopped and knocked on the door.

She wished she had. Maybe if she'd tried a little more with her younger sister, she and Trina wouldn't be in the middle of this mess.

Beth had been angry and exasperated the last time she'd driven past this housing block. Back in Vancouver, Beth had found Trina a charming two-bedroom apartment in a pleasant building with communal gardens. It was a short walk from the nursing home that employed Trina, after Beth had used her RCMP credentials to persuade the manager to give her sister a chance.

Trina had lasted less than a month. Beth didn't know whether they had fired Trina, or she had just not bothered to turn up for work. Either way, she'd followed Beth to

Whitehorse and was living in this squalid building with a new loser boyfriend and was now in all kinds of trouble.

Beth pushed those thoughts to the back of her mind and concentrated instead on watching Trina's apartment. Number five was on the ground floor, the corner furthest from Beth. The squat two-storey building, with faded pink stucco and painted brown doors with frosted glass panes, was in sharp contrast to the smart Vancouver complex Trina had left behind. A wooden staircase led up to the second level, and even from a distance, Beth could see the steps and railings were sagging with age and neglect.

It was late, and the light had faded hours ago. Two exposed light bulbs at either end of the building cast shadows over a row of parking spaces and two overflowing garbage dumpsters. Crows pecked at debris scattered in front of the lower levels, not bothering to take flight even when a door was flung open and a hooded individual left on foot, leaving the door banging in the breeze.

Most of the apartments had their lights on, but Trina's was in darkness. Beth wondered if Trina still lived there. Maybe, after the visit to the hospital, Trina and her boyfriend had left town. Earlier that day, officers had got no response when they'd banged on the door, and a neighbour had told them there had been no signs of life for two days.

Beth shivered. The temperature was dropping, and she needed to turn the engine on to get the heater working. This was useless. Trina wasn't home. She'd have to wait until Trina called — or worse, when her colleagues caught up with her. She should go home and wait for news.

In fact, she shouldn't have come here at all. She'd been under the watchful eye of Inspector Vega all day. He'd assigned her the task of collating and logging information for the investigation as it came in and digging into Virgil's background. Beth's eyes felt dry from hours of staring at a computer screen.

Inspector Vega's instructions had been clear. Wait for Trina to make contact and, when she did, inform the team so they could pick her up.

"We just want to talk to her," Vega had said. "Just find out what she was doing at the hospital."

But if Trina had disappeared, the longer she remained away, the more likely that Trina's status would change from being needed to "help with inquiries" to becoming a "person of interest". Beth wouldn't be able to help her sister then.

She groaned. *What a mess.* She thumped the steering wheel in frustration. If Trina had been involved with Janice's murder and Virgil's shooting, even if only by withholding evidence, how could Beth continue working here? And more than that, how would she ever be able to look her sergeant in the eye again, let alone Julie?

Tears formed in Beth's tired eyes. She let them roll down her cheeks and drip on to her uniform.

Then she rubbed her face. She wasn't behaving professionally. She should follow Vega's instructions and leave the stake-outs for the rest of the team.

She fumbled around for her keys. *Damn Trina.* She was on her own. As she slipped the key into the ignition, a movement out of the corner of her eye made her look up.

Two figures had slipped out of the shadows and were now approaching the apartment building. They were both wearing hoodies and dark clothing, and Beth couldn't see their faces. But they both stopped in front of number five.

Beth took a chance. She got out of her SUV, being careful not to slam the door. She didn't want to spook Trina.

Later, she would pinpoint this moment as the time she should have called for backup.

Instead, she walked briskly over to the apartment building as the two people went through the front door. She hesitated when she reached the door herself. It was still open, and she could hear the muffled voices coming from the inside. Straining to hear, she thought she recognized Trina's voice.

She stepped over the threshold. The hallway was dark. It smelled like mildew and sweat, and as her eyes adjusted to the gloom, she could see stains on the walls and peeling wallpaper.

She cleared her throat. "Trina? Are you here?"

There was a glow coming from a partially open door at the end of the corridor. The voices had stopped, but nobody answered her.

She felt ridiculous. What was she doing, barging into somebody's home? She should have waited for Trina to call. She always did, eventually.

Beth pushed the door open and caught the waft of marijuana. "Excuse me, I'm sorry to barge in, I'm looking for my—"

She spotted the movement, but it was too late. The blow to the side of her head spun her whole body into the wall, and she felt herself slide to the floor, unable to stop herself.

Before she passed out, a face loomed in her blurred vision.

"Shit," the face said. "It's a cop."

* * *

Beth could hear voices again. She tried to listen, but they seemed to come from far away. As she opened her eyes, she instantly closed them again, groaning as a bright light blinded her, and she became aware of a pounding sensation in her temple.

"Whaa . . .?" she croaked, and the voices came nearer. She felt adrenalin flood her veins, and she struggled to move, terrified. *What the hell happened?* She remembered calling out for Trina, and then . . . nothing.

"Beth? Lie still."

Beth recognized the voice. She opened her eyes again and tried to focus. This time, she saw a familiar face.

"Norman?"

"That's 'Sergeant' to you, Stanton." His voice was firm but kind.

"What happened? Why are you here?" Beth was confused.

"I'll explain later. The paramedics are here."

Beth lay still as a medic examined her. She became more aware of her surroundings. She was lying on a carpet, which may once have been brown or green, and her head was resting on an equally grubby cushion.

"Can you sit up?"

Beth nodded her head, wincing, and the paramedic helped her into a sitting position.

"Nasty blow to the head. I'm going to take you in overnight. Just to be sure."

Beth didn't argue.

"I'm so sorry, Beth," a small voice said. "We didn't know it was you."

"Trina?"

For the first time, Beth looked around the small room and saw her sister sitting at a small table, along with her boyfriend. Trina was smoking nervously and darting angry looks at Levine. He was standing beside them, with his hands folded.

"Nice work, Constable Stanton," he said. "You tracked them down."

"I . . . er, I just thought I would check—"

Levine waved his hand. "Save it for later. I had a suspicion you'd try to find your sister."

"You followed me?" Now she knew she was in trouble.

"Don't worry about it now. Go to hospital, and I'll see you in the morning."

"Why are you tracking us down? What did we do?" Trina was back to her belligerent self, Beth noted, the apologies short-lived.

"We'll tell you all about it at the detachment," Levine said cheerfully.

CHAPTER TWENTY-THREE

Vega held back his irritation and smiled at the sullen woman sitting across the table. "How's the coffee?" he asked.

Trina Stanton was nothing like her sister, either in appearance or temperament. Vega had finally figured out why she had seemed so familiar when he had first seen her with Beth. He had observed her and Archie before, at the crappy diner just outside Whitehorse, on his way into town. Trina was just as argumentative now as she was then. Vega was almost feeling sorry for Archie, who was waiting to be interviewed.

Trina ignored his question and the polystyrene cup of coffee in front of her. She was sitting back in the metal chair with her arms folded, staring at Vega, not a hint of nervousness.

Sergeant Levine stood at the door of the small interview room. He'd been short on details of how he'd located Trina and Archie, but Vega suspected Beth had something to do with it.

But that was for later. Right now, he was focused on Trina and Archie. Unfortunately, he wasn't getting very far. Trina claimed she knew nothing.

"Archie was worried about a man in hospital. He wanted to see how he was doing," was her explanation when she saw the video of herself and Archie.

When Vega pressed her on the man's name, how they knew he was at the hospital and why she had made several frantic phone calls to her sister, Trina shrugged her shoulders.

"Ask Archie, it was all his idea," was all she said, and then requested a cigarette.

"No smoking." Vega left the woman slouched pouting in her chair as he went to interview Archie.

* * *

Vega thought Archie looked less like an assassin than just about anyone else he'd ever interviewed. The man's hands were shaking, and unlike Trina, Archie was scared. He was sitting bolt upright. Before Vega could sit down, words were spewing out of Archie's mouth.

"Look, I'm sorry about that, Officer. It was me, not Trina. She had nothing to do with it. Weren't my fault, that woman just came into the apartment. I didn't know she was Trina's sister, and we were scared."

Vega looked at Sergeant Levine, who had followed him into the room, but the sergeant stood at the door and stared straight ahead, as if he hadn't heard a word.

Vega ignored Archie's outburst and sat down. Archie even smelled nervous, Vega thought, as he caught a whiff of pungent body odour. Or it could just be a low standard of personal hygiene. Archie might have been a reasonable-looking man if he had a hot shower and a shave. Instead, his greasy hair was pulled back into a ponytail, and his greying facial hair made him look grimy and unkempt. Interestingly, though, his eyes were clear, and although his hands and fingernails were dirty, there were no nicotine stains on his fingers.

Vega recalled the first time he'd seen Archie and Trina in the diner. He'd sensed they were arguing, and Trina was winning. She was certainly the more belligerent of the two and didn't have any qualms about throwing Archie under the bus. He, on the other hand, had immediately protected his partner.

Archie certainly didn't look as though he had the stomach to shoot and kill anyone. But, Vega reminded himself, looks can deceive. Murderers come in all shapes and sizes.

"Archie, I have something to show you." Vega swung his laptop around for Archie to have the full view. He clicked the mouse and allowed Archie to watch the short video of himself and Trina at Whitehorse General Hospital.

"So, Archie, what's the story here?" He closed the laptop and sat back in his chair.

"That's why I'm here?" Archie said in obvious bewilderment. "Because I wanted to see my dad?"

CHAPTER TWENTY-FOUR

Andi's head ached from lack of sleep, and she felt the acidic burn of too much coffee in her stomach and throat. It was late afternoon, and she was sitting in the kitchen waiting for Hephzibah to return.

After the explosion, Harry had taken a desperate drive to Ed's trailer. "I was dreading finding it empty," he'd said to Andi. "But I knew in my gut that he wouldn't be there."

Later in the morning, Sergeant Beaufort had found Andi, Harry and Hephzibah in the café. One look at his face confirmed the worst possible news.

Andi had sat between the two siblings, while Sergeant Beaufort had confirmed that Ed Brown's body had been recovered.

"I'm sorry," he'd said. "We don't know much at the moment, but it looks like the propane store exploded."

After that, the same BC coroner's vehicle that Andi and Harry had seen at the gas station a few days before parked at Government Dock. People milled around the boardwalk, some involved in the investigation, others curious about another tragedy unfolding in Coffin Cove.

Hephzibah had cried. Harry had sat silently, then without saying a word, got up and hugged his sister tight.

"We'll be all right," he'd said, and then left.

Andi had stayed with Hephzibah, who'd refused to close the café. People had popped in and out, hugging Hephzibah and offering condolences. Andi had left as the afternoon darkened and the crowd dissipated. She'd walked along the dock to the *Pipe Dream*. She had stepped on the deck and called softly, "Harry? Are you there?"

She had peered into the galley. His stateroom door was open, and she had heard heavy breathing.

Harry had been sleeping, fully clothed and still grimy from the morning, on top of the bedclothes.

Andi had backed out quietly and headed for home.

She heard the click of the front door opening. Hephzibah walked in and sat at the kitchen table. She sagged into the seat.

"You look exhausted," Andi said. "Do you want to eat? Coffee? Wine?"

Hephzibah shook her head. "Nothing, thanks. I feel . . . numb. And really, really tired."

Andi reached out and took her friend's hand. "I found Harry sleeping earlier. The two of you have had a terrible shock. Go to bed. Sleep in. Nobody will mind if the café is closed tomorrow."

Hephzibah managed a weak smile. "Everyone, including you, has been so kind. You know, my father was . . ." She hesitated. "He was a drunk and a wife beater. I had assumed nobody in Coffin Cove would care about his death. But all day long, so many people have come into the café, and told me little things about Ed that I never knew. Times he'd helped them out, or funny stories about him, or fishing stories from way back, before the booze got hold of him. The thing is, Andi, there's lots about Ed that I didn't know. And now, it's too late."

Andi sat in the kitchen after Hephzibah went to bed, wondering what she could do to help. Her phone buzzed in her pocket. She'd ignored any calls and messages today.

There was a text message from Jim, and Andi saw he'd called four times during the day. She skipped the message and called him back.

"Jim, I'm sorry—"

She listened as he interrupted her.

"Sure, I'll be there in a few minutes."

It was after eight when Andi arrived at the office. Andi was surprised to see Harry there. He was still dressed in the same clothes as earlier and his hair was tousled as if he had just got up. He kept rubbing his eyes as if he were trying to rouse himself.

Trying to wake up from a nightmare, Andi thought, and her heart ached for him.

Jim was sitting behind his desk. He looked serious. "Thanks for coming in, Andi. We're waiting for someone."

"No problem," she said. She was relieved to see Jim.

At that moment, the office door swung open.

"Clara. Good. We're all here now."

Clara looked around and seemed surprised to see a group of people waiting for her.

What on earth was Clara Bell doing here? Andi knew the elderly, eccentric lady from her previous investigation into the multiple murders in the spring. Clara had been instrumental in finding the killer. She was also the assistant curator of Coffin Cove Museum. Her knowledge of local history was legendary. She was the one woman who commanded respect from the older generation of Coffin Cove men. She was an excellent hunter and knew how to handle a gun.

Clara also lived near Ed Brown. Had they been friends? Andi couldn't remember.

"Why are we here, Jim?" Harry asked. His voice was hoarse. Andi could smell smoke on his clothes from the boat fire that morning.

"Clara thinks Ed's death is suspicious," Jim said bluntly.

Andi looked at Harry to see his reaction, but he didn't look surprised, only tired.

Clara started to talk. "I got a letter from my brother Virgil a while back. He said he was coming to see me. Said he had somethin' he needed to get off his chest, a burden he's been carryin' for years. Somethin' bad. I thought it was about his wife, Alice. She ran off years ago. I showed the letter to Ed. He knew Virgil some, back in those days. Thought he might know what Virgil was talkin' bout. Well, Ed said he didn't remember. But I knew he was lyin'. He wouldn't look at me straight. And the thing is, they found those remains on Hope Island . . . and then . . ." Clara paused and looked at Andi. "Then Ed had that accident. But I don't think that was no accident."

Andi was trying to digest what Clara was saying when Harry spoke up.

"I don't think it was an accident either, Clara. It doesn't feel right."

"So you think whatever your brother needs to get off his chest has something to do with Ed's . . . the explosion?" Andi asked.

Clara nodded. And then, without warning, she bent over and put her head in her hands. "It's all my fault," she wailed. "I shouldn't have shown him Virgil's letter. Poor Ed."

"Clara, stop. It's not your fault," Harry said.

Andi remembered Harry telling her how Clara would look out for him when he was young. Clara took him hunting and showed him how to fish in the rivers and streams. Harry was fond of Clara, and grateful she had remained friends with Ed, despite his drunken, often obnoxious behaviour.

Harry was still talking to Clara, who had regained her composure. "We all know that Ed was into a lot of shady things. But I don't think the explosion was an accident. I kept the *Vera May* in good shape. The stove was nearly new. Plus, I don't think Ed ever used it. He hardly used the boat at all. He used to go fishing on Joshua Moore's boat."

Harry stopped abruptly.

"What's wrong?" Andi asked.

"I don't know." Harry frowned. "Just something about Joshua Moore. I can't put my finger on it."

Andi was silent for a moment. She felt the same about Joshua Moore. Ever since the morning on Hope Island, she'd thought he knew more about the human remains than he was saying. "Clara, why don't you ask your brother what this is all about?" she asked. "When is Virgil coming to see you?"

Clara looked as though she might cry again. Suddenly, this fierce woman looked frail and vulnerable.

"I can't ask Virgil." Her voice was so quiet, it was a whisper. Andi bent forward to hear her. "He was shot. Him and his lady friend. She was killed, and he's just about dead. The police are coming to see me, from the Yukon."

There was a short, stunned silence.

"Jesus, what is this all about?" Harry muttered.

Clara looked at Andi. "Them remains they found on Hope Island?"

Andi nodded. "What about them, Clara?"

"I think it's Virgil's wife, Alice. And I think Ed knew about it. It's what got him killed, and my brother shot."

CHAPTER TWENTY-FIVE

Vega underlined the name on the whiteboard. "Archibald Virgil Bell claims he is the son of Virgil Bell."

There was something about that name. He'd had the same jolt of familiarity twice now. It was a strange sense of déjà vu. Maybe Virgil had a record. He'd find out soon enough.

"His full statement is in today's briefing package."

Vega scanned the room as officers bent their heads over paperwork. He was surprised to see Beth Stanton at the back. She was looking very pale and had a dark bruise on her forehead. After a full interview with Trina and Archie last night, Vega had surmised what Beth had done, and how Sergeant Levine had covered for her.

Their actions irritated him, but he was glad of the result. *Maybe this is how Sinclair feels about me*, he thought, as he decided to turn a blind eye.

He turned his attention back to the report. "What do we know?"

It was the morning meeting three days into the investigation and Vega could already see the telltale signs of tiredness and frustration on the faces of his team. The room smelled of stale coffee, and greasy polystyrene food containers were strewn on desks.

It was always like this. Without quick progress, some officers began to feel the pressure. Not only was this team inexperienced but because Whitehorse was a small town, most of them had a connection with the victims. It took a special skill to keep personal feelings compartmentalized and a professional focus on the investigation.

This morning's meeting was as much about morale building as information gathering, and Vega had his work cut out. He took a deep breath. "Let's start with the preliminary report from the crime scene and see what it tells us and what it doesn't. Then we'll move on to Archie and the interviews from last night."

There were murmurs of agreement and the sound of shuffling paper. Vega waited until all eyes were on him before he continued.

"OK, the forensics team has a lot more work to do, so I'll pick out some significant highlights. First, nothing seems to have been stolen. Apart from the kitchen and the dining room, where some kind of scuffle took place, nothing seems out of place. This preliminary report suggests the attack wasn't about robbery. We'll know more once Julie Levine has walked through the house, after Forensics has cleared out today."

Vega paused as another murmur went around the room. He knew what they were thinking. *Why kill Janice or Virgil?* But one step at a time. Take it too fast, and they'd miss something.

"The weapon used to kill Janice and injure Virgil was a Beretta .22 caliber pistol. Semi-automatic. One casing was found underneath the kitchen table, but the killer must have retrieved the others. He took the time to do that. He was careful. Sergeant Levine, what's your take on the gun?"

Vega noted how Norman Levine weighed his answer. He was bearing up well under the stress and heartache he must surely have been feeling.

"The Beretta? Not a popular weapon in this town. Most gun owners have rifles for hunting. I can check the ranges, and local gun collectors," he said.

Vega nodded. "Good." He moved back to the white-board and tapped at the horizontal line he'd drawn at the beginning of the investigation. "We know Janice spoke to her daughter on Saturday morning around ten a.m. We did not discover Janice until Monday morning, Thanksgiving Day, and the pathology report says the time of death is between nine p.m. Saturday evening and the early hours of Sunday morning. Now, this is important, so listen up."

He paused, making sure he had his team's full attention. "The estimated time of death is significant for two reasons. Janice died over twenty-four hours before Virgil arrived. We have him on the security camera at the gas station, and the attendant had a conversation with Virgil about his journey. It tallies with the time his buyer said Virgil left Dawson City, and the length of the journey. So Virgil *did not* kill Janice."

Vega looked around the room to make sure his words had sunk in. He noted some of the team looked downcast, probably because they'd been hoping the case would be neatly solved. But it rarely worked that way.

"Virgil wasn't anywhere near the house when Janice died," Vega continued. "If we assume it was the same person, Janice's killer either waited an entire day to shoot Virgil or came back to do it. Either way, the killer took a huge risk. Anyone could have visited and found Janice before Virgil arrived."

Vega heard an intake of breath and looked at Sergeant Levine. He guessed the man was running through scenarios in his head: what if his wife had driven out there? What about their baby? But there was no time to consider what might have been.

"It must have been extremely important for Janice's killer to wait for Virgil. One explanation is that Virgil was the intended target and Janice was in the way — *or* it was important to kill them both."

"Then why leave Virgil wounded? Why not finish the job, if Virgil was the target?" an officer asked.

"Good question. The clips for these pistols only hold seven rounds. My guess is that the shooter didn't anticipate

178

having to kill the dog or chase Janice before killing her. It was a chaotic scene in the house. Six shots were fired, which only left one for Virgil. The killer either thought Virgil was dead, or assumed he probably wouldn't last that long, given the weather conditions. And it was a reasonable assumption. Virgil is a tough old guy, that's for sure."

There were nods and murmurs of agreement.

"Motive for this attack is key."

Vega marked Janice's time of death and Virgil's estimated arrival on the timeline. He turned back to the officers. "This is where your knowledge of the victims is crucial. When IHIT is called in to run an investigation, we rarely know much about the victims unless they're in the system. But most of you here know Janice and Virgil. So I need you to think about anything you know about them — even if it feels insignificant — that would have led to this violence."

Vega drew two columns, headed with the victims' names, and wrote one word under "Janice".

"Money. What do we know about Janice's finances? Was she in debt? Wealthy? Any major changes in spending recently?"

Some officers shifted awkwardly until Norman Levine spoke up. "Janice was comfortable. Not wealthy. Her house has been in her family for generations. She bought the restaurant with the life insurance payout when Julie's dad died. When she retired, she sold the restaurant to Julie, but we didn't pay for it all upfront. We made payments. Janice had some savings and her Canada pension. She wasn't much of a spender. We had to talk her into buying a new washing machine."

He gestured to a pile of paperwork on the desk beside Vega. "When it first happened, I thought you'd want to know all the financial stuff." He cleared his throat. "There's a copy of Janice's will and her life insurance. Julie is the executor and the main beneficiary of Janice's estate. There's the house, but not much else. But—" he took a breath — "I know Janice talked to Julie about changing her will. Virgil proposed to

179

Janice last spring. I don't know when they were intending to get married, but Janice said she and Virgil would do their wills together and include the baby."

Vega nodded. "Nothing strange about that. OK, what about Virgil?"

Levine shrugged. "We know his claim was doing well. He has more than one, I think, up at Indian River. He didn't talk much about business at all, except Janice said he was thinking about retiring and selling his claims. I think he wanted to do one more year. And as I said, he'd already discussed his will."

Vega thanked him. "Sergeant, assign one of the team to look into all of Virgil's finances: bank accounts, investments, life insurance, everything. And let's check into all of Virgil's crew and anyone connected with the claim — buyers, contractors, anyone he's associated with in Dawson City. This could be all about gold."

An officer spoke up from the back of the room. "Maybe Janice was killed because someone knew Virgil was leaving all his money to her? Maybe Virgil has other family or business associates who thought they would get control of Virgil's claims."

"Wouldn't that put Archie in the frame?" another officer asked.

Vega was silent for a minute. He'd thought of this, but something didn't add up for him. It was just a feeling in his gut. He decided to voice his thoughts. "First, we need to establish that Archie is indeed Virgil's son. He claims he found his original birth certificate along with other letters and papers when he moved his mother to a nursing home."

Vega's eyes met Beth's, and she dropped them, her pale face staining red.

"Archie met Trina in the nursing home. They both say they came up to visit Virgil, just to make contact and hopefully get to know him. Archie said he did not know of Virgil's existence until he moved his mother."

"Sounds far-fetched," Levine said. "He must have seen his birth certificate lots of times. Doesn't make sense."

Vega nodded. "I agree. But Archie says his mother is — well, *was* —secretive, and given to making up sob stories to benefit herself financially."

"A con artist, you mean?" an officer asked.

"Yes. It seems that way. Recently she's been diagnosed with dementia and has forgotten most of her lies. According to Archie, she's spewed all kinds of information about her life and his childhood, including the identity of his father."

"So Archie has recently found out his father is a gold miner and conveniently turns up for a reunion just as Virgil is shot and his soon-to-be wife is killed," an officer commented.

"A huge coincidence, yes." Vega frowned. "And I don't believe in coincidences. But there's something not right. Archie was genuinely scared. He doesn't seem to have the confidence and sheer *nerve* to kill a woman in cold blood and then hang around to make another kill. Plus, he claims he didn't know about Janice, or where she lived."

"How did he know Virgil was in hospital?"

Vega sighed. "He says Trina overheard someone talking at the Klondike. After Julie was told about her mother." He held up his hands. "No, not one of us. One of the staff. PC Stanton did a good job and kept as much under wraps as possible." He nodded at Beth. "But this is a small town. Gossip happens. Archie and Trina didn't know for sure if it was his father at the hospital, or a different Virgil, hence the visit to the hospital to find out."

"If they didn't know Virgil's address, how did they know Virgil lives in Whitehorse? Or that he's a gold miner? Has he ever spoken to Virgil?"

"No." Vega answered the last question first. "He says he's never spoken to Virgil before. All he knows about his father — if all of this is true — is from his mother's documents and what he could find out online." Vega sat on the edge of a desk facing the room. "We have more questions than answers at the moment. Archie and Trina are still helping us with our inquiries. They have voluntarily agreed for us to search their apartment, so if there is any evidence to connect them to the shooting spree, we'll find it. Archie says all the paperwork is there. So, if their story is true, soon we'll be able to eliminate them and progress to other leads, which are sparse. Sergeant, let's allocate some tasks, please."

While Levine delegated work, Vega walked over and sat facing Beth Stanton. She looked apprehensive and opened her mouth to say something, but Vega waved his hand. "PC Stanton, I know it must be difficult to have a family member right in the middle of an investigation. Especially one this serious. However, I appreciate your efforts in finding your sister." He lowered his voice. "And I don't want to know what happened last night, all right?"

She nodded.

"OK. I'm giving you an important assignment. I want you to take Julie Levine back to the house. The crime scene guys are done, and it should be cleaned up. I want you to walk her around to see if anything is missing, out of place, or if she notices anything strange at all, OK? Can you do that?"

"Yes, sir." Beth Stanton nodded, and Vega could see the look of relief on her face.

"And while you're gone, Constable, we'll work on finding out if your sister and her boyfriend are telling the truth, OK?"

Beth Stanton nodded again, but this time her face clouded over. Vega felt sorry for her. Without thinking, he reached out and grabbed her hand. "Don't worry," he said. "It'll be all r—"

An officer interrupted Vega. "I've just heard back from Dawson City, sir. Clarence held Virgil's mail. He gave a letter to Virgil the last time he saw him. He says Virgil said the letter was from his sister. She lives on Vancouver Island somewhere. He said the name was Coffin something. He doesn't know her name."

Something clicked in Vega's mind. He understood now why Virgil's name was so familiar.

"It's OK, Constable," he said. "I know her name. It's Clara Bell."

CHAPTER TWENTY-SIX

Julie Levine stood on the porch of her mother's home. Although the log cabin was as familiar to her as her own face, she felt lost and alone as she stared at the front door.

A scrap of yellow crime-scene tape flapped in the wind and Julie felt the sting of snow against her cheek. She couldn't stand here much longer.

PC Beth Stanton was waiting in her cruiser. She'd offered to come in, but Julie had refused, terrified if she didn't do this alone, cross the threshold and face the tragedy head-on, then somehow this home and all the memories would be lost along with her mother. She pushed the door, and it swung open.

The smell of disinfectant was overwhelming. Someone had tried hard to remove bloodstains from the hardwood floor, but Julie could see footprints. She'd insisted that Norm walk her through the details of the last moments before Janice was killed. Could she make sense of it? Was there something here that everyone had missed, but maybe she could see?

Julie had been sitting beside Virgil at the hospital, watching his chest rise and fall rhythmically and the array of tubes and monitors holding death at bay. She did not know how long she'd been there. Norm had tried to coax her away, but when she'd refused, he had brought her food and coffee.

"Eat," he'd said. "If not for you, then for the baby."

So she'd obeyed.

Inspector Vega had pulled a chair up beside her and taken her hand.

"Julie," he'd said gently, "you can't help Virgil at the moment. Everything possible is being done for him. But you can help me."

He'd asked her to walk through the house. "We don't have many leads. Anything you find or see, however small, could help us find who did this to your family."

Julie had felt her husband bristle at Vega's suggestion, his default need to protect her on full display.

"Yes," she'd said. "I'd like to help."

It was true. She needed to do this for her mother. So she'd gone home and eaten a full meal. She'd taken a shower, dried her hair and put on warm clothes, and allowed Beth to drive her out to her mother's house.

She must find something. Something that made sense.

Julie stepped around the stains on the floor. She went into the living room and faltered again.

A blanket was thrown back on the couch, creases in the seat where Janice used to sit. A book was open and upturned on the side table under a lamp, which still glowed dimly. Janice's glasses were beside it. It was as though her mother had just got up to make herself a cup of tea.

Julie sank down where Janice had been sitting and held her head in her hands. *What happened here? Why would anyone want to hurt you?*

She took a deep breath. She had to stay focused. This was the only thing she could do for her mother now. She must be observant, take in every detail.

There was nothing missing in the living room. The drapes were partially open. Maybe Janice or Buddy had heard something outside that made her pull back the curtains a little?

Julie frowned. She'd have to check if the motion light on the porch was working. If Janice had seen someone she knew, then she'd have gone to the front door. But then, the killer could have shot her in the foyer, along with Buddy. So Janice cannot have known the person who'd killed her.

Satisfied with this small insight, Julie walked into the hallway. Janice had run into the kitchen. That made sense. Julie walked into the kitchen and looked around. The forensics team had cleaned up, but there were still smears of white dust on the door jambs and the kitchen table.

Why didn't Janice run out the back door? Why did she head to the dining room?

Julie took a careful look around the kitchen. Her grandmother's old cast-iron pots were arranged on the shelves. The everyday china was still on display on the oak dresser. Julie picked up and set the overturned chair back at the kitchen table.

The heavy tick of the kitchen clock echoed around the room, breaking the silence. Julie couldn't remember a time when the kitchen was quiet. Most of her childhood memories were tied to this room.

She felt a wave of emotion, and then at the same time a tiny flutter from her stomach. She must hang on.

Come on. Focus.

She walked through the kitchen and into the dining room. A cabinet held all the precious fine bone china dinner service, a family heirloom that dated back to the first generation of Janice's family, who had emigrated to Canada from Europe in the nineteenth century.

"Imagine," Janice had said in wonder many times, "our ancestors travelled across Canada carrying all that china, and not one piece was even chipped."

The cabinet door was closed, but the drawer had been pulled out, and the wood had splintered. Vega's team had left the contents on the floor, and silver cutlery was strewn everywhere. Surely the killer hadn't been looking for silver knives and forks?

The rug was old-fashioned, covered in a floral pattern, which nearly disguised the bloodstains, but not quite. Janice had died here, gunned down in cold blood. But nothing had been taken, as far as Julie could see.

She walked slowly around the room. A picture hung to one side. Janice didn't have a safe. She never kept much cash at home. Did Virgil have a stash of money somewhere? Did he keep it in the dining room?

Julie was about to leave when her eye caught sight of a tiny flash of something on the corner of the rug. She bent down and picked up a key. It was a dull bronze and was almost indistinguishable from the floral pattern.

She held it up and knew immediately why her mother had died in this room. In the corner was an upright metal cabinet, which held three shotguns. Virgil had always been pestering Janice to keep the guns more accessible, but she'd always laughed and said she'd never had need of a loaded gun.

"Except this time," Julie whispered. She finally allowed her tears to roll down her face unchecked.

Her mother's instinct hadn't been to run away. It had been to fight and defend herself. And it had cost her her life.

"Julie?" Beth was standing in the doorway, a worried expression on her face. "I was getting worried. Are you OK? What did you find?"

Julie wiped her face and explained her theory. "It's not much. But I definitely think Mum didn't know her killer."

Beth nodded. "That's good, Julie. It helps a lot. And we can be fairly sure this wasn't a burglary gone wrong. Whoever did this intended to kill your mother."

Julie looked at her for a moment. "Or Virgil. Or both of them. I still don't know why my mother would have been the target. Virgil was the one with all the money, and most of it was tied up in the gold claim."

"Would you like to leave now?" Beth asked.

Julie shook her head. "No. I haven't looked upstairs yet."

Janice's bedroom was tidy. The bed hadn't been slept in.

"Mum always went to bed early. Before ten, anyway. The blanket downstairs on the couch is usually folded up on the end of the bed."

"So everything must have happened earlier in the evening," Beth said.

Julie nodded. "Nothing missing in here." She sat down on the side of the bed. The bedside table was covered in framed photographs of herself. She absent-mindedly picked one up and dusted it off with her sleeve.

"No pictures of Virgil's family?" Beth asked.

"I've never seen any," Julie said. "Virgil didn't talk about his family, or his past. Not to me, anyway. Mum said he had a sister somewhere in British Columbia, but I don't know if she's still alive. He's a really private man. I think he was married once before. But he's been the only dad I've ever known, and . . . and I don't know what I'll do if I lose him too . . ." Julie couldn't help it now. Emotion and tears overcame her exhausted body.

Eventually, she felt Beth's arms around her shoulders, and she regained her composure.

"I think it's enough for today," Beth said. "Let's get you home. My sergeant told me to look after you." Her tone was mock severity, and Julie attempted a smile.

"There's just my old room left. There's not much in there, nothing of any value, but I'd like to check it, anyway."

She heaved herself off the bed and straightened the bedcovers, trying not to think that her mother would never sleep here again.

Julie's childhood room was across a wide mezzanine floor, which overlooked the foyer and front door. There were two easy chairs and a large bookcase full of Janice's novels arranged in the space, and a carved coffee table. Julie pointed to it. "Virgil made that." She remembered the hours he'd spent in the woodshed, carving and sanding, and then oiling the natural wood until it had a deep burnished sheen. "He loved making things for us."

Julie pushed open the door to her old bedroom and stood aside to let Beth in. It had been a while since anyone had used the room, because there was a thin layer of dust on bookshelves and the chest of drawers. The single bed was made with Julie's patchwork quilt, and a teddy bear was perched on the pillow.

Virgil had made the desk for her so she could study but still have a view of Grey Mountain. The desk was built in under the dormer window.

"Virgil used this room as his office sometimes," Julie explained to Beth, "but he took his laptop and files with him when he went to the claim. Mum left his mail here. Do you think your team took it? Or maybe the man who . . ." She trailed off.

"I'll call it in and ask," Beth said. "Did Virgil have any business records here? Any personal papers anywhere?"

"I don't . . ." Julie started to answer and then stopped.

"What is it? Is something missing? Or out of place?"

"No, nothing like that." Julie went over to the desk and knelt beside it, feeling along the log wall.

"What are you doing?"

"It's somewhere here. Oh, here it is." Julie let out a small laugh. "See these logs? It looks like this side of the desk is an extension of the wall. But if you look closely, they don't match. Virgil made me a secret cubbyhole to put all my secret stuff — you know, all my teenage diaries and pictures of boys I didn't want Mum to find. He said everyone needed a private spot to keep their treasures."

"Oh, that's lovely." Beth smiled back at Julie. "But nobody knew it was here?"

Julie shook her head. "Not as far as I know. I cleared it out when I left home. Oh, look . . ." Julie opened the false log panel, and she felt inside. Her hand touched something metal.

"This isn't mine." She pulled out a large metal cash box and stood up, showing it to Beth. "Oh no. Do you think it's Virgil's? Do you think whoever it was was looking for cash? Or knew he had cash in the house?" She felt lightheaded suddenly, and moved towards the bed, sinking down as the room spun.

Julie felt Beth take her arm and help her lie on the bed. She closed her eyes and waited until the vertigo and nausea subsided.

When she opened her eyes again, Beth had on thin latex gloves and was attempting to open the cash box.

"It's locked," she said to Julie. "I'll look for a key."

Julie sat up slowly. She felt sadness seep over her again. "Oh, Beth, do you think Mum lost her life for that? A pile of cash?" She started to cry all over again.

Beth found a tiny key in the corner of the cubbyhole. She opened the tin. "No cash." She held the box open for Julie to see. "Just old photographs and some newspaper cuttings."

Julie forgot her nausea. She took out some black-and-white photos. "Look at this one," she said. "This must be Virgil's sister. She looks like him."

Beth glanced through the papers. "We'll have to take them back to the detachment. You never know, maybe this has a connection to the . . ."

Julie noticed Beth had hesitated, not wanting to say the words. "To Mum's death," she finished for her. "I know. But Virgil will want them back." She refused to contemplate another loss.

Beth nodded. "Of course."

Julie peered at another photograph. "This lady isn't the same as the other one," she said thoughtfully. "I think this must be Virgil's first wife."

CHAPTER TWENTY-SEVEN

"Here you are, Alice. A nice cup of tea, dear. Let's get you sitting up. Take your pill now, that's right. It's a big day today, remember?"

Alice didn't remember. The nurse knew that. Some days, the old lady didn't know her own name. Dementia had withered her brain first, and then her body, so Alice's nod of her head came from long-programmed responses, rather than any remaining cognitive ability.

Occasionally, Alice was fully alert and would chat with the nurse. These moments were flashes of clarity, like clouds parting to reveal the sun. It was not one of those mornings.

The nurse gently lifted Alice to a sitting position in bed. Her patient was as frail and light as a bird. She chatted to Alice in a singsong voice as she moved around the small room, pulling back the curtains and removing the debris left by the last shift. She enjoyed working here, at the Cheriton Assisted Living Facility. Staffing levels were more than adequate, and the patient's "suites", as management liked to call them, were comfortable, if a tad on the cramped side. There were more spacious VIP suites for very wealthy clients. This care home was in sharp contrast to others the nurse had worked in, where elderly folk were crammed into tiny rooms on their own for twenty-three hours a day and fed slop.

She liked working the afternoon shift. Very often, grateful sons and daughters would press a twenty-dollar bill in her hand, whispering to take extra special care of their loved one. The nurse would at first protest, but then relent, patting their hand and promising a little extra attention. It never happened, of course, but the relatives could hurry off, safe in the knowledge that they'd gone the extra mile in their duty to their elders.

As the nurse plumped up Alice's pillows and checked her blood pressure, she made inane remarks about the weather and her drive in to work that morning. She liked to think her cheerful banter brightened the days of her geriatric patients, even if they did not know what she was saying. Sometimes they gratified her with a smile or a squeeze of her hand, but not this one. No, Alice was mostly unsmiling and stared blankly into space.

The drugs kept emotions in check. Some patients in her care got agitated and hit out when they first moved into the care home. She could see the fear in their eyes as they were moved into unfamiliar surroundings. Mild sedatives and kindly words helped them settle into their new routines, and gradually, all memories of their lives before faded into the background.

Alice was different. She was still new and settling in. At first, she'd been compliant, eating whatever was put in front of her, and allowing the staff to wash and dress her without a murmur. But when she'd started having her meals in the dining room with other clients, the trouble had started. At first, small personal items had gone missing. One elderly lady had been missing a brooch. A gentleman had been wearing his watch at lunchtime, but inexplicably, it was missing in the afternoon. Puzzled staff had watched the closed-circuit cameras, and to their amazement, had seen Alice nimbly removing small items from her fellow residents when she'd thought no one was looking.

Alice was smart. She had sidled up to other clients and held their hands, talking to them. Sliding her hands back, she had removed bracelets, rings, and watches. She was sly and, worryingly, she had seemed to know that a camera was watching. It was only an eagle-eyed security guard watching the footage in slow motion who had spotted Alice tucking something up her sleeve one lunchtime.

A quick search of Alice's room had found a stash of treasure under a corner of her mattress. All items had been quickly returned to their rightful owners before relatives complained, and they had confined Alice to her room for all her meals. It was then that Alice had displayed her mean streak.

The nurse rubbed her arm, recalling a purplish bruise from one of Alice's vicious pinches. Alice wasn't averse to grabbing stray locks of hair when the nurse bent over the bed to straighten a pillow. She'd twist the locks around her bony fingers and pull and jerk until tears were streaming down the nurse's face.

"Not so crafty now, are you?" the nurse carried on in her fake, childlike voice. "All drugged up now, aren't you? Stuck in your room like the naughty girl you are."

The nurse had a theory. As a person sunk further and further into dementia, all that remained was a person's raw personality, laid bare without the layers of societal niceties to blur the edges or smooth the roughness. If a person was truly kind, or truly horrible, dementia would reveal it.

In Alice's case, "horrible" was her core personality, the nurse had decided, and the only course of action to contain Alice's spitefulness had been a shitload of drugs.

Maybe the theory was sound, because the one time the manager had relented and allowed Alice to dine with her fellow clients, she had stuck a plastic knife into the frail hand of the unfortunate lady sitting next to her. The force of the blunt edge had pierced the victim's papery skin and fragile vein, and Alice had sat watching, expressionless, as blood had seeped over the dining-room table. So now Alice's meals were delivered on a tray.

The nurse had only been assigned to Alice for a short while. The previous carer, Trina Stanton, had left suddenly under a cloud, and although the manager was tight-lipped, it was rumoured that Trina had run off with Alice's son.

The nurse had seen Alice's son. She didn't like to judge people by appearances, but the man's wispy blond hair, scraped back in a greasy ponytail, and his grubby shirt and jeans screamed "grifter" to her. As he fiddled with his phone — the latest model, the nurse noted — she had caught sight of a gold watch. Maybe it was fake, she couldn't tell. Drug dealer. Or some kind of petty criminal. He couldn't wait to get out of the home, either. Not the kind of person she'd get involved with. But she didn't know Trina very well. There had been rumours about her, too. Some of the other nurses had whispered about drug-taking.

Since Trina had abruptly left, Alice's visits from her son had ceased as well, adding to the potential validity of all the rumours. Still, it was not an unusual occurrence for visits to become less frequent. At the start of a client's residency, visitors usually overwhelmed them, family members attempting to assuage their guilt for dumping their "loved one" in a home, by pledging weekly, even daily, visits. It never lasted for long. Soon, clients may get a monthly visit if they were lucky, often after monthly statements were sent out. Other than that, senior citizens were "out of sight, out of mind", once the burden of their care had been lifted.

The nurse wondered where the money was coming from to pay for Alice's care. Her son didn't look particularly well off, but the mystery had been solved when the manager had winked at the nurse and whispered, "All the money is in a trust for Alice's care."

The management of Cheriton Assisted Living loved clients like Alice. The monthly payments were guaranteed from an unbreakable trust, overseen by the family lawyer. No chance of Alice being moved to a cheaper facility to safeguard the family inheritance.

The nurse had seen it all before. An elderly relative moved into a comfortable, upmarket home for their last days of their life, by tearful relatives. But the final phase of a person's life, once they were receiving round-the-clock care, could stretch out a lot longer than the family had expected or budgeted for. An old person, practically at death's door, could perk up considerably with balanced nutrition and daily stimulation.

Then the phone calls would start. Is it really necessary to have a physio in three times a week? Can the dry-cleaning bill be reduced? The nitpicking over the monthly bill would continue until, finally, notice would be given that the "well-loved" senior who deserved the "best care money could buy" was to be moved to a cheaper facility, which was entirely "adequate".

The nurse shuddered as she remembered some of those "adequate" care homes. Clients left for weeks without a proper wash, cleaning and laundry at a minimum, and food slopped into bowls that she wouldn't have fed to her dog.

But that was not for Alice. Her last days were secure, and she wanted for nothing, and it showed. Sparkling white bed linens, fresh flowers and all the drugs necessary to keep her quiet.

The nurse patted Alice's hand, and then drew back quickly as a light flickered in Alice's lifeless eyes.

It goes to show, the nurse thought, *how seldom we get what we deserve in life.* An obnoxious old bat like Alice lives in the lap of luxury, while the sweetest of old people suffer without proper care or respect at the end of their days.

It had been decided that Alice was too unpredictable to be one of the chosen clients for the VIP visit later this week.

"A politician and his wife," the manager had informed the staff at their weekly meeting. "You know the drill."

They did. They'd had visits like this before. Cheriton Assisted Living Facility received public funding for all kinds of programs for the clients and was often showcased in the media by local elected officials eager to show their support for seniors.

The nurse fussed around the room before escorting Alice to the shower. Enough time had elapsed since Alice had taken her pill for the nurse to briskly strip her naked and wash her body from top to toe with no resistance. Finally, she helped Alice on with a colourful dress and dried her wispy hair.

According to the ledger, Alice had a visitor that afternoon. It was essential that Alice look her best and be in a good mood.

"There you are." The nurse smoothed down Alice's dress. "You're ready for your visitor."

When the nurse was finished, she propped Alice up in a high-backed chair. The woman smiled vacantly at the TV.

The manager popped her head in just as the nurse was leaving to go to her next client. "Good morning, Alice, you look lovely, dear," she cooed. "All ready for your visitor?"

Alice said nothing, but bobbed her head up and down, staring straight ahead.

"Is it her son?" the nurse asked.

The manager shook her head and pressed a finger to her lips. "I can't say."

CHAPTER TWENTY-EIGHT

Andrew Vega stared at the papers on the desk in front of him. He'd borrowed an office from one of the civilian staff at the detachment and was trying to make sense of everything the team had discovered in the last twenty-four hours.

He was aware of Beth Stanton fidgeting in her chair from where she faced him on the other side of the desk. He closed his eyes for a second, trying to ignore the dread he'd felt since he had discovered Virgil Bell was Clara Bell's brother.

How was this possible? How could he have found himself in the middle of an investigation connected with Coffin Cove *again*? That place had nearly cost him his career, and now it looked like he'd have to go back.

Beth Stanton broke into his thoughts. "Are they significant?"

Vega heard the anxious note in her voice, and he looked up. "This is good work, Beth. At the moment, I'm not sure how significant these documents are, or if we can connect them to the shooting. But we don't have any other leads at all, so we need to investigate thoroughly. We must follow up on everything. Now, if you'll excuse me, I need to make a phone call."

Stanton left and closed the door, leaving him alone.

It was true. They had no other leads. As much as he wished the reason for Janice's death and Virgil's injury was as straightforward as greed for gold, there was nothing in the investigation to point to that.

Virgil's crew was solid. None of them had records, and they all had firm alibis. Only Clarence Bailey seemed aware that Virgil was thinking of selling his claims. Virgil's doctor had said the man was as fit as an ox, except for arthritis, and his lawyer had confirmed the appointment, but did not know what the meeting was about.

Everyone in town seemed to know Janice and her family. She was well-liked, no lingering resentment from old employees and no significant financial worries or recent windfalls. Julie and Norm were aware of Virgil and Janice's intention to marry, and they had no objections.

No, this tragic event was either an act of random violence by a madman, or there was something else they were all missing. Vega's gut feeling was that the puzzle would be solved in Coffin Cove.

Virgil's newspaper cuttings dated back to 1975. Some were about a missing person inquiry, a young native girl from the interior. Missing native women had commanded little attention back then, so this was strange.

Only recently, the Murdered and Missing Indigenous Women report by the RCMP had found that thousands of women had disappeared or had been murdered, and so far, almost no perpetrators had been brought to justice.

Why had Virgil been so interested? Virgil had saved other photographs, and Vega hoped Clara Bell could help him make sense of it all.

He picked up his phone to make a call.

* * *

Vega arrived at Whitehorse airport early the next morning. He'd contemplated driving back to Vancouver, but it would have taken two whole days if he was really pushing it. Plus, PC Beth Stanton was coming with him. He hoped she was already at the airport.

He was getting used to the climate, he thought, as he eased his truck along the frozen tarmac and parked in the short-term parking lot. But he didn't think he would ever get used to the lingering darkness of the fall and winter mornings. When he arrived in Vancouver two hours later, Whitehorse would still be enveloped in velvet blackness.

Superintendent Sinclair had been skeptical of Vega's reasoning. "Seems flimsy, Andrew," she'd said. "I will not tell you how to run your investigation, but if you screw up again . . ."

She hadn't finished her sentence, but Vega had known what she'd meant. She wouldn't go out on a limb for him. He was on his own. Again.

Superintendent Carter at the Whitehorse detachment hadn't been impressed either, especially when Vega had told him they had no reason to detain Archie and Trina any longer.

They still had a few hours, he'd informed Vega, and had insisted Sergeant Levine continue investigating.

Vega understood. Once someone was brought in for questioning, the excitement levels were high. It was deflating for the team to release a potential suspect. Reluctantly, Vega had agreed Norm should continue probing, but he had requested PC Stanton be assigned to accompany him.

Beth had been surprised, but relieved to get out of Whitehorse, Vega thought. He'd sensed some hostility towards Beth in the detachment. Probably because of her sister. It wasn't Beth's fault, but she had one other black mark against her. She was an outsider.

There was another reason for Vega to travel to Vancouver. Virgil Bell was being transferred to Richmond hospital for surgery.

"It's a long shot," the doctor had said simply, "but it's Virgil's best hope." He wouldn't speculate whether Virgil would wake up and be able to recall anything, but Vega wanted to be near, just in case.

Beth Stanton was waiting for Vega in the airport foyer. "Good morning, sir," she said. "I've already checked in."

Half an hour later, Vega settled into his seat and clicked his seatbelt. Only then did he allow himself to think about Andi Silvers. Coffin Cove was a tiny community. He was certain news of his arrival would be transmitted quickly on the active gossip network. He'd already decided to ask Jim Peters, Andi's boss, to accompany him to see Clara Bell. The news he had for her wasn't good, and Jim was a good friend to the old lady, as he remembered.

It was entirely possible he'd run into Andi.

This time, he thought, the investigation was of no interest to her. He could keep everything professional.

The engine roared into life, and Vega sat back as the plane taxied towards the runway, which was lit with floodlights. In a few moments they were in the air, and Vega reached for his laptop. It was two hours to Vancouver, plenty of time for some work. As Vega went over his notes, he wondered what the future held. If he couldn't get answers, his days at IHIT may be numbered.

CHAPTER TWENTY-NINE

Joshua Moore raised his empty glass and gestured to Walter for a refill. He rarely had more than one beer at the pub, preferring instead to buy a couple of six-packs and take them back to Hope Island. He could drink in peace there. But today was different. He had time to kill.

He'd checked at the dock when he was tying up his boat and had seen, with relief, the *Pipe Dream*'s usual mooring spot was empty. Harry must have been out fishing. He had been avoiding Harry since the explosion. He had given his statement to the cops, but he knew that wouldn't be good enough for Harry. Harry had been in shock when he had seen Joshua that night, but given time, it might occur to the man to ask more questions.

Joshua slapped his hand on the bar in frustration, making Walter look round and frown at him. He'd gone over and over the events of that night, and it had gone so well, until Harry had bumped into him. He should have stayed out of the way until later in the morning, but he had needed to make absolutely sure that Ed hadn't somehow survived the blast. When the commotion had died down, he'd asked one of the sport fishermen to take him back to Hope Island. He had been sure to reiterate the same story to him too — that

Ed had given him a ride to get more fuel and had offered to take him back. He'd been as shocked as everyone, but then Ed was known to drink heavily, and those propane stoves were dangerous if you forgot to turn them off.

The fisherman had nodded. "Yep, the way Ed drove that old truck when he was three sheets to the wind, well, surprising he didn't kill himself years ago."

The more Joshua thought about it, the better he felt.

"Here you are then, Joshua." Walter set his drink on the bar and removed his empty glass.

Joshua nodded his thanks to Walter and sipped his fresh pint. He took a quick glance around the pub. It was lunchtime, and he was the only person sitting at the bar. There was a couple sharing a plate of fries in a booth, but other than that, the place was empty.

He slid his hand into his jacket pocket and wrapped his fingers around the cell phone. He'd plugged it in the cigarette charger on the boat. It was Ed's. He could only use it for a short while longer, before someone missed it, or discovered it had been used after Ed's death. It mustn't lead back to him. The screen had three little green bars, so he knew he could receive a call. The cell phone reception on the island was spotty, so his plan was to wait for the call after he'd got his week's supplies.

Joshua checked the time. He still had half an hour to wait. He hoped Harry would be out fishing for a while.

Not for the first time, Joshua silently thanked Ed Brown. It was a shame that man had got greedy and lazy over the years. They'd both made good money together, grifting and poaching. Enough to keep life comfortable. But Ed had always wanted more. A "retirement package", he'd called it, and finally he'd figured out a way to get it.

At first, it had seemed a good idea. Ed had the proof, he said, about that body. If he threatened to go to the papers, they might pay up. They have a lot to lose, Ed had said. People like that made payouts all the time to keep their names clean. He'd make a few phone calls, issue a threat, and see what happened.

Joshua had thought it was all talk. Ed had grandiose schemes all the time, and they never came to anything. Then Ed had found out that Virgil Bell had grown a conscience after all these years up north. He had wanted to cash in quickly, before it all went wrong, before the complete story came out.

Ed had made a call. At least, that's what he had told Joshua. The recipient of the call had laughed. Ed had been angry. He'd even threatened to go to the newspapers, to that new reporter who had stirred up all the trouble since she'd arrived in Coffin Cove. She was seeing his son, he'd said. She'd definitely put out a good story, and once it was out, that'll be the end of the Hope Island development and other people's pension plans and lives would be over.

But Ed hadn't thought it through. Forty-five years later and people had changed. Some had become powerful with influence and money and weren't intimidated by the rambling threats of a drunk failure.

Joshua had often thought of that day back in 1975. He'd believed he'd never feel the same way again. But thanks to Ed Brown and his "insurance", Joshua felt free and awakened. Killing Ed had been a walk in the park.

Joshua finished his second pint and left the empty glass on the counter. Walter was talking to another customer, so he slipped out the door without acknowledging him. He walked around the back of the pub, out of sight of passers-by. He hovered by the dumpsters for a minute, and then worried about Cheryl, Walter's wife, coming out with garbage. He ducked behind the dumpsters and sat on the bottom step of the stairs leading up to the apartment over the pub.

Then he waited.

The phone buzzed at exactly the planned time.

"Yeah," Joshua said, flatly.

"Well done, Thomas. I read about the accident in the paper," the voice said. The voice was familiar, even after all these years.

Joshua grunted in reply.

"Mr Brown mentioned insurance. Items that may be a nuisance. These need to be located. Can you help me with that, Thomas? You don't mind me calling you Thomas, do you?"

Joshua shivered and smiled but didn't want to seem easily manipulated. "I don't know what you're talkin' about," he answered, but there was some hesitation in his voice. "Ed's dead. Ain't my problem anymore."

"Yes, it is, Thomas. The statute of limitations doesn't run out on a crime like yours, and Montana still has the death penalty. In fact, the state hasn't had an execution in over a decade, so they're overdue for a state-sanctioned killing."

"You don't know nuthin'," Joshua growled into the phone.

The voice laughed. "You don't believe that, Thomas. I think you and I understand each other perfectly. Now, this part is simple. Locate the insurance. I will call you on this number in three days, and I expect the task — this final task, Thomas — to be completed for me. I'm counting on you."

The phone went dead.

Joshua sat still, looking at it. He sighed. He hoped Harry hadn't cleared out Ed's trailer yet.

He'd have to make a plan. He had no intention of sitting out his final years on death row. And besides, he wanted to do this, even if he had to kill again. *Especially* if he had to kill again. He'd missed it.

CHAPTER THIRTY

The weather finally broke in Coffin Cove. Andi nursed a mug of coffee and watched Hephzibah wipe down tables and rearrange chairs as fat drops of rain slid down the windows. Andi contemplated everything that had happened in the last week.

Life changes in an instant, she thought, as she looked at Hephzibah's face. Grief and tiredness had replaced her friend's usually cheerful countenance.

Nothing prepared you for losing a parent. Even though it was expected that parents would die before you and eventually the pain had to be endured, it was still a shock. Andi had had weeks to prepare for the death of her mother, and she still remembered her disbelief when her mother had finally died.

"Can I help?" she asked. She wished she could hug away her friend's pain.

Hephzibah shook her head. "It's OK. I need to keep busy."

Ed's death was terrible enough, but news from the BC coroner had confirmed Harry's suspicions. Jim's contact at the coroner's office said the explosion had not been an accident. A salvage team was still working to retrieve the *Vera May* and a diver had found fragments of a beer bottle with traces of a fire accelerant among the charred remains of the wheelhouse.

Andi had told Harry and Hephzibah the news.

"It's not official yet," she had said. "But you'll get notification in a few days. Someone deliberately set the boat on fire, so Ed's death is murder or manslaughter at the least."

Harry had asked, "What now?"

"The coroner will authorize an investigation once she's officially confirmed the death as a homicide."

"No, I meant, what do *we* do now?"

"We find out who did this," Andi had said. "It's all we can do." But Andi did not know where to start.

"Can I sit down?"

Andi had been lost in her thoughts and hadn't noticed Bob Hinton ordering coffee.

She instantly felt awkward. She hadn't spoken to her father since her outburst in front of Ruth Cloutier. Andi's anger had been short-lived, and now she was just embarrassed.

Her father must have sensed her discomfort because he held up his hand and said, "Truce?"

She nodded and gave him a weak smile.

"You look deep in thought. Anything I can help you with?" Her father sat down facing her and waited for her reply.

"I don't think so."

"Anything to do with the death of your friend's father? That's tough, I'm sorry."

Andi looked at him.

"Jim told me. Actually, he's joining us in a few minutes. I just wanted a chance to apologize."

Andi was stunned. Her father, apologize?

"I guess there are lots of things I should apologize for," Bob said, "but I'd like to start by saying sorry for not telling you I was on the island, and not explaining why. It's perfectly understandable why you'd think . . . but I can assure you, my relationship with Ruth Cloutier is entirely professional."

Andi wasn't sure what to say. "Bob, I . . . er—"

"'Dad', please."

"OK, Dad, look, I shouldn't have lost my temper. I'm sorry too."

Hephzibah delivered two mugs to their table. Andi and Bob sat in awkward silence and sipped their coffee.

"Dad, why—"

"Andi, I have—"

Bob smiled. "After you."

"Why are you here, Dad?" Andi asked.

"Ruth Cloutier's sister went missing in 1975. We believe she came to Vancouver Island. We were following a lead."

Andi stared at her father in amazement. Investigating a missing person from decades ago? This wasn't the man she remembered. Then she thought of something. "Joyce Mayfield? Was she your lead?"

It was Bob's turn to stare in surprise. "How did you know?"

"I covered the shooting. You left your business card, and the cashier remembered your phone call. You made quite an impression on Joyce."

"And now she's dead," Bob said. "I don't think the shooting was a coincidence."

"Really? You think she was killed because she knew something about Ruth's missing sister?" It seemed far-fetched to Andi.

Her father nodded. "I'm working on that theory. We believe Joyce helped Essie — that's Melissa, Ruth's sister — and we think Essie ended up on Hope Island, at the women's commune."

Andi felt a chill. And it wasn't just because the café door had opened.

She remembered Ruth's reaction when they had heard the news about the human remains when they were on Hope Island. There was something else about that day too, but Andi couldn't put her finger on it.

Jim had walked into the café. Andi waved at him, and he joined them. She turned back to her father, eager to know the rest of the story. "Dad, does Ruth think the remains found on Hope Island belong to her sister?"

"Yes, I'm afraid so. She's given a DNA sample, and is hoping they can tell her definitively, one way or the other."

Andi turned to Jim. "What about Clara's theory? She thinks the remains belong to her sister-in-law."

Jim told Bob about Virgil Bell, Clara's brother, and her fear the remains belonged to Virgil's wife.

As Bob Hinton listened, Andi watched his face. There was a flash of recognition when Jim mentioned Virgil's name. She mentally filed away a note to herself. There were a few things she needed to get straight with her father.

"I'm due to meet Clara in a short while," Jim said. "I'm just waiting for someone. Oh, here he is."

Andi looked up and felt a flutter of recognition as Inspector Andrew Vega walked in.

"Jim, how are you?" Vega walked over and shook Jim's hand. "Hi, Andi, nice to see you again," he said.

"You too," she said and felt her face get hot. Internally scolding herself for behaving like a teenager with a crush, she introduced her father. "I hope you have some better news for Clara," she said, hoping to divert further attention from her blushes.

Vega sighed. "I'm afraid the news isn't good. But I need to talk to her directly. Jim, are you ready?"

Jim got up to leave. He turned to Andi. "I'll at least tell her she might be wrong about the remains."

"What remains?" Vega asked.

Jim explained about the discovery on Hope Island. "Clara's worried they might belong to Alice Bell, Virgil's estranged wife."

"I can put her mind at rest about that," Vega said. "Alice Bell is alive and well in a nursing home in Richmond."

As Jim grilled Vega about this new information, Andi looked at her father again. He didn't look the least bit surprised.

* * *

An hour later, Clara, Jim and Inspector Vega were sitting around the table in Clara's trailer.

Vega had thought it best PC Stanton didn't attend this interview. He remembered Clara to be fiercely private. He thought she'd be more open if only he and Jim were there.

Clara's face was hard to read, but Vega could see the pain in her eyes. Anger, too, he thought as he told her everything he could about Janice's death and her brother's injury. He tried to be gentle but direct. He thought Clara was the type of person who wouldn't want to be patronized.

At first, Clara was quiet, seeming to process the information, and then she asked Vega to explain Virgil's condition again. He did so without sugar-coating it. He didn't want Clara to have false hope.

She nodded, as if relieved, when Vega explained that Alice Bell was still alive. He also told her about Archie, although he stressed they hadn't yet confirmed he was Alice's son. Of course, he said, Archie might not be Virgil's son. It would take time to establish the truth.

Clara listened carefully, and then wordlessly got up from the table and went over to an open cardboard box. She brought back a handful of black-and-white photographs and laid them on the table in front of Vega.

Jim said he'd already seen two of these photographs. One was of Virgil as a young man, laughing with a friend as if neither of them had a care in the world. The other was Virgil in his fifties, a brooding, intense man. Clara had two more pictures.

Vega picked up one and looked at it closely. It was a wedding photo. Virgil was standing stiffly, his hair slicked back, a fixed smile on his face as he looked directly into the camera. His arm was around his bride, who was laughing. Her head was thrown back, and her hair had come loose from her veil. She was tiny. Her waist was pinched in, and she clutched a posy of flowers. It was a charming photo, Vega thought. A newly married couple, blissfully happy, ready to take on the world.

He put the photo down and looked at the other one. The subjects of this picture seemed unaware of the camera. The same girl sat on a porch step in front of a small clapboard house. Vega thought it must be somewhere in Coffin Cove. He recognized the style of house. The girl wasn't laughing in this photo. Her hair was tied back, and her face was unsmiling as she watched a toddler splash in a tin bath. The girl's shouldered sagged a little. Like many new mothers, she looked exhausted.

"Is this Virgil's wife?" Vega asked.

Clara nodded. "Those are the only pictures I have of her and the child." She sighed. "Virgil was a fool over that girl."

Vega studied both photographs. "You said Virgil had something on his mind? A burden?"

Clara handed Vega an envelope. He recognized the return address as Clarence Bailey's house in Dawson City.

Vega scanned the letter, then passed it back to Clara. "Virgil wasn't specific about his burden," he said. "Do you have any idea what he meant?"

Clara shrugged. "As far as I knew, his only troubles were brought on by that girl. I don't know much about his life since then. I just hoped he was happy. And now—"

For the first time, Vega heard a catch in her voice. He rubbed his face and then picked up one photo and studied it again. "Who is this? A friend of Virgil's?"

"His best friend, once upon a time. Till they fought over Alice. I don't know if Virgil ever spoke to him after they both went looking for her."

"They went looking for Alice together?"

"Yep. The two of them came to some kind of truce and went looking for Alice. Right before Virgil left. Come to think of it, Ralph must have been the last to see Virgil before he went north."

"Ralph? Where is he now?"

Jim answered for Clara. "Ralph Stewart. You must have heard of him. He's one of Canada's most successful businessmen. His development company is in Steveston. I've been trying to contact him for Clara, but he won't return my calls. Why do you want to know?"

"Same reason as Clara. Maybe Ralph Stewart knows what burden Virgil was carrying," Vega said. "Maybe Virgil wrote more than one letter."

CHAPTER THIRTY-ONE

Andi sat in the office alone, staring at the wall. Jim and Andrew Vega had gone to visit Clara. Maybe she had some information or insight about the shooting in the Yukon. She knew Vega was a deft interviewer. He extracted vital information from interviewees, knowledge or details they didn't know they had. Often something that seemed irrelevant might blow a case open.

Before heading to the office, Andi had walked down to the dock and found Harry watching a marine salvage company hauling the last pieces of the boat wreckage from the water.

He was standing with his hands in his pockets and his shoulders hunched. "This doesn't make sense to me," he had said, almost to himself. "I just can't figure this out."

Andi had left him alone. She had recognized his need for space and time to think, to let details settle in his head. Even in her own mind, the strands of stories and strange events were tangled. Like Harry, she couldn't make sense of it all. She couldn't see a pattern, just a collection of weird coincidences and connections.

Andi flipped through her notes. Her gut instinct was telling her that Virgil, Joyce, Ed and Essie were connected, that their threads were intertwined, but she was questioning herself. Her father had added another layer of intrigue, and now she sensed a story. She needed a place to start.

The presence of her father always gave her a severe case of imposter syndrome, she realized. Every time she clashed with her father, she felt as if she wasn't worthy of calling herself an investigative journalist.

It's time to get over that, she scolded herself. *I have to let all these old feelings go.*

As if she'd manifested him through her thoughts, she heard someone clear their throat and she turned around to see her father in the doorway. He was carrying a briefcase.

"May I come in?" he asked. "Am I interrupting?"

"Yes, to the first question and no to the second," Andi said. "I'm just thinking, that's all."

He came in and sat on the edge of a desk. "You used to do that when you were little," he said. "If you had a problem, you used to stare into space, thinking hard until you figured it out. You mother worried about you, but I could see you were just—"

"Well, I'm all grown up now," Andi said, suddenly irritated at his reference to her childhood and her mother.

"Yes, of course." He seemed deflated for a moment.

Andi regretted snapping at him, remembering their truce. Maybe he was only trying to find some common ground. She sighed. "I was thinking through these stories, these cases, and trying to establish connections. But I'm worried I'm making something out of nothing. Maybe Virgil, Joyce and Ed are separate events, tragic but unconnected incidents. But then . . ."

"Then you can't get rid of that gut feeling that tells you they are all connected?"

Bob Hinton stood up and opened his briefcase. It was full of files and documents. He extracted one sheet of paper and walked over to the blank wall.

"This is a picture of Essie George," he said. "Do you have tape?"

Andi handed him a roll, and he attached the picture to the wall. She gave an involuntary gasp. "That could be Ruth," she said. She peered closer. The picture was grainy, but the resemblance to Ruth Cloutier was uncanny. Andi felt as though this was important to the investigation, but she didn't know why. There was something buried in the back of her mind she couldn't comprehend yet.

Her father was taping more pictures and documents to the wall. "I do this so I have a visual of the entire story," he explained. "I can see connections and patterns."

Andi laughed. "I do exactly the same thing."

"Of course you do." Bob grinned. "You watched me do it a thousand times. I used to worry you'd get nightmares from looking at crime scene photos, and your mo—" He broke off, for once sensitive to Andi's feelings, she thought.

She rescued him. "I remember," she said, although she didn't. She brought over her stack of documents and notes. "Let's see what we've got here." For the next few minutes, they forgot the awkwardness between them as they worked.

Andi stood back to survey the pinned photos and documents.

"Let's start with the facts." Bob tapped Essie's picture, which was now in the centre of their story wall. "In the summer of 1975, Essie George, Ruth's sister, left her home to go camping. She didn't tell her grandmother, Nora, she was going, because she'd arranged to go with a boy. The boy's name was Michael."

"And how do we know this?" Andi asked. Her job was to fact-check every detail. She did this when she was working alone, questioning assumptions, making sure she had a corroborating story from another source.

"Ruth's aunt said she saw Essie physically get in the van with Michael and his friends, and Michael apparently confirmed this in a later statement but said they had let Essie out just as they left town. This—" Bob tapped the picture — "is Michael, Essie's camping friend."

Andi felt a jolt of recognition. "Is that . . . ?"

"Yes," Bob finished for her. "Michael Halwell, aspiring prime minister, currently campaigning for your soon-to-be vacated seat. The Nanaimo–Ladysmith Riding."

"OK, Dad. I hope you've got more than the coincidence that the Halwells were in the same area as Essie George?"

Bob Hinton held up his hand. "Of course."

Andi nodded for her father to continue. He tapped another picture on the wall. "This is Michael's camper van. Ruth's aunt described a van that was covered with flowers and psychedelic patterns, same as this one."

Andi felt herself get impatient, just like when she was a child and had needed help with homework. Her father loved making a performance when a simple explanation would do.

"Here's another picture of the van in 1975, the summer of Essie's disappearance, with Michael and his friends in Tofino," Bob continued. "Halwell released this picture on social media to set the scene for his campaign next year."

Andi recognized the picture and remembered the conversation she had had with Jim about Michael and Elizabeth Halwell. "I don't see Essie in that picture," she commented. "All this proves is Michael Halwell and friends were on the island. It kind of confirms his story, that Essie didn't go with them. Not all the way, anyway. Do you have a copy of Halwell's statement?"

Bob nodded. "Yes. Based on that statement, Ruth Cloutier spent years looking for Essie in the wrong place."

Andi thought of something. "Did Michael say where he and his friends went after they left Essie? And is it possible Essie travelled on to Vancouver Island without him?"

"No, nobody followed up, or checked on Michael Halwell's statement at all. But that's not unusual for those times. Remember, Michael is from a family of influence, and Essie was a young native girl. It's likely the police just took Michael's word for what happened. It is possible that Essie travelled here on her own, or with another group of people, but not probable."

Andi stood in front of the wall. "She was very beautiful." Despite the grainy quality of the photograph, Andi could see Essie's fine features and wide smile. "No wonder Michael Halwell was attracted to her." She turned her gaze to Halwell's picture. Even in his sixties, the politician was a handsome man. "They would have made a striking couple," she mused. But Elizabeth was beautiful too. Two blond, blue-eyed, laughing teenagers looked out from the picture, exuding confidence and optimism. They didn't have a care in the world. Was it likely Michael Halwell would have invited Essie George along on a camping trip? Something didn't feel right to Andi.

"Michael Halwell has an eye for beautiful women," Bob commented, as if reading Andi's thoughts. "There are rumours he was quite the womanizer when he was younger, but they are unsubstantiated."

Andi felt herself get hot again as she recalled the angry insults she'd hurled at her father. "Dad . . ." she began, but her father had moved away and was staring at Andi's article and photograph of Joyce Mayfield.

"Our investigation took us to Tofino and Ucluelet, the two coastal villages. Ruth and I and showed Essie's photo to as many locals as possible. It was a long shot, but we did get a lead."

"Joyce Mayfield."

"She had the answers," Bob said. He turned to face Andi. "I don't believe her death was a coincidence. Andi, I've read your reporting on Joyce's death. Was there anything you left out?"

Andi sighed. "Yes." She told him about Ryan and her promise to him and his father.

She thought her father would be dismissive of her decision. Instead, he said, "Poor kid. It's hard to get the balance, isn't it? Between reporting the truth and not making it worse for innocent victims."

Andi found her notes from Ryan's interview and handed them to her father. "I have a photo, too. Harry asked Ryan about the gun the shooter used." She found the picture on her phone, and in a couple of clicks, the printer was whirring.

As her father taped up the new pictures, Andi thought it was time to grill her father a little. She was certain he was holding something back.

"Dad, how did you get involved in this?" she asked. "I mean, how did you meet Ruth Cloutier and why did you agree to help her?"

She saw Bob hesitate for the briefest of moments, and then he said, "Andi, I will tell you, but I'd rather work through this first, OK?"

Andi felt some irritation. "Look, I know you dislike sharing information in case anyone gets the scoop first, but I'm damned if I am going to do the grunt work on this and then let you walk off with the story."

Bob held his hands up. "Whoa, stop right there. It isn't like that. Andi, I've been working on something for years — an overlapping investigation that led me to Ruth Cloutier and her missing sister. This—" he gestured at the wall — "is a part of it, I'm sure. Once we've worked through this, I promise I'll share more with you. But until then, you'll have to trust me. I'm sorry."

Andi sat in silence. She had little choice. Her father had pieces of the puzzle and she needed them.

She nodded. "OK. I'll wait. But answer me this. How did you make the leap from Joyce Mayfield out on the West Coast to Hope Island? Why would Melissa have gone there, and how did she get there? It doesn't make sense."

Before Bob Hinton could reply, Andi heard footsteps on the stairs and Jim opened the office door. He came in with Andrew Vega and a woman Andi didn't recognize.

"How did it go with Clara?" Andi asked.

"She's relieved Virgil didn't kill his wife, and she confirmed he was worried about some kind of 'burden' before he was shot, but apart from that, she didn't know much," Jim answered. "But she thinks his old friend Ralph Stewart might know."

"We'll interview him," Vega said.

"Sir, look at this!" The woman was staring straight at the picture of Essie George. "This is the same woman in the newspaper clipping, I'm cert—"

"PC Stanton!" Andrew Vega cut her off. Andi could see he was annoyed.

"You found a newspaper article about Essie George in Virgil's things?" she asked the woman, who had flushed red.

"Andi, we can't talk about our investigation. You know that," Vega said.

"Andrew, come on, this isn't just about your investigation. Ruth Cloutier has been looking for her sister for years. If Virgil knew something—"

"He knew something," Bob Hinton put in. "Virgil Bell wrote to me. He said he could help Ruth Cloutier, and he was supposed to meet me here, in Coffin Cove. Except he was shot before he could talk to me. Same as Joyce Mayfield."

There was silence in the room. Andi saw it all now. That was how her father had connected Essie to Hope Island. What else did he know?

Vega was first to speak. "Mr . . . er, Hinton, is it? I hope you still have that letter. I'll have to see it and I'll have to ask you to make a statement." He looked at the wall. "Who is Joyce Mayfield?"

Andi found her voice. "Another person who knew something about Essie George's disappearance. She was shot and killed during an apparent robbery."

PC Stanton pointed to the printout of the gun. "Is that the gun used to kill Joyce Mayfield?"

"Not that gun exactly, but similar. A witness to the shooting identified it from this picture."

PC Stanton looked at Andrew Vega. She was obviously reluctant to say anything after his earlier rebuke.

"Was Virgil shot with a gun like this?" Andi guessed.

The expression on Vega's face was all she needed to know.

The door swung open and Harry came in. He looked around the room and seemed surprised to see so many people.

217

Andi went over to him. "Are you OK?"

"I know why Joshua Moore has been bothering me," he said.

"Go on."

"I bumped into Joshua that morning when I was looking for Ed, during the fire, before we knew he was . . . Anyway, I thought it was weird, him being over here so early. He told me Ed had picked him up so he could get diesel, and he was carrying a can, but there was something wrong."

Harry looked up and saw that everyone was listening. He carried on. "The smell. He didn't smell like diesel. He smelled of gas. Petroleum. It's a different smell. And there's no reason for him to have gas. His old boat doesn't run on it. But I was distracted, worried about Ed, so I didn't think anything of it."

"He might have misspoken?" Jim said. "It was a wild morning. He might have been confused."

"Who is Joshua Moore?" Vega asked. "What does he have to do with anything?"

"Joshua Moore lives on Hope Island. He's an old draft dodger from the Vietnam War," Jim explained. "We had lots of them hiding out on the Gulf Islands. Joshua's been there for decades."

"And you think he has something to do with your father's death?" Vega directed his question to Harry.

Harry shrugged. "I don't know. There's something off about the whole thing, and I think Joshua knows more than he's letting on."

"Clara thought Ed knew something about Virgil," Andi chipped in.

Vega rubbed his eyes. "Let me get this straight. Clara Bell thinks Ed knew something about whatever's been bothering Virgil enough to want to meet a reporter in his childhood home — and this Joshua Moore guy was somehow involved in Ed's death? Is that right?"

"Yes," Andi and Jim spoke in unison.

"OK." Andrew Vega sat down on the edge of the desk and was quiet for a minute. "I'm not here to investigate a cold case about a missing girl, unless it's connected to my investigation. And so far, all you have is speculation and theories. No firm evidence." He looked pointedly at Andi. "I'm not here for wild goose chases. I don't see anything here that helps my case."

"Except the gun, sir," Beth Stanton said.

Vega sighed. "You're right, Constable. Please liaise with Sergeant Levine and whoever is in charge of the investigation into the Mayfield shooting. Do you know who that is?"

"Diane Fowler." Andi pulled a face.

"Inspector Fowler," Vega corrected her. "I'd like to speak to you in the morning, Mr Hinton, about Virgil's letter." He pointed at Andi's father, who nodded.

Vega turned to Harry. "Please talk to Sergeant Beaufort at the detachment. I'm sure he can help you with your concerns."

"Sure," Harry said, but Andi knew from his tone that Harry would rather talk to Joshua Moore directly.

"What about Ralph Stewart?" Jim asked.

"I'll be speaking to Mr Stewart in the morning. Right now, I'm going to get something to eat and an early night."

Vega's phone rang. He answered it and walked over to the other side of the room.

Andi turned to her father. "You have a letter from Virgil Bell? Why didn't you say?"

"I was coming to that," Bob Hinton said. "But this is excellent news about the gun. Good work."

Andi felt a flush of pleasure slide up her neck, but she wasn't about to let her father off the hook.

Vega finished his call. "Good news," he said. "Virgil Bell is out of surgery and awake."

* * *

It was late, but Andi didn't want to go home just yet.

Vega had left in a hurry with PC Stanton to arrange an early flight to the mainland. If Virgil could talk, he might provide a break in the case.

She could tell Vega was hoping for a result. He looked uncomfortable being in Coffin Cove again. Andi couldn't blame him. The last time he was here, the investigation had resulted in his suspension.

Harry had marched off with purpose. Andi knew he'd wouldn't talk to Sergeant Beaufort. He'd look for Joshua Moore himself.

Andi sat in the office, gazing at the wall, which was covered with photographs and notes. Although she could see the investigation taking shape, her father had left her most important question unanswered.

Why was Bob Hinton helping Ruth Cloutier? Why was the infamous reporter, once feared by politicians and celebrities alike, working on a cold case of a missing and murdered native girl?

Just before Bob had left the office that evening, he'd taken a call from Ruth. The DNA test had proved the human remains on Hope Island were definitely related to Ruth Cloutier, and therefore most likely to be those of Melissa George, her long-lost sister.

Ruth was very emotional, Bob had said, and had left the office to be with her. Andi didn't recall another time in her life when she'd seen her father so considerate about someone else's feelings. Either he had changed, or maybe she'd never really known him at all.

She turned her attention to their investigation. She stood and stretched and walked over to the wall, carrying a red marker pen. At least one theory was now fact. They had a positive identification for the human remains. Andi put a tick mark on the picture of Essie George. But solving one mystery had created several more.

Why and how had Essie been on Hope Island? What had Virgil Bell kept secret all these years, and what had he wanted to reveal to Bob Hinton? And how was Michael Halwell involved? Even if Halwell had brought Essie to Vancouver Island, how had she made her way to Hope Island if they'd been camping on the West Coast?

Joyce Mayfield and Virgil Bell had answers, but now Joyce was dead and Virgil was barely clinging to life. Andi traced her finger over the picture of the gun, still taped to the wall. She hesitated before she ticked the gun and the pictures of Joyce and Virgil. She didn't have the ballistics report, and it was unlikely she'd ever see it, but Andi had seen the look that had passed between Vega and Stanton, and that was good enough for her.

Vega had grudgingly left copies of Virgil's newspaper clipping with Andi. "*Only* because they are in the public domain," he'd said.

Andi looked through them all, carefully looking at each one. She stopped when she found an article about Essie George's disappearance. It was a brief summary of facts and included a quote from Michael Halwell.

Elizabeth and I are heartbroken for the family. I wish I had driven Essie back home that day, instead of dropping her off as she insisted. We both feel terrible.

Andi checked the byline. It was written by "B Silvers". It must have been her father. But Silvers was Andi's mother's maiden name. Andi had taken it when her mother reverted to her maiden name after Bob left. Why would her father have used a pseudonym?

Frustrated, Andi moved along the wall to the picture of Virgil Bell. Clara had been so convinced the terrible burden in his past was his disastrous marriage to Alice. Clara had even been willing to believe her brother was capable of murdering his wife. Now they knew Alice Bell was in some nursing home, so Virgil was not a murderer. But Clara had told Jim about Virgil and his friend Ralph looking for Alice on Hope Island, so Andi ticked Virgil's picture. Plus, he'd had the article about Essie George in his possession. Maybe Virgil's burden was the death of Essie George? If Clara had thought him capable of killing Alice, maybe he'd killed Essie? But why?

Clara also thought that Ed Brown had known about Virgil's burden. But now Ed was dead. Andi put a tick on Ed's photograph, too.

She stood back from the wall. Her red ticks leaped out at her. But she wasn't looking at them. She was studying the pictures she hadn't marked — the old photograph of the Halwells and the black-and-white picture of Ralph Stewart. Andi grabbed a blank piece of paper from her desk, wrote "*Joshua Moore*" in large letters and taped it to the wall.

Andi surveyed the wall again. She might not have answers, but she had three clear leads to follow. She picked up her phone. After a brief call to her father, she had a plan in place for the next day.

Her stomach growled. It was nearly midnight, and she hadn't eaten. She shoved her cell phone in her pocket and walked over to the door, intending to switch off the lights and leave.

She took one last look at the wall and stopped.

A missing piece of the puzzle slotted into place. It had been floating at the back of her mind, just beyond her grasp, but now something else made sense. She smiled to herself and mentally ticked it off. Maybe her father hadn't changed that much, after all.

CHAPTER THIRTY-TWO

Ralph Stewart stared at his phone. The ping had interrupted his morning coffee. He disliked modern forms of communication. He particularly disliked the intrusive nature of technology, which allowed all kinds of people to send messages whenever they liked, even at 6.30 a.m.

Usually, Ralph kept his phone turned off and his laptop closed outside of office hours, and even when he was behind his desk, he still depended on a personal assistant to carefully monitor his schedule and arrange in-person appointments for him to conduct his business. He preferred face-to-face meetings, where he could study body language and listen to telltale changes in tone of voice.

It was old-fashioned, he knew. But he didn't care. He still dictated letters and made sure important business was kept off the internet. He'd seen too many powerful people brought to their knees because of a software breach or an embarrassing email made public. It wasn't that he was too old to keep up with the relentless march of technology, not at all. He'd made careful investments to keep his businesses at the forefront of efficient changes over the decades, sometimes to the dismay and opposition of unions and politicians, who seemed to think their opinion should matter to Ralph.

This morning, Ralph had missed his Saturday walk. He didn't usually spend time at the office during the weekend, but today was different. He had a meeting. Ralph conceded to himself that his annoyance with his phone had probably been exacerbated by a lack of fresh air and the disruption of his morning routine.

Routine and discipline. Two of the "four pillars of his success" as a businessman. At least, that's what it said in his biography. The other two pillars were fiscal responsibility and the ability to embrace change. When his ghostwriter had presented Ralph with the first draft of his book, Ralph had been amazed.

"People don't know this shit already?"

The writer had shrugged. "You're a powerful businessman. Your readers want to know the secrets to your success."

"Taking a walk and looking after your money shouldn't be fucking secrets to success. They're goddamn common sense."

"Well, sir, you came from humble beginnings. Lots of people want to emulate your journey. This book is a kind of . . . roadmap for them. If you could do it, so could they — that's the premise of the book, sir."

Humble beginnings. Local boy made good. Ralph was used to these epitaphs. Every damn interview he gave, they harped back to his days as a fisherman. He hadn't even owned a boat. He'd been a deckhand on someone else's. He always said the same about his meteoric rise in the business world: "Just hard work and a little luck. And a successful businessman is only as good as his word."

It was the usual bullshit, which people lapped up. The truth was Ralph's success was because of some powerful people in his life, who expected him to keep his mouth shut in return for lucrative opportunities. It was a cut-throat world he inhabited.

His survival had depended on his ability to embrace whatever was in front of him and to leave the past behind without a moment's thought. Or at least, the part of the past that didn't serve him.

Ralph ignored the second ping from his phone and walked over to the window, taking his coffee with him. The ache in his bones reminded him of his impending birthday. He didn't mind getting older. His mind had never been so sharp. Physically, he was still in good shape. He'd given up drinking and smoking years ago, he ate well and exercised, even took yoga lessons.

Ralph looked over Steveston Harbour from his office and drank his coffee. He did this most mornings. The view of the boats on the muddy Fraser River reminded him of those early days fishing out of Coffin Cove. Those were still the best days of his life — even the day he'd made his first million dollars didn't compare with a good day of fishing.

He wished he could open the window and breathe in the briny air. But none of the windows opened, and the office was air-conditioned to the perfect temperature at all times.

He felt trapped, suddenly, yearning for freedom from constant business decisions and worrying about his profit margins. In the last few weeks, he'd had plenty of reasons to worry.

This morning when he'd arrived at the office, he'd had an urge to walk along the waterfront and grab a coffee from the fishermen's café. Maybe sit in the corner for a while and listen to the banter.

But that would never happen. As soon as he was recognized, there would be an awkward silence. Ralph Stewart owned several high-profile businesses in Vancouver, including the development company that had transformed much of Steveston from a busy fishing port, smelling of fish slime and seaweed, to one of the most sought-after residential enclaves in the Vancouver area. He'd been instrumental in replacing riverfront warehousing with smart condos and hardware stores with artisan boutiques. Newcomers from the east didn't care that the water view was of the muddy Fraser River. It was waterfront, and they'd paid small fortunes to look at it from their living-room windows.

The fishing industry had been pushed out. The warehouses and net sheds had downsized and relocated to a site further down the river — inconvenient for the fishermen, but out of sight for the new residents. Ralph predicted it would be less than a decade before that site would also be ripe for development. He'd already purchased options on the property. He didn't want to see his legacy reduced to nothing but a second-rate autobiography.

His desk phone rang. Ralph walked back to his desk, picked up the receiver, and listened.

"That will be fine," he said, and replaced the receiver. He sat heavily on his chair and took a shaky breath. Then he unlocked and opened his desk drawer. He felt around the bottom and pressed a small indentation, which revealed a secret compartment. He pulled out an envelope. It was handwritten.

He held it for a moment before removing the contents and laying them on the desk. He smoothed out the folded letter and looked at the single photograph of two young men laughing at the camera without a care in the world.

"Damn it, Virgil," Ralph murmured. "Why couldn't you let things be?"

CHAPTER THIRTY-THREE

Bob Hinton beamed at the receptionist at Stewart Developments. "Lovely," he said. "And the brooch, of course." He added a wink, which Andi thought was rather overdoing it.

The middle-aged, severe-looking woman who'd glared at them when they'd pressed the buzzer on the office door — not happy about working on a Saturday, Andi suspected — relaxed as Bob flirted with her. She even blushed and giggled, before picking up the phone.

"Seriously, Dad?" Andi hissed.

Bob shrugged and grinned. "It still works," he said. "You'll see."

In a few minutes, Andi and Bob were following the receptionist down a corridor and into an elevator. Andi was relieved that her father talked only about the history of Stewart Developments and refrained from making the poor woman swoon.

Ralph Stewart was sitting behind a desk. The office had floor-to-ceiling windows and Andi's attention was immediately drawn to the view of the Fraser River.

"Magnificent, isn't it?" Ralph said. He got up from behind the desk and held out his hand.

Andi could see the trace of the young man in Clara's photograph. He'd aged well, and although he was dressed casually, his clothes were expensive. *A far cry from the boy on a fishing boat*, she thought.

Bob Hinton shook Stewart's hand first, then Andi.

"Thank you for seeing us, Mr Stewart, especially on a Saturday," she began, but he interrupted.

"Miss Silvers, I imagine you knew I wouldn't refuse you, given the message you imparted to my receptionist. I was very disturbed to hear about the tragic events in the Yukon. But I haven't been in touch with Virgil Bell for years, so I'm not sure how I can help you."

His tone was even as he walked to his chair and sat down again. He gestured for them both to sit in chairs facing him across the desk.

Straight to business. But if he really didn't have any information, Andi was sure he'd wouldn't have bothered to see them.

It was Bob's turn. "Do you know who I am, Mr Stewart?"

"Of course," Ralph said. "And I'm not sure why a *celebrity* journalist would be interested in me."

Bob smiled back, seemingly unfazed. "How well do you know Michael Halwell?" he asked abruptly.

Ralph's expression darkened for a moment, but he shrugged. "Fairly well, I suppose. We've met at various charity and business functions over the years."

"When did you first meet him?"

"I can't remember. What does this have to do with—"

"Did you meet him in 1975? On Hope Island?" Bob Hinton fired back.

"Where? I'm not sure what you two want—"

"You were good friends with Virgil Bell?" Andi asked in a soothing tone, changing the subject. The man was getting agitated. She shot a warning look at her father. *Don't go too hard on him. We'll get thrown out.*

"Yes, I was. But that was years ago when we were boys. I was sorry to hear about the shooting accident."

"It wasn't an accident, Mr Stewart. You and Virgil had a falling out. Is that correct? Over his wife, Alice?"

A smile formed on Ralph's face, but his eyes darted back and forth between Bob and Andi.

"You've been talking to Clara. She was always a little . . . *eccentric*, shall we say? I have to admit, I flirted a little with Virgil's wife, Alice, and he was rightly upset. But that was a long time ago, and I believe the marriage didn't work out."

He sounded calmer now.

"You recently got a letter from Virgil Bell. You and he share a secret about a day on Hope Island in 1975. A secret which resurfaced at the same time human remains were found on Hope Island, earlier this year. Virgil wanted to clear his conscience. And that's what got him shot, Mr Stewart."

"I don't know what—"

"You received the letter, and you put into motion a series of events designed to keep that secret, Mr Stewart." Bob Hinton wasn't asking questions anymore.

Ralph stood up. "This interview is over."

"How often do you visit Alice?" Bob Hinton asked. "Have you been looking out for her, all these years?"

Andi stared at her father. How could he possibly know that?

Ralph was staring at him, too. He was silent for a moment.

"I don't know what you are talking about," he said in a measured tone. "But it sounds like a shakedown to me, one that my lawyer will deal with. I suggest, Miss Silvers, you rethink your journalistic methods. You have already been fired from one job, and I guarantee I won't stop at destroying your career. I will destroy the *Coffin Cove Gazette* at the same time. It would be a shame, of course, because Jim Peters is a good man, as I remember."

Andi didn't answer. *Interesting*, she thought. His speech sounded rehearsed. He must have spent the last hours digging into her past.

"Mr Stewart," Bob said calmly, "Virgil Bell is awake. He's talking to the police right now. This is your opportunity to get your story out there before we publish our article."

Ralph's face drained of colour.

"And once we're done with this story," Bob continued, "we'll be digging into all those contracts Stewart Developments has been awarded over the years, until we find the evidence of corruption and the connection to Elizabeth Halwell."

Elizabeth Halwell? Andi stared at her father.

Ralph Stewart slumped back into his chair.

"Come on, Ralph." Bob Hinton leaned across the desk. "Your old friend is fighting for his life. His partner was shot and killed, and an innocent woman was gunned down. How many more lives will be lost or ruined, just so you can protect . . . this." Bob waved his hand around the office. "Do the right thing, and we'll do our best to keep your name out of it."

Ralph appeared to think, holding his head in his hands. He looked up. Tears glistened in his eyes.

"I can't go on the record." He said it so quietly, Andi had to lean forward to hear him.

"Just tell us your story. It will be OK." Bob Hinton's tone was kind now, Andi observed. Promising to help, bringing Ralph in as though they were both confidants rather than reporters. She'd used that tactic before, and it worked. But it was ruthless. She knew as well as Bob if Ralph Stewart knew anything incriminating, the police would have to be informed.

"Just keep Alice out of it. *Please.*"

"We will," Bob said. "Why don't you start by telling us about Alice?"

Another strategy, Andi thought. *Get him talking about a comforting subject first.*

"She was always Virgil's girl." Ralph gazed out of the office window as if he were looking back into the past. "Virgil was taken with her from the first moment he saw her."

He looked back at Bob and Andi. "When she was young, she was wild, you know? Fearless. Beautiful. She just turned up in Coffin Cove one day, and Virgil fell for her right from the start. She loved him, I think. Anyway, I was smitten too, and Alice, well . . . she was a free spirit. Virgil wanted to marry her, and finally she agreed after she was pregnant, but his family didn't like her. His father was strictly religious. When the baby was born, Alice struggled. She was lonely when Virgil went fishing, and I . . ." His cheeks reddened. "I . . . visited her."

"You had an affair?" Andi asked.

He nodded. "Yes, I was sleeping with her."

"Did Virgil know?"

"Not at first. Then he came home and found us. She stopped seeing me for a while. I got on with my life and tried to stop thinking about her, and then I bumped into her again. Well, I suppose it wasn't an accident. I convinced myself Alice had tried to do the right thing but wasn't really happy."

He looked sadly at Andi. "Terrible, isn't it? Hoping the person you love isn't happy? But I was obsessed, I suppose."

Andi silently agreed. She wasn't in a position to judge. She'd been blinded with obsession in a previous relationship, too.

"You started seeing Alice again?"

"Yes. Virgil was still fishing and was away from home a lot. I started seeing Alice regularly."

"But this time someone else found out?"

Ralph nodded. "Virgil's sister, Clara. She used to look after the baby. One day she brought the baby back to Virgil's house early and caught us both."

"Did she tell Virgil?"

"No. She insisted we did."

Andi visualized the small, fierce woman and imagined there would have been no arguing with her. "So, you told Virgil? How was that?"

"We did. Alice wanted to tell him herself, but I had to be there. I wasn't that much of a jerk. It was awful. At first, Virgil was in shock. Then he got angry, and we had a fight."

"An actual physical fight?"

Ralph laughed, but without humour. "Yes. I was bigger and a better fighter, but Virgil was really mad. When we were finished, both covered in blood, Alice was gone. Just disappeared. She'd grabbed some things for the baby and left the house. We thought she'd gone to Virgil's parents or a friend, and she would be back. Virgil waited for days. I waited for word from her, but nothing."

He lapsed into silence. His face turned again to the window.

Andi waited for a few moments before prompting him. "Mr Stewart? What happened next?"

"Well, Virgil looked everywhere, even the mainland. Alice didn't have any family. Then I got wind that she was on Hope Island, that she'd joined the women's commune — you've heard about that?"

Bob and Andi nodded, and he went on.

"I went to tell Virgil. I knew he was distraught. I said I'd go with him and when we found Alice, we'd ask her who she wanted to be with, and both of us would respect her decision."

"What if she didn't want either of you?" Andi couldn't help asking.

Ralph flashed her a genuine smile. "We were so young and arrogant, of course, that didn't occur to either of us. It was a different time back then. We couldn't comprehend that a woman could be perfectly fine on her own."

Andi smiled back. "Go on, please."

"Well, we found Alice. We took Virgil's boat over and Joshua Moore met us. He had a gun — I think he thought he was some kind of bodyguard, but we persuaded him we only wanted to talk. Alice came to see us. We talked for hours. She was very upset about a lot of things. She was on the verge of coming back with us, when we heard a commotion, lots of shouting."

Ralph rubbed his eyes, as if trying to erase the memory. "What happened next haunts me every day. It changed the course of my life."

Andi stole a quick glance at her father. He was riveted.

"We were sitting away from the dock, near Joshua's cabin. There were a few rundown cabins, and Joshua had fixed one up. The main commune was further away, hidden in the woods. A young native girl came running, and she was clearly terrified. She was looking for somewhere to hide. She was followed by a young couple, both white. The native girl looked like she'd been beaten badly. She was covered in bruises.

"Virgil and I tackled the man to the ground, and the native girl ran and hid. We were holding him down, thinking we'd saved her. But then we heard screams coming from one cabin. I ran in and Alice was there, screaming. The white girl had a knife in her hand and was standing over the native girl, and Joshua Moore was just standing there."

Andi was shocked. "It was the girl who killed her? She killed Essie George?"

Ralph nodded. "Virgil still had the man on the ground, screaming to be let up, and we realized he'd been chasing his girlfriend, not Essie. He had been trying to save her."

"And that girl — you know who she is, don't you?" Andi thought she knew, but she wanted him to say it.

Ralph swallowed. "Of course I do. We got Elizabeth Halwell to stop, finally. She was like an animal. She scratched and attacked us as we dragged her away. There was blood everywhere. So much blood. And it was too late. Essie George was dead."

Ralph was sweating. He wiped his forehead, and his breath was coming in short gasps. Andi leaned forward, concerned the man might have a heart attack, but he waved her away.

"I — I'm fine." He said at last. "It's just that I haven't thought about this for a long time."

Andi took a deep breath, thrown completely by Ralph's revelations.

Ralph seemed calmer, and Bob prompted him to continue. "Can you tell me what happened next?"

"We were all in shock, I think. Joshua, he was in a state, pacing around, saying it would all come back on him. Michael was grabbing at Elizabeth, just shouting that they needed to get out of there. He turned on Virgil and me and said it was our fault for holding him down. Alice was crying. Elizabeth was the only one who was calm. Essie had fought back and had ripped Elizabeth's dress. She was covered in blood, but she acted as though it was nothing. *Nothing*. It was grotesque."

Ralph looked at Andi and then at Bob. "What happened next was the defining moment of my life. I should have been courageous, but I wasn't. I was a coward."

"You didn't call the police," Andi stated, unable to keep the accusatory tone out of her voice. She was here to get the story, not make judgment, but it was impossible to feel anything but disgust for the men who had conspired to cover up this murder.

"No. Virgil wanted to, but Michael Halwell stepped in. He said that Elizabeth's father was a diplomat, and he'd know what to do. He said the best thing for everyone was to go home and forget about it. He told Joshua to get rid of the body. Then Ed Brown arrived. I think he'd brought Michael and Elizabeth to the island. We couldn't hide what had happened, and Ed saw everything.

"Anyway, we left Joshua to get rid — take care of the body. I always thought he had dropped the body out at sea. I had no idea he'd — he'd just put her under the floorboards to rot."

"So you just left?"

"Ed Brown took Elizabeth and Michael back to shore. Virgil wanted to take Alice home, but she refused to leave that night."

"Didn't she tell anyone else at the commune?"

Ralph shook his head. "No. At least, that's what she told me." He was in tears now. "You have to understand, everything was a blur after that. I could hardly believe I had witnessed such a — a brutal act. I was in shock," he pleaded.

"I went home and expected the police to knock at the door at any moment. I was sure that Virgil would report everything. I hardly left the house. I was living with my parents in Coffin Cove back then. They thought I was ill. I had to go back to work. My father wouldn't let me lie around the house for more than a day or two. I tried to find Virgil, but his sister told me he'd left town, and nobody knew where he'd gone.

"I began to believe it was all a horrible dream. Life in Coffin Cove was . . . normal. I went to the pub, nobody said anything about any trouble on Hope Island, I just — just got on with my life, as callous as that seems now. Eventually I left Coffin Cove and came here. I started my business, and I almost forgot about that day."

Ralph walked around the desk to the window and stood with his back to them.

"Business was going really well. I was bidding for lots of development contracts and getting them all. I expanded the business, took on more staff, made more profit. Then, one day, I got a call from Elizabeth. She and Michael had married by then. She told me, in enough detail so I knew she wasn't lying, that she had made sure I won all those contracts, or most of them. She told me she could take away everything I owned just as easily as she had given it to me, if I ever breathed a word about that day on Hope Island."

He turned to face them. "So that's what I did. I kept my mouth shut all these years. And then someone dug up the body. I imagine Virgil must have heard about it, and the next thing I knew, I'd received a letter from Virgil saying he couldn't live with it anymore and he was going to the police."

"What did you do, Ralph?" Bob's tone was calm, but Andi could see her father's hand shaking a little.

"Believe me, I did not know what she would do."

Bob raised his voice. "What did you do?"

"I made a phone call." Ralph looked desperate now. "And then I got a call from Ed Brown. He wanted to talk to Elizabeth. Apparently, he'd picked up the knife and a piece of material from Elizabeth's dress and kept them all these years."

He looked disgusted. "Ed was going to blackmail Elizabeth, threaten to go to the police with his 'insurance', as he called it."

"So you told her?"

Ralph nodded. "She told me to take care of it. But I didn't know how. So I contacted Joshua Moore. I told him he owed Elizabeth and all of us for not getting rid of the body, like he'd promised. So he had to make it right by shutting Ed up and finding his 'insurance'. Elizabeth called him to make sure he did it. She had something on him, too."

Andi looked at Bob. "We need to—"

"We have to go." Bob Hinton got up.

"But . . . but what happens now?" Ralph asked, wringing his hands.

"We have to find Joshua Moore. And tell the police he is responsible for killing Ed Brown," Bob said. "And you'll have to testify, Mr Stewart."

Ralph started to sob.

Bob Hinton carried on talking, his repulsion evident in his tone. "All you wanted to do was protect your profit. You let a family suffer for decades, not knowing what happened to Melissa, and innocent bystanders have lost their lives. All you had to do was speak up."

A thought struck Andi. "Mr Stewart," she said urgently, "where's Alice?"

"What?" he said, as if he hadn't heard her correctly.

"Alice. She's the only other person who knows what happened on Hope Island."

* * *

Andi and her father stood in the rain as they waited for a floatplane to take them back to Vancouver Island. She had made an urgent phone call to Vega, telling him Ralph Stewart's story and now she was anxious to get back to Harry before he found Joshua Moore.

She turned to her father. "Your investigation, your *real* investigation, is about Elizabeth Halwell, right? The article that got you fired, all those years ago? That was her. And you met Ruth Cloutier because of Elizabeth Halwell."

Bob Hinton nodded. "I promise, I will tell you everything. But Elizabeth Halwell is a dangerous woman with a lot of influence. We need to be careful."

He sounded worried and Andi was surprised. "You've never worried about an investigation before, Dad. If everything Ralph Stewart says is true, and Virgil backs him up, then she's guilty of murder. We have to report the truth."

"People like her have their own truth," Bob said. "She twisted the truth enough to ruin my career. And she had enough influence to ruin yours, too."

As Andi stared at him in astonishment, she heard the rumble of the floatplane. The other passengers joined them in the drizzle, and she knew she'd have to wait before she could ask her father what he meant.

CHAPTER THIRTY-FOUR

The motorcade glided to a stop in front of Cheriton Assisted Living Facility. Sebastian Romero, head of security for Michael and Elizabeth Halwell, slid quickly from the front passenger seat and moved swiftly around the black sedan to open the door for his employers. To an outside observer, he looked like a dapper fifty-something executive assistant. But Sebastian, while smiling broadly at the manager and staff of the seniors' home, was scanning the parking lot and shrubbery for any threats to the politician and his wife.

The staff clapped politely as the couple got out of the car. Michael, as always, rushed over to the nearest staff member and started pumping her hand. The man was exuding energy and enthusiasm. People always warmed to the sixty-something Robert Redford lookalike. Sebastian didn't doubt for a moment Michael Halwell would be the next prime minister. Fucking moron.

Staying alert for any hint of danger from the small crowd, Sebastian allowed himself to appreciate Elizabeth Halwell. Dressed impeccably in an elegant sky-blue dress that hugged her curves, Elizabeth smiled warmly at each nurse and member of staff. They looked in awe of her. One young nurse even bobbed a curtsy. Sebastian understood.

Elizabeth was glorious. Her blonde hair brushed her shoulders and shimmered like silk in the October sun. Any forty-year-old woman would be proud to have her body, and Sebastian knew Elizabeth was a month older than her husband. Just a hint of a crease around her neck gave away her age. But Sebastian could testify that every inch of her skin was smooth and firm. He'd inspected Elizabeth's naked body many times.

God, that woman was the best fuck he'd ever had.

Ever since he started working for the Canadian ambassador to Argentina, he'd protected Elizabeth, the ambassador's daughter. He recalled his first day. Elizabeth was nineteen, wild and belligerent.

"Keep her safe and out of trouble," her father had demanded. "At all costs. Stand in front of a bullet if necessary. Kill for her."

Sebastian had grown up in Buenos Aires' La Boca area, and had been fully immersed in the crime culture, mostly robbing tourists at gunpoint. He'd joined Galtieri's army to fight the war to liberate Las Malvinas in the eighties and had survived. His military record had convinced the ambassador to hire Sebastian as his daughter's minder.

Sebastian had no problem killing for Elizabeth. Especially after he'd bedded her for the first time.

The golden couple moved among the line of staff. Just before they all entered the foyer, Elizabeth Halwell turned her head, caught Sebastian's eye and held his gaze for just a moment. Then she was gone.

Sebastian moved the car away from the entrance, then got out and slipped on a jacket. Making sure nobody was looking, he tucked his trusty Beretta .22 handgun in his belt at the small of his back. He didn't need it for this task, but the feel of hard metal and weight of the weapon was reassuring. In his jacket pocket, he placed a small plastic bag.

He entered the building. He could hear the voices of the throng of people in front of him, and he hung back until they faded away. He smiled and winked at a young, round-faced receptionist who was half-hidden by bouquets of flowers. She blushed and giggled.

He tapped at the plastic card on a ribbon around his neck, identifying himself as the Halwells' security officer and gestured that he was going to follow them. She nodded.

Once out of the foyer, he faced a flight of stairs. To the left was a lounge area. Sebastian assumed it was some kind of communal space for the residents. Beyond that was a dining area, and he could hear the clink of china and smell coffee mixed with a faint aroma of boiled cabbage. To the right was a narrow corridor, made gloomy by panelled walls and an orange-and-brown patterned carpet that was wearing thin in places. Attached to the wall was a plaque reading *Residents' Rooms 1–44*.

Sebastian stole down the corridor, happy for the carpet to hide the sound of footsteps. If anyone stopped him, he was looking for the washroom.

Nobody was around. Ammonia and the faint odour of urine replaced the smell of cabbage. Sebastian passed an open door and caught sight of a gnarled old man, bent almost double in his chair. He was dribbling, unable to wipe his face, and he was making faint moaning noises. Sebastian shuddered. What was wrong with these people? In his community they took care of their elders, respected them. They didn't shove them in "facilities" and drug them until they died.

The names of the residents were printed on card in plastic holders on each door. Sebastian stopped at number thirty-seven. He was in the right place.

The door to the room was slightly ajar. He pushed it open and looked in. Immediately to the left was another door, which Sebastian assumed was the bathroom. He waited and listened in case someone was in there. When he heard nothing, he stepped into the room and closed the door behind him.

A high hospital bed was in front of him. It was neatly made. Beyond the bed was a chair with its back to him and Sebastian could see wisps of grey hair and the top of the head of its occupant.

Sebastian felt in his pocket for the plastic bag. He pulled out a syringe.

His instinct was to jab it in her neck from behind. But he'd already made mistakes. The big screw-up in the fucking snow with the woman and the dog, and his failure to kill the old guy. He winced as he recalled all his errors. He just hadn't been prepared for the cold, and he'd waited all fucking day in that woodshed. And then speaking in front of that young cashier. Why didn't he just shoot the kid, too?

He couldn't get anything wrong this time. Elizabeth's vicious temper was legendary, and he'd already been on the receiving end of her cruelty.

Sebastian cleared his throat and put on his most winning smile. "Good afternoon," he called and walked around the chair to face the old lady. She was small and shrivelled-looking, and she was huddled under a thin blanket.

"Hello," he said. "Are you Alice?" He crouched a little, so he wasn't bending over her.

Her eyes were bright and alert, and she nodded.

"My name is Sebastian." He held out his hand, holding the syringe concealed in his other hand by his side.

Alice slowly and shakily removed one hand from under the blanket and grasped his. Her grip was firm.

Sebastian brought up his free hand, ready to jab the syringe in her arm, but she was too quick. With a high-pitched cackle, she moved her other arm from under the blanket and slammed a fork into the top of his hand. He dropped the needle and howled with pain. He tried to pull his hand back to extract the fork, but Alice had him in a vice-like grip, laughing like a hyena.

Sebastian could hear a commotion in the hallway and he tried desperately to get free, but Alice hung on.

"You can't barge in there!" a woman's voice shouted. "You have to be on the list to visit."

The door flew open, and a dark-haired man rushed in with a nurse behind him.

"Oh, my goodness!" she shrieked, when she saw the blood gushing and the fork embedded in Sebastian's hand. "Alice, what have you done now, you naughty girl!"

Alice still hadn't let go of Sebastian's hand.

"Well, it's nice to meet you, Alice," the dark-haired man said. "And your friend here. My name's Inspector Andrew Vega."

CHAPTER THIRTY-FIVE

Joshua Moore cursed as he stumbled over a rusty iron gate concealed by blackberry bushes.

What a fucking mess.

Ed Brown's trailer stood on a quarter acre of dirt surrounded by tall fir trees. The trailer was set back just a few feet from the rutted track that zigzagged up the hill towards Clara Bell's place.

Few people used it. Ed had never had many friends, and Harry had visited his father infrequently. Clara never encouraged visitors, so no passers-by would have seen the pile of junk nestled in the shadows behind the dilapidated trailer.

Joshua had parked Ed's truck out front. The old beater had been left at the dock since the explosion. The keys were always in it, so Joshua had decided to brazen it out. He was doing a good turn for his dead friend's family. Helping in their time of sorrow. He'd have to walk back to town, but if he found Ed's tin box with the valuable "insurance" he didn't care. It would be worth it.

But time was running out. If he didn't locate Ed's secret stash soon, then not only was Montana State Prison beckoning, but he would never kill again. And now he'd got the taste back, he had a powerful urge to keep going. It was his destiny, and he'd pushed it away too long. He had to find Ed's box.

He started with the woodshed. Logs were scattered everywhere. An axe was buried deep in a stump but looked like it had been there for some time. He squeezed around the piles of bark and kindling and felt his way to the back of the structure. Light glinted through cracks at the back and fell on sheets of rusty tin. Had they been disturbed recently? Joshua couldn't be sure. But the tin box wasn't here.

He worked his way around the outside of Ed's home. Old garbage bags, bins overflowing with beer bottles and old cans, rusty tools and other debris filled the fenced-in yard at the back. At one time, Ed had kept chickens and maintained a vegetable garden, but now waist-high weeds obscured a crumbling chicken coop.

The front porch of Ed's trailer was rotten. Paint was peeling off, and the planks sagged. Ed's old canvas chair sat next to the front door, beside a bucket half-filled with brown liquid and cigarette butts. An empty beer can rolled towards Joshua as the porch groaned under his weight. The movement made him jump. He half-expected to hear Ed curse and throw open the door.

Shaking off the feeling, Joshua pushed at the door. As he expected, it opened. Ed had never bothered to lock it. It smelled musty inside but was cleaner than Joshua expected. There was a small kitchen with mustard-coloured stove and fridge in an open-plan room. A round table stood in one corner and in the other was a sofa with shiny patches on the arms from decades of use. Apart from that, there was a flatscreen TV — probably a gift from Harry — and a bookcase with no books, but an assortment of small tools and a tin.

Joshua picked up the tin and opened it. Inside was a photograph of Harry when he was a boy, standing beside his mother, who was holding baby Hephzibah. Neither Harry nor Greta was smiling at the camera.

Joshua remembered when Greta had arrived on Hope Island. Then, the commune was only made up of a few women hiding from their drunken, abusive husbands and trying to survive. Then more and more arrived. They had set up some kind of network on the island. Women came from everywhere.

Joshua had tried to make them go away at first. He didn't need company. Those women had assumed he was a draft dodger, and he'd let them believe it. It was common in those days to find Americans hiding out in the bush.

Thomas Keaney, convicted murderer, had become Joshua Moore, draft dodger, when he had escaped from Montana State Prison in 1969 and sneaked across the border into Alberta. He'd had help from people who told him never to come back. He'd hitched rides over the Rocky Mountain range into British Columbia. Nobody had paid him much attention. Some Canadians who opposed the Vietnam War had even given him money. He'd eventually arrived in Coffin Cove and got some work in the McIntosh sawmill. He'd slept rough around town mostly, hoarding as much cash as possible. One evening, he'd found an aluminium boat half-hidden under driftwood on the beach. The outboard had been rusty and jammed, but Joshua had worked on it every evening until it had fired up on one pull.

Hope Island was deserted back then. Joshua knew little about the natives up here in Canada, but he had assumed the rounded heaps of shell-and-beach debris were middens, which showed that years previously, Hope Island had been a native settlement.

There had been other signs of human occupancy — the crumbling base of a lighthouse on the east side, a few abandoned cabins in various stages of decay, and a well with a hand pump, which had actually produced fresh water.

It had been the perfect place. For months, Joshua had chugged back and forth to Hope Island and worked his job at the sawmill. Nobody had seemed to care he was living on the island. He became a fixture in the town. Thomas Keaney was just a bad dream, a man he had known a long time ago. The only hint, the only time Thomas reappeared briefly, had been that chaotic day on Hope Island.

Joshua put the photo back. If the box was here, Ed would have put it somewhere safe and well-hidden. Somewhere locked? A gun cabinet? He moved through the trailer, opening cupboards and running his hand along top shelves.

Nothing.

The door of the gun cabinet swung open. A few stray bullets were left in an old canvas bag. *Harry must have taken Ed's gun*, Joshua thought. Maybe a long time ago, for Ed's own safety.

He was becoming frustrated. Fuck that old drunk. Why hadn't he kept Ed alive and tortured him until he'd given up his precious "insurance"?

Ed's bedroom smelled stale. The bedclothes looked as though they hadn't been changed in weeks, and there was a large grease stain on the pillow. Apart from the bed, there was only a battered chest of drawers. Joshua pulled out each drawer and tossed the contents on to the floor.

Still nothing.

It was no use. Joshua looked around wildly. *It must be here somewhere.* He looked at the bed again. He crouched low and pulled up the bedclothes to look under the bed. It was dark and dusty, but there was something in the back corner.

He lay on his stomach, trying to avoid breathing in dirt and grime from the carpet, and stretched his arm as far as he could.

His fingers touched metal.

CHAPTER THIRTY-SIX

The day hadn't started well. Beth Stanton woke after a miserable night's sleep in the Wilson Motel. It took a moment for her to realize where she was. So much had happened in the last few days. She had lain awake for hours, wondering whether she'd ever be able to go back to Whitehorse. Although Trina had effectively been cleared of any wrongdoing, her stupid sister had led the team on a wild goose chase and wasted valuable time.

Beth recalled the expression on Sergeant Levine's face when he'd told her she was going to Coffin Cove with Inspector Vega. Was it relief? Was he glad to get rid of her? And why was she with Inspector Vega? She'd already screwed up — was this trip a punishment?

Beth knew she was being self-absorbed. Norman and Julie had enough to worry about without being concerned about Beth's feelings.

When Beth discovered there was only stale instant coffee available in the room and lukewarm water for her shower, her self-pity threatened to overwhelm her.

She'd arrived at the Coffin Cove detachment at eight o'clock. Vega had left her with a to-do list, which included liaising with an Inspector Fowler from IHIT, and Sergeant

Levine. She was also tasked with delving into Ralph Stewart's background, as well as finding anything out about the mysterious Joshua Moore.

Sergeant Matt Beaufort was helpful, at least. He showed her into a small windowless room, which he described as the "conference room". Beth had thought the Whitehorse detachment was archaic, but here it was as if she'd travelled back in time to the 1950s.

Despite the aged working conditions, Sergeant Beaufort was professional and courteous. He made sure she was connected to the Wi-Fi, on a computer that looked several decades old. "Sometimes we have to reboot it three or four times before it sticks," he said cheerfully. "And if you want coffee, it's best to walk down to Hephzibah's Café. There is a vending machine, but the coffee sucks. Is there anything else you need?"

Beth shook her head and thanked him, and Beaufort looked at her with an expression of awe. "How did you get assigned to Vega's team?" he asked. "I'd love to be part of IHIT."

She avoided his gaze. "It's probably because I'd become a bit of a liability back in Whitehorse."

His expression changed to sympathy. "It's hard being posted to a small community," he said. "It was tough here at first. I doubt anyone thinks badly of you. You can't help your relatives. And besides, you found Virgil's papers, and that brought you to Coffin Cove. If you do a good job here, and help find Janice's killer, I'll bet you'll be a hero in Whitehorse."

Beth had felt better after he'd left. She was here to do a job, and she would throw herself into it. But first, she needed something to eat and a decent cup of coffee.

Hephzibah's Café smelled of freshly brewed coffee and cinnamon. Beth got a wide smile from Hephzibah, who waved off Beth's proffered payment for a large cappuccino and a muffin.

"On the house," Hephzibah said. "We're glad you and Andrew are here to sort all this mess out. He's a legend around here, you know."

248

Beth thanked her and turned to walk out, nearly bumping into Ruth Cloutier. "Sorry," she said. Ruth nodded at her without smiling. She was a beautiful woman, Beth thought, but so serious looking.

"Ruth, good morning!" she heard Hephzibah say behind her. "I'm so glad to see you. I wanted to ask if you were free for dinner this evening?"

Maybe the cheery Hephzibah could make Ruth smile, she thought and then felt a little ashamed. How would she feel if her sister had been missing for years? Thinking of Trina, Beth wondered if she should call her. Maybe later. She had a lot to do.

Back at the detachment, Beth scoured all available RCMP databases for information about Ralph Stewart and Joshua Moore. Nothing.

She then searched public information on the internet and found articles about Stewart's business accomplishments over the years. There were many references to his humble beginnings in Coffin Cove, but no details about his early life. Most of the information posted a picture of a successful businessman who donated regularly and generously to local charities. Just one article caught Beth's eye for its critical content.

Who is behind Stewart Developments' Lucrative Contracts? the headline read. The article insinuated that someone with influence was making sure that Stewart Developments had an unfair advantage when tendering for federal projects. The article was more of an opinion piece, but she printed it out anyway.

There was no sign of Joshua Moore in any database or on the internet. That was strange. How did someone drop off the grid? She dug further and found that Joshua Moore had a bank account and a social identification number. How had he managed that, Beth wondered, given that everyone thought he was a draft dodger? If he was, he would have been considered a fugitive in the USA but protected as an immigrant in Canada. Either way, there should be some records somewhere.

Beth thought for a minute. What if Joshua Moore had left the USA for another reason?

On an impulse, she tapped in the website address for Interpol. While the slow Wi-Fi and ancient computer loaded the website, Beth left the room and found a microwave in a tiny office. She reheated her coffee and went back to the conference room.

The website was fully loaded, and Beth scrolled through the picture of the most dangerous criminals in the world, paying most attention to the American escapees. She was about to give up when she spotted a black-and-white photograph of a convicted criminal from 1967. The man had a crew cut and was wearing prison clothes. There was something about his eyes that kept Beth's attention. Dark, brooding. She picked up the printed picture of Joshua Moore, which Andi Silvers had taken with her cell phone. Joshua was staring past the camera in the shot, and although he had a shock of white hair, the eyes looked eerily familiar.

Beth read the details of the man on the Interpol website. *Wanted for multiple murders, escaped from Montana State Prison in 1969.* His name was Thomas Keaney.

Beth looked back and forth between the pictures of Joshua Moore and Thomas Keaney. She was certain they were photographs of the same man.

CHAPTER THIRTY-SEVEN

After finding the shotgun under Ed's bed, Joshua sat for a while, just thinking. Then, he walked into Ed's grubby bathroom and rinsed his face. The cold water cooled him and cleared his head.

He grinned at his reflection in the tarnished glass. It was time for Joshua Moore to go. It was Thomas's time now.

He'd missed Thomas. Thomas Keaney enjoyed killing. For him, it was almost spiritual, a connection to a higher power. As life left his victims, Thomas Keaney felt invigorated, as if their vitality transferred to his body.

It had started with the cashier at the First Madison Valley Bank in Ennis, Montana, in 1965. The bank had been open for six months. The cashier was a young woman with blonde hair and the type of face that rested in a smile.

Her pretty mouth had contorted into a round "O" of shock when Thomas had pointed his shotgun at her. But she had maintained enough calm to hand over all the money she had, while a terrified young man had run to the other tills and emptied all the cash into a bag.

As the man had handed it over, Thomas had seen his beads of sweat and he had breathed in the pungent aroma of fear. He'd liked it.

Thomas had felt suspended in time. He could have backed out, still training the shotgun at the counter and the terrified staff. In a minute, he'd have been in the truck, and in five, he'd have been on Highway 287 on the way to Texas.

The jury that had convicted him of murder and sentenced him to death had commented on the cold-bloodedness of Thomas Keaney's next action.

He had raised the shotgun, pointed it at the cashier and blasted her pretty blonde head clean off her shoulders.

Nothing had ever compared to his first kill. Thomas had tried to replicate the rush of adrenalin and euphoria many times, but he'd never come close. Not until a warm summer's evening on Hope Island a full ten years later. He'd seen something beautiful.

His whole life, Thomas had assumed he was a freak. This love of extinguishing life, the overwhelming desire to kill — he knew this was abhorrent to other people who lived in normal society.

But that night, he had seen someone else who felt the same. There was no mistaking the pure pleasure in the woman's eyes as she had plunged the knife into that native girl, again and again. Blood was splashing up her arms and neck, and the small cabin was full of the metallic aroma of it.

When the woman had stopped, Thomas had realized she was not much older than her victim. Her face had been splattered with red, and there were small clumps of tissue in her hair. Her eyes had met Thomas's and she had smiled.

He had wanted to fuck her right there, in the pool of congealing blood, next to the lifeless body. He had held her eyes in a long gaze until hysterical screaming had shattered the moment.

He'd offered to dispose of the body. He'd run his hands reverently over the wounds and gashes in the flesh, some of them so deep, the knife had marked the bones.

He'd tried to hide his awe as the shocked onlookers had negotiated and apportioned blame as they attempted to distance themselves from this beautiful murder.

When everyone had left, Thomas had cleaned up and piled the rags, along with the victim's bag, on top of the corpse and wrapped it in old sacks. Instead of dumping the body in the ocean, he'd carefully placed it under the boards in the old caretaker's cottage. A part of him had hoped the woman killer would return someday and they could relive the moment with her trophy.

Thomas had never forgotten her.

As he sat on Ed's dingy sofa, running his hand over the shotgun, Thomas realized this moment had been coming for days. Ever since he had seen that woman on the island. He thought he'd seen a ghost. The woman looked exactly the same as that native girl long ago.

The more he thought about it, his destiny became clear. He'd been given an opportunity to re-enact the greatest kill he'd ever witnessed.

Joshua Moore had arrived at Ed Brown's trailer, but it was Thomas Keaney who emerged two hours later. He had a plan. He needed uninterrupted time if he was to savour his kill.

Thomas hunted around the edges of the trailer and found an old gas canister. He shook the gas around the rotten porch and rummaged in Ed's truck until he found an old cigarette lighter. He lit an old piece of cardboard and tossed it into the pool of fuel.

He waited until the fire took hold. There was still some fuel in the canister, so he put it in the truck and shoved the lighter in his pocket.

Reflected in his rear-view mirror, the porch collapsed as flames consumed the wood and licked at the trailer roof. Black smoke billowed into the afternoon sky. Soon, the fire would attract the volunteer fire brigade, police and nosy members of the community.

It was a perfect distraction. It would give Thomas the time he needed, and if Ed's tin box was anywhere in that trailer, it would be destroyed.

* * *

Hephzibah Brown moved around her garden, picking ripe fruit from the apple trees and harvesting pumpkins. In a couple of weeks, she thought, she'd be carving the oversize pumpkins and lighting them up for Halloween. Celebrating a night to remember the dead.

She shivered. There had been too much death in her life. Too much death in Coffin Cove. Hephzibah still couldn't fully grasp that her father had been murdered. At night she lay awake, unable to escape the images of Ed Brown burning alive. She worried about her brother too.

Harry had said little since Ed died, but Hephzibah knew he'd been struggling with guilt about the explosion. But Ed's death hadn't been a drunken accident with a propane stove. It was a deliberate act.

Now there's just the two of us, Hephzibah thought. *How would I have coped without Harry?*

Maybe Ed's legacy was his wonderful son. That thought made her feel better.

She gathered up the apples and pumpkins and took them inside. Gardening and cooking, these normal daily activities that she'd recommended to Andi, were now keeping her grounded.

She busied herself with making pastry for pies. Soon her kitchen was full of the sweet aroma of cinnamon and sugar. Outside, the wind was blowing off the ocean, and maple leaves were already carpeting the lawn. It grew darker, but a warm glow lighted the kitchen.

There was a knock at the door. Hephzibah smiled. Right on time.

Ruth Cloutier stood on the porch, awkwardly clutching a bottle of wine. "Hello," she said, holding it up. "I wasn't sure—"

"Ooh, lovely, wine. Come in!" Hephzibah opened the door wide. "You don't mind early-afternoon pie and wine, do you?"

In exactly fifteen minutes, Hephzibah watched Ruth Cloutier hungrily attack a large slice of apple pie and ice cream.

She must have felt Hephzibah's eyes on her. "I'm hungry," she said, as if it had just occurred to her. "I haven't been eating properly, not since . . ." She couldn't finish her sentence and she let her spoon drop on the plate. Her eyes filled with tears.

Hephzibah handed her a tissue.

"I'm so sorry. You've just lost your father. You don't need my—"

"Nonsense," Hephzibah said. She felt the woman's pain, and she knew Ruth wanted answers from her. She needed something, anything, to help make sense of her sister's death.

Hephzibah topped up Ruth's wine glass. "I was very young when I lived in the commune," she said, "so memories are fuzzy, you know? But I do recall being anxious. I remember being surrounded by lots of women, different hands touching me, different smells. Sometimes I felt safe. Other times, it felt scary and chaotic." Hephzibah hesitated, trying to find the right words.

"I know you want to know something about your sister. I don't remember her, I'm sorry. Those periods of panic and chaos? When I got older, I realized these times were when men had arrived on the island, often a husband looking for his wife, and all the women would be forced to defend themselves. I am sure one of these times was when your sister was there. But I can't . . . Maybe it was something I blocked out. I've conditioned myself to only remember the good times, take the positive out of my memories. Life in general, I suppose."

"That's a good trait," Ruth said.

"Is it? I'm not sure. I think I blinker out the ugly stuff. I don't always live in the real world. When something terrible happens, I'm forced to admit the world isn't always fairies and unicorns, and it comes as a complete shock."

Ruth laughed. "I think I'm the opposite. But then, we come from different worlds."

Hephzibah didn't know what to say. She'd been horrified at the blatant racism from some of the Coffin Cove community. Although she'd known those attitudes and prejudices existed, she'd chosen to ignore them. But Ruth Cloutier couldn't. She had to face that ugliness every day.

As if reading Hephzibah's thoughts, Ruth Cloutier started to speak. "I lived with my grandmother, growing up. She had a little diner, just on the edge of band land. I still do not know how or why she managed to operate that diner. Or how she kept me and Essie out of residential school. Maybe she had some leverage over someone powerful, I don't know. Essie should have been picked up in the Sixties Scoop . . ." She paused. "I hate that expression. It makes that time sound trivial, like scooping up a mess, cleaning up." Her voice took on a bitter edge. "But they were scooping up babies, sometimes before their first birthday and putting them in prisons. Except white people called them 'schools'."

They sat in silence for a moment before Ruth carried on. "It broke my grandmother's heart, to lose Essie. She'd already lost my mother to alcohol and drugs. My mother had Essie and dropped her off with my grandmother to raise, and disappeared. Fifteen years later, she came back with me, and did the same thing. My grandmother said my mother couldn't cope."

"How much have you found out about Essie?" Hephzibah asked.

"Not much. I promised my grandmother and my auntie I'd keep looking. My grandmother worked very hard for me to get an education. After I qualified as a lawyer, I thought doors would open for me, but they remained firmly shut. Things have got a little better recently, because of the National Inquiry into Murdered and Missing Indigenous Women, but there are thousands, Hephzibah. Literally *thousands* of women ripped away from their families, just like Essie. The lucky families are those who at least know what happened. But the rest . . ." Her voice trailed off for a minute.

Then she smiled. "And then one day, Bob Hinton contacted me. I'd got nowhere. I had the police report and interview with Michael Halwell. He'd said Essie had got out his camper van just a few miles from home. He'd said she was worried about her grandmother and asked to be dropped off.

We'd always worked on the assumption that she must have been taken, or . . . Anyway, I put an ad in the paper asking for information. I described the camper and the day and time, and nobody responded. Until Bob Hinton." She grew more animated as she spoke of him. "He started helping me and the investigation wound up here. Then an opportunity opened with Three Cedars band, and it felt like the right thing to do. I could work, and in my spare time I could focus on finding Essie. When the human remains were found right under my nose, I knew they were Essie. It was as if she was sending me a sign. She sent me Bob, and she led us here."

Without knowing why it was suddenly important, Hephzibah asked, "Are you and Bob . . . ?" She blushed. "God, sorry, that's none of my business."

Ruth looked at Hephzibah steadily. "No. Bob and I are not together. He's . . . he's not my type. I think you know what I mean?"

Hephzibah stared at her for a moment. Then, Ruth reached out and touched Hephzibah's hand and smiled at her. Suddenly, with that small gesture, everything made sense. She understood perfectly what Ruth was saying. Hephzibah squeezed Ruth's hand and started to speak, but then a rumble sounded from outside and she jumped. She said, a bit self-consciously, "That sounds like a truck." She left the kitchen and went into the living room to look out the window.

"That's strange," she said to Ruth, who had followed her. "That's Dad's truck. Maybe it's Harry. But why would he have Dad's truck?"

The driver's door opened.

Hephzibah opened the front door. "Is everything all right? Why have you got Dad's—"

She tried again. "Joshua," she said, surprised and annoyed, "why have you got Ed's truck?" And then her legs went weak.

"Get in." Joshua Moore's voice came from a distance. Her whole focus was on the shotgun pointed at her.

CHAPTER THIRTY-EIGHT

Beth answered the phone at the detachment.

"Where's Matt?" the speaker asked.

"He's attending a 911 call," she said.

Beth had been printing out as much information as possible about Thomas Keaney. She'd tried calling Inspector Vega, but she'd got his voicemail. She'd decided not to leave a message. She would keep digging and explain to the inspector when he was free. She didn't want them chasing down a case of mistaken identity. Vega had been clear about one thing. This investigation had to be mistake-free.

Sergeant Beaufort had rushed into the detachment, and then out again within minutes, as he had received a call about a fire on the edge of town.

"It's Andi," the voice on the phone said.

As Beth listened, she walked back to the computer and refreshed the screen. She looked at the image of the wanted man, and her heart sank. She *should* have told Vega.

Andi's urgent voice said, "Tell Matt, we need to find Joshua Moore. We're about an hour away."

"His name's not Joshua Moore," Beth said, but Andi had already finished the call before she could explain.

Beth immediately called Vega. His phone went straight to voicemail again. She called Sergeant Beaufort, and the same thing happened.

Beth fought down the urge to scream. What should she do?

She tried Beaufort again. This time, to her relief, he picked up the call. The line was crackling, so she bellowed into the phone, and finally he understood he needed to return to the detachment.

Feeling calmer, Beth returned to the computer and printed out everything she could find about Thomas Keaney.

Besides the Interpol information, she found a Wikipedia page and old newspaper reports. A true crime blogger had done extensive research about Keaney's murders, and as Beth read it, she felt chills. If even half of this was true, Thomas Keaney was a true cold-blooded killer, and he was roaming around Coffin Cove.

"Excuse me," a voice called from the reception area, "is there anyone here?"

An annoyed-looking middle-aged lady stood at the counter. Beth recognized her as the owner of the motel.

"Oh." Peggy Wilson's face softened a little as she recognized Beth as a paying client. "I was looking for Sergeant Beaufort. I want to report a stolen truck."

Beth explained Sergeant Beaufort was not available and offered to help.

"Do you have the registration?"

"Oh no, dear. Everyone knows Ed's truck, it's the old red one."

"It's not your truck? How do you know it's stolen?"

"I've just seen it driving at high speed into town," Peggy said.

Beth looked at her questioningly. This still wasn't making sense.

Peggy sighed impatiently. "Ed Brown died in that explosion. It wasn't Harry driving the truck, because I saw him leave the dock this morning. Hephzibah doesn't drive, and dead men don't drive either, far as I know," she snapped. "So who could it be?"

Beth stared at her. She had no idea what this woman was talking about. This day wasn't getting any better.

CHAPTER THIRTY-NINE

Hephzibah stood close beside Ruth, their backs to the kitchen window. The late-afternoon sun had broken through the clouds, and Hephzibah felt the warmth on her neck, but she couldn't stop shaking.

Ruth must have noticed, because Hephzibah felt Ruth's fingers curl around her own. It made her feel a little better, but her legs were still weak from the shock of Joshua Moore pushing into her house, holding a gun to her head.

On the other side of the kitchen table, Joshua Moore stood with the shotgun casually slung under his arm. For some reason, he'd been carrying an old gas canister, and he'd put it on the kitchen table. He was leering at Ruth and talking gibberish, as far as Hephzibah could tell. It was hard to hear him over the *whump, whump, whump* of her heart beating against her ribcage. It was so loud, Hephzibah was sure the sound was resonating around the kitchen.

"Look at you, all grown up," he muttered.

Hephzibah was confused. Did he know Ruth?

"Not so frightened this time." Joshua giggled. It was a grotesque sound. "It'll make it more interesting, eh?"

"Joshua . . ." Hephzibah's voice croaked with fear. "Why—"

"Shut up," he roared, swinging the gun up to his shoulder and making her jump. "You shut the fuck up!"

Hephzibah did as she was told. She dropped her eyes to the floor, not wanting to stare down the barrel of his gun. She took deep breaths to stop herself from screaming.

Joshua chuckled again. "Ol' Thomas is gonna cut the pretty Indian girl into strips, just like *she* did before, that's right."

Thomas? Who was Thomas? Who was "she"?

Hephzibah lifted her head enough to see Joshua unsheathe his hunting knife and lay it on the kitchen table. She tried to think calmly. Where was Harry? She remembered him saying he was going to look for Joshua. Harry was certain Joshua had something to do with Ed's death. *He must be right about that*, she thought. Maybe Andi would come home. God, what if she walked in on this? Joshua would have the three of them trapped here. What could she do?

She had to keep Joshua talking or distract him somehow. He clearly meant to hurt Ruth — if she could just buy them both some time . . .

* * *

Andi and Bob Hinton arrived at the detachment, just as Sergeant Beaufort's police cruiser pulled into the parking lot.

Matt hopped out of the cruiser and ran into the detachment.

"Something's happening," Andi said, and they followed the sergeant.

As Bob pulled the door open, Andi could hear Peggy Wilson's shrill tones. That woman was always making a damn nuisance of herself.

Sergeant Beaufort was trying to calm Peggy. PC Beth Stanton looked agitated. Finally, he persuaded Peggy Wilson to take a seat, with promises that he'd look after her complaint as soon as he was able. Then he invited Beth, Andi and Bob into the small conference room where Beth had been working.

"What on earth is going on?" Beaufort asked.

Andi ignored the question and directed her attention to Beth. "Where's Vega? And Harry?"

"Vega's still on the mainland," Beth replied. "I have no idea where Harry is."

"He's been out to Hope Island, looking for Joshua Moore," Beaufort said. "I called him to tell him about the fire at Ed's place."

"What?" Andi asked, and Matt told her about the fire that had been started at Ed's trailer.

"Deliberate?"

"Looks that way. There was a strong smell of gasoline. I don't know who would want to torch Ed's trailer, though."

PC Stanton said suddenly, "Ed? Is he the man who recently died?"

"Yes, why?" said Beaufort.

Beth got up and rushed out of the room.

"Can someone please tell me why you are all here?" Beaufort asked again.

Bob Hinton briefly filled him in. He then told him about the information they had got from Ralph Stewart and how it pointed to Joshua Moore.

"He knows more than he's letting on," Bob Hinton said. "He might be a witness or accomplice to the murder of Melissa George. And Ed Brown."

Beth burst back into the room, breathless. "I think Joshua Moore stole Ed's truck. Peggy Wilson—" she gestured behind her — "she saw—"

"I saw someone driving Ed's truck," Peggy said, pushing past Beth into the room. "And I said to myself, 'That's not right. Who would have Ed's truck? Not Harry, because I saw him leaving the dock, and not Hephzibah, because she—'"

"When?" Andi cut in. "When did you see the truck?"

Peggy shrugged. "A while ago. A good *long* while, I've been kept waiting here," she said pointedly.

"Where was it going — did you see that? It would be really helpful," Beaufort asked. "Then I think we've detained you long enough."

Peggy sniffed. "Let me see, the truck was coming into town — quite fast — and I think it turned into Seaview Road."

"Could it have been Joshua Moore driving?" Andi asked.

"Maybe. I don't know."

"If it's Joshua, he's going to Hephzibah's cottage," Andi said.

My home. My sanctuary, she thought. She didn't want any part of this investigation intruding into her home. Not after last time.

"Remember what Ralph said about Ed's 'insurance'?" she said. "Maybe he thinks Hephzibah has it."

"Let's check," Bob said. "Andi, you and I will go to Hephzibah's, and the sergeant here can decide how to deploy his resources—"

"No!" PC Beth Stanton broke in. "No, you can't go. It's too dangerous. *Look*."

Andi and Bob followed Beth over to a computer in a corner. Andi's heart sank as she saw the screen and read the information.

"Jesus. I have to phone this in," Beaufort said.

"This changes everything. I have to check on Ruth." Bob made for the door.

"She's at Hephzibah's house," Beth said. "I overheard Hephzibah invite her for dinner."

"Right, let's go."

Andi and her father raced out of the detachment while Matt Beaufort was still on the phone. Andi could hear PC Stanton shouting after them, but she didn't care. She had to make sure Hephzibah was all right and she could tell from his expression that her father was worried about Ruth.

As his father drove, Andi called Harry.

"I'm a few minutes from the dock," he said. "I'll be there."

CHAPTER FORTY

Thomas Keaney was irritated.

At first, he hadn't believed his luck when he'd found Ruth at Hephzibah's house. His plan had been to set fire to the cottage and then do the same to Harry's boat. Those were the only two places Ed could have stowed his tin box of insurance. After that, he was going to look for his prey.

When he'd found them both, he was elated. He didn't have to hunt down Ruth. She was right here. But the situation posed some problems.

He didn't want to kill her in the cottage. No, he wanted her all to himself on Hope Island. He wanted to slit her throat while she was kneeling in the same spot as the last kill. He wanted her blood to soak the same earth, as he watched the life drain away from her body. It would be a fitting tribute.

Hephzibah was the problem. The fucking woman wouldn't shut up.

Then an idea came to him. Why not follow the same plan? He'd just kill Hephzibah right here, and if Ed's tin was here, he'd take care of that, too. He cocked the gun and pointed it at the tall woman whose lips were still moving, pleading with him.

"Shut up. Sit on that chair."

Hephzibah obeyed.

Thomas pulled open the drawer nearest him. It was full of knives and forks. He jerked it angrily and let the contents spill out. He found what he was looking for in the next drawer. Nylon gardening twine.

"You." He pointed to Ruth. "Tie her up."

Ruth tied Hephzibah's arms behind her, and her legs to the chair with shaking hands.

When she was finished, he pushed her out of the way and checked her work. "Stand over there."

Then he took the gas canister and shook the remaining fuel around the chair.

"Dear God, no! *Please*!" Hephzibah screamed.

The noise didn't bother Thomas anymore. He shoved the gun into Ruth's ribs. "Turn around. Move."

"Please don't do this," Ruth whispered, but Thomas moved the gun so the end of the barrel was pressed into her cheek.

"Do you want your brains all over the wall?" he hissed.

As Ruth shook her head, Thomas pulled the lighter from his pocket along with a wad of kitchen paper. He tossed the lighted paper on the floor and heard the *whoosh* as the single flame found the fuel.

"Fucking move!" he screamed at Ruth.

* * *

"Stop, that's Ed's truck," Andi said, and Bob parked his car a few yards from the cottage. The police cruiser turned in behind them and she got out of the car to wave Beth down.

"He's inside," she said. "Perhaps it's better we don't alert him?"

Beth nodded. "Yes. Please wait in your car. Sergeant Beaufort is on his way, and it's best you—"

"Dad!" Andi's attention was drawn away from Beth as her father ran towards the cottage.

"I see smoke!" he shouted. "Is there a back door?"

Beth grabbed her radio, and Andi hurried after her father.

"This way." She climbed the fence into the backyard and Bob followed.

"Andi, look!" he shouted.

Andi felt the heat before she saw the flames.

She grabbed the door handle and tugged, ignoring the pain as the metal burned her. "It's locked!"

Bob looked around the garden. "I need something heavy."

He bent down, grabbed a loose brick from the patio and hurled it through the kitchen window.

Through the smoke, Andi could see the outline of a person. Hephzibah was on a chair, her face contorted with pain and fear.

"Help me!" came Hephzibah's voice.

Bob Hinton hauled himself through the window. Flames obscured her view.

"Oh God!" she heard herself scream.

She looked around the garden. *Stay calm*, she forced her mind to think. *Stay calm and do something.*

Harry's axe was leaning against his smoke house. She rushed over, grabbed it, and ran back to the kitchen door, where she swung the axe with all the strength she had.

* * *

Beth Stanton was still shouting into her radio when a truck pulled up behind her cruiser.

"What's going on?" Harry yelled. "Where's my sister?"

"Mr Brown, please stand back. Help is on the way."

Harry glared at her. "Fuck that. Is Joshua Moore in there?"

Before she could answer, the front door of the cottage burst open and Ruth Cloutier came out, closely followed by Moore.

"What the fuck have you done with my sister?" Harry bellowed.

"Stay there or I'll kill her," Moore shouted.

Beth noticed the shotgun pressed up against Ruth's back.

"Harry! Stay where you are!" She ran over to the cottage gate, her hand on her firearm.

"Sir, let Ruth go," Beth said as calmly as she could. Her heart was practically beating in her throat. "Backup is on the way. There's no need for anyone to get hurt."

"Get the fuck outta my way," Moore growled.

"Where did you get that gun?" Harry said. "You steal that from my dad? Before or after you killed him?"

Beth looked at him. What was he talking about? Why did it matter where he got the gun?

Joshua Moore laughed. "Your daddy burned and your sister's burning, so I reckon it's *my* gun now."

Beth heard sirens. "Harry, stand back—"

But it was too late. Harry was running straight at Ruth and Moore. Beth knew she had no choice. She pulled out her gun, aimed at Joshua, and fired.

* * *

The wooden door gave way with a sickening crack. Intense heat forced Andi backwards, and she sank to her knees. She couldn't get through the flames.

Then she saw the outline of a figure emerge through the flames, dragging something.

As the smoke cleared a little, Andi made out the shape of her father and Hephzibah, who was stuck somehow to a smoldering chair.

"Get on the ground!" she screamed. Her father was on fire. "Roll over, roll over!"

Andi pulled off her rain jacket and ran to Hephzibah, and began beating out the flames, while her friend lolled forward, unresponsive.

Andi tugged but couldn't free her. Finally, she pushed Hephzibah and the chair sideways, and turned Hephzibah's head to find her mouth.

She did not know how long she tried to breathe life into Hephzibah, but finally a voice said, "Stand aside, we'll deal with this." A man grabbed her shoulder and firmly moved her away. One paramedic cut Hephzibah loose and worked on her, while the other rushed over to Bob Hinton's still body.

"Can you stand up, Andi?" Sergeant Beaufort was standing over her.

Andi nodded and got to her feet. She swayed, and Matt Beaufort grabbed her.

"My dad . . ." she croaked. "Hephzibah?"

"They're in good hands now," Beaufort said. "You need to go to the hospital. You've been burned."

Andi looked at her hands. They were red raw and blistering.

Sergeant Beaufort helped Andi walk to the front of the cottage, standing back to let firefighters rush past, dragging hoses.

Flashing lights blinded her and she felt dizzy. There were people running and shouting.

"Joshua Moore?" she asked. "Did he burn? What about Ruth?"

"Joshua Moore is dead," Matt Beaufort said. "And Ruth is safe."

"Andi?" Harry was running towards her.

"Oh God, Harry," she whispered, "I'm so sorry about Hephzibah."

CHAPTER FORTY-ONE

On a dark afternoon in December, Andi huddled beside Harry under an umbrella in the Coffin Cove cemetery.

The drumming of the relentless rain drowned out the pastor's words and drenched him as he stood at the head of the open grave.

Bob Hinton stood beside them, his hands still bandaged. Jim Peters held an umbrella over him. Her father was still moving stiffly. He'd suffered third-degree burns on his hands, legs and back. He'd been in hospital a whole month.

Clara Bell stood on the other side of the grave. Her eyes were on the pine coffin, which was lowered slowly into the earth. She wasn't alone. A young woman holding a baby stood on one side of her, and a young man had his arm around Clara's shoulder. Behind them was an older man, who bent his head. He was unkempt and needed a shave, Andi thought.

"Who are they?" Andi whispered to Jim after the ceremony was over.

"You remember Virgil had a partner who was killed? That's Julie, her daughter, and Norman Levine from Whitehorse. They've kind of adopted Clara, now that Virgil's gone," Jim whispered back. "I'm glad. We all need family, doesn't matter if it's blood or not."

"And the other man?"

Jim shrugged. "Apparently Virgil's son."

Virgil had regained consciousness for a few hours but had not been able to talk coherently. He'd finally succumbed to his injuries after weeks of fighting. Clara had arranged for his burial in Coffin Cove after asking his adopted family in Whitehorse if they minded.

After Virgil's funeral, Harry had left Andi and her father to go back to Hephzibah's cottage. He'd been repairing the fire damage while Hephzibah remained in hospital, although he wasn't sure his sister would want to ever live there again.

"She's still shook up," he'd said to Andi after his last visit to the hospital. "But Ruth is helping."

Ruth Cloutier had barely left Hephzibah's side, even when she was transferred to Victoria's burns unit.

They had released Andi from hospital after a couple of days. Harry had collected her and taken her to the *Pipe Dream*, where she'd stayed.

He'd told her what had happened to Joshua Moore.

"I recognized the shotgun," he'd said. "It belonged to Ed. He never looked after anything, and he always relied on me to fix things. The shotgun jammed up because he would never clean it. When I saw Joshua holding it, I took a chance. I figured running at him would be the last thing he'd expect, and I just prayed the gun would jam. I didn't expect that young constable to get a shot off like that, though," he'd added admiringly. "He went down before he had a chance to pull the trigger."

"He was a cold-blooded killer," Andi had said, leaning on his shoulder, and she told him all about the history of Thomas Keaney, the killer who'd lived in their midst for decades.

Vega had visited Bob Hinton and Hephzibah in hospital and had asked to meet Andi. "I don't have good news for you," he'd said when they'd met in Hephzibah's Café, which Harry and Andi were managing to open for a few hours a day.

He'd arrested the Halwells' security guard and charged him with the Whitehorse shootings of Janice and Virgil and Joyce Mayfield's murder. They'd also charged him with the attempted murder of Alice Bell.

"He'll probably get away with that one," Vega had explained. "He hadn't actually done anything when we caught him, and he has a high-priced lawyer. Unfortunately, despite your interview with Ralph Stewart, we don't have any direct evidence that connects Elizabeth Halwell with Essie's murder, or any other murder or shooting. Virgil couldn't give a statement. Alice has dementia, and the security guard insists he acted alone. Unless any other evidence shows up, it's just a story. Ralph Stewart says he made the whole thing up."

"What about the contracts he won because of the Halwells?" Andi had demanded. "Isn't that some kind of corroboration?"

Vega had shrugged. "Not really. And not only that, I've been told to stand down on any further investigation of the Halwells. They have friends in high places, Andi. Unless concrete evidence is found, the murder of Essie George remains unsolved. I'm sorry, I really am."

Andi had sighed. "It's not your fault. At least you got someone for Virgil's murder. And you got Joshua Moore — I mean, Thomas Keaney — off the streets."

"That was all PC Stanton. She takes the credit for that. I'm very proud of her," Vega had said. "I've recommended her to apply to IHIT."

Andi had already known that. Inspector Fowler had found the time to call Andi and let her know that Inspector Vega was "very taken" with PC Beth Stanton. "He's even helped her sister get into rehab," she'd added smugly.

"Will you let me know if there are any developments?" Andi had asked as Vega got up to leave.

"Probably not. I'm considering changing my career," he'd explained to Andi, and then he'd sat down again and leaned towards her. "It will mean that I'll be free," he'd said. "If you ever change your mind about living in Coffin Cove . . ." He'd let his words trail away.

Andi had smiled and squeezed his hand. "Good luck, Andrew," she'd said.

* * *

Andi collected her father from Nanaimo Hospital and brought him back to Coffin Cove. Jim had offered the use of his guest room, and Andi brought over Bob's things from the apartment and helped her dad settle in.

As they watched TV with Jim, a news anchor announced that Michael Halwell had decided not to run for the Nanaimo–Ladysmith special election the following year.

"Andi, I owe you that explanation," Bob said.

Jim got up to leave the room, but Bob waved for him to sit down. "You need to hear this too." He paused. "I first met Elizabeth Halwell when she was Elizabeth Consuales."

"Consuales. Why do I know that name?" Jim asked.

"Nicholas Consuales, ambassador to Argentina back in the seventies. He's her father. He's still around, somewhere in the murky shadows. I was interested in him because of all the corruption back then, mainly because of the oil wealth in that country. I'd got the sniff of a scandal involving him, but at the time, the only scandals I was writing about were celebrities behaving badly."

He smiled ruefully at Andi. "The celebrity stuff paid better. And at the time, your mother and I, well, we were partying hard and the bills were mounting up. Anyway, one evening I heard from one of my contacts at a well-known nightclub in Ottawa. Elizabeth Consuales had been seen snorting cocaine with some rock star. I went there immediately, first because a photograph would pay well, but I thought I might be able to leverage an interview with Nicholas Consuales. Elizabeth was a teenager, she was underage, and by all accounts, she was wild and out of hand, and I thought I might get a foot in the door."

Bob shrugged. "It was the way things worked back then. Still is, sometimes. Anyway, when I arrived, Elizabeth was passed out in the alley behind the nightclub with the rock star, so I got my picture. The next day, I called her to make the offer. She told me to fuck off, so I printed the picture and the article."

"I remember, I think," Andi said.

"It was 1973. You were young." Bob smiled. "Shortly after that, I was fired. Someone had leaned on my editor. But I was always getting fired and rehired because of some celebrity threatening to sue, so at first, I wasn't worried. Then I got a call from my contact at the nightclub. She had been threatened, and she was mad as hell because she thought I'd thrown her under the bus. I hadn't, but she didn't believe me. The next thing I know, her body was found in a ditch. She'd been the victim of a hit-and-run."

Bob Hinton sighed. "I didn't know what to think. I don't believe in coincidences now, and I didn't then. But my sources were drying up as I effectively became blacklisted in the industry, so it was hard to investigate. I was only getting jobs for gossip rags, and I started drinking heavily. I was consumed with self-pity, and in the end, as you know only too well, honey, I screwed up my marriage, too. And when your mother died—"

Andi saw her father was emotional. "Dad. None of that matters now. Finish your story."

He nodded. "Over the years, I got the whiff of a story about Elizabeth Consuales. There were stories of her being violent, just rumours at first. But then I heard she'd gone to South America after a housekeeper for the family mysteriously died in an accident. She fell off the radar for a while and then later, she reappeared and married Michael Halwell, her teenage sweetheart. It was easy to follow her after that, because the Halwells were and are an influential political family and Michael was their big hope for the top job."

He hesitated. "You know, I often wondered why it took so long for Michael Halwell to fulfill his destiny. Maybe Elizabeth was too volatile, too much of a risk. Anyway, a few years back, I saw an article about Ruth Cloutier and her search for her sister. The article briefly mentioned Michael Halwell, and I contacted Ruth."

"Did you tell her about Elizabeth?" Andi asked.

"Not at first. I thought she would think I was helping purely out of revenge. To start with, I was." He paused again, to get his emotions in check. "But when I witnessed Ruth's commitment, and I learned more about all the thousands of indigenous girls and women who go missing every year, I wanted to help. *Really* help. So I wrote articles and helped other investigations, and all the time kept digging for leads for Essie and, of course, Elizabeth Halwell."

"Virgil must have seen one of your articles," Jim said.

"He did. But he didn't contact me until he saw the TV report about human remains on Hope Island. Around that time, Ruth applied for a job with Three Cedars band, and we carried on the search. Unfortunately, he also contacted Ralph Stewart, who tipped off Elizabeth. That's when she arranged the murders of Virgil Bell and Joyce Mayfield. She wanted to wipe out anyone who could connect her to Essie back in 1975. When Ed tried to blackmail her, she got Joshua — Thomas — to kill him, too. Alice would be dead if Ralph hadn't spilled the beans."

Andi sat in silence, letting it all sink in.

"Did you know Ralph Stewart was supporting Alice?" she asked.

Bob laughed. "No. I just put it together when I heard Clara's story. It was a guess, really."

"Why didn't you contact me when you first came to the island? Why did you wait?" Andi had wanted to ask that question for a while.

Her father looked at her sadly. "Because I think it was my fault you got fired," he said. "And I didn't want to jeopardize your job at the *Gazette*."

"What do you mean?" Andi and Jim asked almost at the same time.

"Every time I've got close to Elizabeth Halwell, I've received a warning. Or a threat. One of those times, she — or whoever she used — threatened to destroy you. I didn't take it seriously enough and then I discovered you had been fired. And I wanted to meet Jim first. To make sure your job was secure."

Andi sat back, shocked. "But that's impossible. I got fired because I didn't verify a source. It was my fault." She didn't want to mention her affair with her married editor.

"You may have contributed, but you were getting close to exposing a corrupt businessman who happened to have ties to the Halwells. I'm sorry, Andi."

"Don't be," Andi said. "It was the best thing that ever happened to me." She meant it.

"So what happens now?" Jim asked. "We've got Ralph Stewart's interview, but nothing we can corroborate. If we want to nail her, we need to have a lot more."

"I think I'm done," Bob said. "If she can get away with all these murders, she can get away with everything. And I've run out of funds and energy, I'm afraid. I'm not sure what I'm going to do next."

As Andi looked at her father, she felt her anger grow. *She* knew what she was going to do next. She was going to investigate Elizabeth Halwell and help bring her to justice, if it took a lifetime.

Bob Hinton smiled at Andi, as if he knew what she was thinking. He said to Jim, "For now, I'd like to heal and spend some time with my daughter. Is that OK?"

"Stay as long as you like," Jim said. "But there's something I need to tell you both. Andi, I should have told you this a while ago."

* * *

On a rare dry day just before Christmas, Mayor Jade Thompson declared the Fish Plant open for business. Mayor Thompson asked Jim Peters to cut the ribbon.

A small crowd, including Harry and Andi, gathered to watch the ceremony and listen to Jim's very short speech.

"I shall miss all of you," he said, "but while I'm on my travels, I know the *Coffin Cove Gazette* will be in good hands with Andi Silvers and Bob Hinton at the helm, and I'll be keeping up with local events. I wish all of you a prosperous time, and I'll see you in two years!"

Andi smiled and clapped, but she couldn't help the tears running down her cheeks. She would miss Jim terribly.

"I don't have much time left, Andi. I want to travel while I still can, and I want to write a book," he'd said simply, "I won't be gone for ever, and you are more than capable of running the *Gazette*, especially with your father to help you."

Andi saw Peggy Wilson in the crowd. The newly formed Coffin Cove Business Association was still very much against any development on Hope Island. But Peggy had stopped complaining so loudly since she and several other businesses had qualified for a new grant to upgrade their facilities. Peggy had started renovations, and Walter and Cheryl were finally planning a new conference room.

"Stewart Developments kindly donated the grant money," Jade Thompson had told Andi.

Harry nudged Andi. "Look over there."

Hephzibah was standing with Ruth Cloutier, smiling and greeting people. Andi could see some red scars on her hands, and she knew Hephzibah had a long road of recovery in front of her, but she took Harry's hand and squeezed it.

"I'm so glad she's here," she said, "And I'm glad I am too."

EPILOGUE

Harry eased himself out of bed, so not to disturb Andi. She was in a deep sleep, her arm flung over her pillow, and she didn't move, even as the boat creaked while Harry pulled on some clothes and then moved around the galley.

He set the coffee pot on the stove, opened the door, and stepped out on to the deck.

It was early. The sun was just a promising glow on the horizon, and the ocean rippled gently like grey, billowing silk.

He looked over at the boardwalk and saw a light on in Hephzibah's Café. Harry stood in the cool winter air, waiting for the coffee pot to splutter. After a few minutes, he poured himself a strong black coffee using a tin mug he'd once given to his father. *World's Greatest Fisherman* it said on the side in chipped black letters.

Harry had found it when he had cleared the charred remains of Ed's trailer. In the spring, he'd clean up the land and sell that too, and give the proceeds to Hephzibah. He didn't need the money.

"It's as though we erased him," Hephzibah had said, surveying the black ground where her father's home had been.

Harry thought of all the times during his life when he'd wanted Ed to be erased permanently from his life. Ed's drunken rages after Greta had left, hauling his father out of the pub when his drinking sparked arguments and fights, paying off Ed's bar bill, the embarrassment of hearing about Ed's thieving or corrupt dealings — all these times Harry had wished his father was anyone else other than Ed Brown.

But now Ed was gone, he felt more alone and abandoned than he had when his mother had disappeared with Hephzibah.

Hypocritical? Maybe. But he'd tried to be a good son, even when Ed had made it difficult.

Harry heard Andi moving about in the stateroom. He went back inside and poured her a coffee. He knew Andi felt the disappointment of not bringing Elizabeth Halwell to justice. "It wasn't your decision," he'd told her.

Andi still felt she'd let Ruth Cloutier down. She'd written a great article about Essie George's disappearance and the years it had taken to discover her fate. It had helped to revive other cold cases of missing native women.

"It helps," Ruth had told Andi, "to know what happened to my sister. I have peace when many other families don't. Thank you."

Harry and Andi had attended a memorial service for Joyce Mayfield. After Andi's article was published, other women came forward and told their stories about Joyce. Essie wasn't the only girl she'd helped and directed to Hope Island.

Harry sighed. It had been a sad time. He and Andi needed to look forward now. But today? Harry looked around the deck. Today, he'd do some long-neglected boat maintenance. Tasks that required little mental energy. And he'd start by moving all his fishing gear into the hatch.

Harry pulled open the hatch door and lowered himself into the dark space. He felt around for his flashlight but couldn't find it.

He groped in the darkness and his hand touched something hard. Something metal.

What was that?

* * *

Andi woke to the smell of coffee. She stretched out her arm to the other side of the bed. It was still warm. How was it Harry managed to get out of bed without waking her up? she wondered. Maybe she was sleeping better. It was nice to sleep next to someone, she admitted to herself. Nice to sleep next to *Harry*.

She'd moved on to the *Pipe Dream* while Harry repaired the smoke damage at Hephzibah's cottage. Andi could have moved back after Christmas, or moved in with her dad at Jim's house, but she hadn't wanted to leave the boat. *Not yet*, she thought.

The living space was cramped on the *Pipe Dream*. Andi only had one bag of clothes and her laptop. She'd left the rest of her belongings in Hephzibah's cottage. At some point, she'd have to decide what to do next. She'd been putting off that conversation with Harry. She was just enjoying his company and the simplicity of living on a boat. Harry hadn't said anything about his new living arrangements either. But he always had coffee brewing for her when she emerged from the stateroom in the morning, and he seemed happy to see her after work.

That thought, and the gentle list of the boat as Harry moved outside on the deck, motivated Andi to leave the warmth of the bed for the galley.

As usual, Harry had left a pot of strong coffee waiting for her. Andi had just poured herself a mug when she heard Harry call to her.

Out on the deck, she saw the hatch door was open. She peered into the opening.

"Morning. What are you doing down there?"

"I was just cleaning up the deck. Here, can you take this?" Harry held up an old black tin container.

Andi put down her coffee and leaned over to grab it.

"What is it?"

"No idea," Harry said as he hauled himself back on to the deck.

"It's locked," Andi said, as she tried to open the lid, "or jammed shut."

Harry used a screwdriver to pry the tin box open.

"Let me see," Andi said, as Harry started to laugh. "What's so funny?"

She looked down. In the box were scraps of faded fabric and a crude knife. The wooden handle was lashed to a metal blade with frayed rope. It was covered with dark brown stains.

"Don't touch anything," Harry warned, still grinning.

Suddenly Andi realized what she was looking at.

"Ed's insurance. I don't believe it! He must have hidden it here."

Harry nodded. "Ed came through in the end. You know what this means?"

"Evidence. Justice. Justice for Essie. Finally." Andi didn't know whether to laugh or cry. "We can finish the story. *Essie's* story." She looked around for her phone. "I have to call Ruth."

"You had better call your Inspector Vega first," Harry said, still smiling. But Andi detected a sharper note in his voice.

"No need," she said briskly, "Inspector Fowler's in charge. Besides, Vega is not 'my' inspector. He never was and he never will be," she added in a softer tone.

Harry nodded. "OK. Sorry . . . it's just . . . well, I like having you around. All the time, I mean."

Andi knew it was time.

"You know Ruth has been spending a lot of time with Hephzibah?"

Harry nodded.

"You know why, right?"

He nodded again.

"The problem is, I feel a bit like a third wheel. And I know there's lots of room at Jim's place, but I don't really want to live with Dad." Andi knew she was stalling and felt herself flush with embarrassment.

"Are you staying?" Harry asked abruptly. "I mean, are you staying in Coffin Cove? Because I want you to stay here, but . . ." He spread his hands open. "I don't just want to be a temporary fix, Andi." His voice was gentle, but firm.

There it was: the question Andi had been turning over in her mind for months.

"You're not, Harry. And neither is Coffin Cove," she said, and she truly meant it. "This is home."

THE END

AUTHOR'S NOTE

A special thank you goes to Si'i'mithiye Tammie Myles, who generously provided her knowledge of the Hul'qumi'num language, helped my research and generally added to the authenticity of this story.

ALSO BY JACKIE ELLIOTT

COFFIN COVE MYSTERIES
Book 1: COFFIN COVE
Book 2: HELL'S HALF ACRE
Book 3: HOPE ISLAND

Thank you for reading this book.

If you enjoyed it please leave feedback on Amazon or Goodreads, and if there is anything we missed or you have a question about, then please get in touch. We appreciate you choosing our book.

Founded in 2014 in Shoreditch, London, we at Joffe Books pride ourselves on our history of innovative publishing. We were thrilled to be shortlisted for Independent Publisher of the Year at the British Book Awards.

www.joffebooks.com

We're very grateful to eagle-eyed readers who take the time to contact us. Please send any errors you find to corrections@joffebooks.com. We'll get them fixed ASAP.